BIANCA
TORRE
IS
AFRAID
OF
EVERYTHING

Bianca Torre
IS AFRAID OF
EVERYTHING

JUSTINE PUCELLA WINANS

CLARION BOOKS
An Imprint of HarperCollinsPublishers

Clarion Books is an imprint of HarperCollins Publishers.

Bianca Torre Is Afraid of Everything

Library of Congress Cataloging-in-Publication Data
Names: Winans, Justine Pucella, author.
Title: Bianca Torre is afraid of everything / by Justine Pucella Winans.
Description: First edition. | New York: Clarion Books, [2023] | Audience: Ages 14 up.
| Audience: Grades 10–12. | Summary: "Nonbinary teen birder Bianca Torre must face
their large list of fears to solve a murder they witnessed or they might be next"
—Provided by publisher.
Identifiers: LCCN 2022007886 | ISBN 9780358721642 (hardcover)
Subjects: CYAC: Murder—Fiction. | Fear—Fiction. | Bird watching—Fiction.
| Gender identity—Fiction. | LCGFT: Novels.
Classification: LCC PZ7.1.W5833 Bi 2023 | DDC [Fic]—dc23
LC record available at https://lccn.loc.gov/2022007886

Typography by Joel Tippie
23 24 25 26 27 LBC 5 4 3 2 1

First Edition

To all my queer readers:
whether you have known for years
or are just meeting yourself for the first time,
whether you are afraid of nothing or everything,
thank you for being you
and for taking a chance on me.

BIANCA TORRE IS AFRAID OF EVERYTHING

ONE

LESBIAN SHEEP DO EXIST

There are many things we are uncertain of on this planet, like what happens after death, the possibility of life outside our solar system, and the existence of lesbian sheep.

Maybe that last one isn't widely regarded as one of life's great mysteries, but it is. I read an article about homosexual male rams but found no mention of homosexual ewes. It goes back to their mating patterns. When female sheep, so I'm told, are feeling some kind of way, they go still so a male sheep can mount them. Apparently, it's highly unlikely for any ewe to mount another sheep.

So it isn't that there aren't any lesbian sheep, it's that we can't figure out if there are. Somewhere out there, a lesbian sheep is frozen and horny, waiting for the ewe of her dreams to top her.

I really relate to lesbian sheep.

Not because I would love for a hot girl to mount me—although I most definitely would—but because no matter what I want, it's like nature prevented me from being capable of chasing it. I was programmed to be too afraid, too uncomfortable to do anything. I'm not the kind of person that takes risks. Or makes the first move.

I'm the person who goes still and waits, even though I know nothing ever happens for sheep people like me.

There's a lot I don't like about myself, but sheep don't stop being sheep because it's unlikeable. They don't suddenly go against nature and mount whatever they want without consequence.

It's the way we're wired.

Ewes don't get to hump other ewes like they want, and I spend all my time alone in my room.

Sure, I have to go to school and mandatory dinner with my family, but even when I'm outside, the sheep personality is still prominent.

There are people who can do whatever they want, say whatever they want, and there are people like me who have a full CVS-receipt-long list of fears.

And, by the way—

FEAR #24: SHEEP

Those soulless eyes hide something more than just lesbianism, I'm sure of it.

I know a lot about hiding. I do it constantly. Whether it be my sexuality, my personality, or the literal hiding happening right now.

I'm standing in front of the large window, wedged between two tall bookshelves that are filled with novels I've never opened and birding bibles I've well worn out. Interacting with the world safely behind a piece of glass, I adjust the position of my telescope to dip below the sky. Point it at the weathered red brick of the building across the little alley. There's enough of a distance to be subtle about it, but not enough to prevent me from seeing everything clearly. This telescope works great for constellations or shooting stars too far away for small wishes like mine to reach. At night, it provides a fantastic view of the open sky, filled with endless possibility, reminding me that when facing the bulk of the universe, everyone is tiny, not just the fearful ones. It's a comforting thought.

In the daytime, however, it's great for being a total freaking creep.

I position the telescope to Queen Elizabeth's apartment. Obviously not the late queen. I call her that because she's a white lady in her late seventies who wears formal dresses like she's going to an opera. Though whatever sound spins on her record player by the window can only be heard by her and her two cats. She lives on the second floor, which is about level with my bedroom window, in the apartment farthest right. The third floor is too high for me to see anything. I may get bored, but I haven't gotten to the point of staring at someone else's ceiling fan.

I would at least have to exhaust the option of staring at mine first.

Queen Elizabeth doesn't seem to be near her big-ass bay

window today. I spot one of the cats, the fluffy white one with the permanently pinched face, as he licks his paw before rubbing it over his nose. He glances in my direction, almost like he knows he's being watched.

Cats. Nothing gets past them.

"You think I'll be like her in fifty years?" I ask Puck, my own ginger cat currently curled up on my bed.

Being as she's a cat, she doesn't respond. Although the fact that I asked her kind of speaks for itself.

Swallowing that thought, I slide the lens over to the next window. Mr. Conspiracy has his curtains drawn shut during the day, so it's not like I actually watch him. Which is almost a bummer, since he's directly across from my window and would offer the best view. I only know that he looks like a thirtysomething-year-old white man because one time, there was a manhunt nearby, and the LAPD had a helicopter circling real close. He happened to have the curtains open just enough to see if someone was hopping buildings.

It was a really lucky break. We get a decent amount of helicopters circling in this area of North Hollywood, but that was the one that took him over the edge. He didn't have aluminum foil on his head like I expected, but he had a phone that seemed like a burner from Walmart. And what looked like an alarming amount of Post-it notes on the wall, hence the nickname.

But we have a different kind of connection. He knows I'm looking. Maybe he doesn't care because I can't see him anyway. Or maybe he thinks I'm only doing it for birdwatching, based on the feeders I fastened outside my window with sheer hope and loads of duct tape.

Either way, he's taken to leaving little bird drawings for me on occasion, which is actually kind of sweet. Right now I can make out the familiar, slightly grayed white paper taped to the very top and center of his window, where he always leaves them.

I twist the focus to give the drawing some clarity.

With the rosy coloring on the neck and crown and a beautiful blend of emerald and lime on the body, it's unmistakably a male Anna's hummingbird.

A smile creeps up on my lips. Mr. Conspiracy may be a weird dude, but he's a great artist. And sadly enough . . . he might just be one of my closest friends. Sure, I've only seen him once, but there isn't anyone else drawing birds for me.

Romeo and Juliet live below Mr. Conspiracy. I don't care about Shakespeare like my mom, with her classical theater obsession, but being named after a character from one of his plays is a pain I know too well. Though, as far as Shakespearean names go, I kind of got lucky with Bianca.

I tried to fight Mom when it came to naming the cat, but she won.

She always wins.

Romeo and Juliet bring it upon themselves, though. They're all over each other 24-7 with the curtains wide open, like they get off on the idea of someone watching. I try to avoid it. Sure, they aren't bad looking, and I'd be lying if I said Juliet wouldn't have me freezing my sheep self any day, but even creeps have to draw the line somewhere, and mine is at the PG rating.

Romeo stands by the window, about to say something to Juliet. He smiles, pulling off his shirt to reveal a large tattoo over his brown skin that I think says Aguilar. I don't really get the trend of tattooing a last name on your body, but some of Dad's favorite UFC fighters ride that bandwagon hard.

I catch some welcome movement to the upper left—a window sliding open. Immediately, my telescope lens follows, as I push it in the direction of a very familiar frame—the last apartment on the second floor.

It's the apartment of Anderson Coleman, the only person in the building I actually know, because he's kinda my only real-life friend.

He leans his head out the window, making him clearly visible. He's Black, with deep brown eyes, and he currently wears a huge smile as he looks right in my direction.

And flips me off.

I watch as he lifts his phone to his cheek, and my own phone buzzes from next to me on the shelf. I pick it up.

"You're stalking people again, huh?" he says as I see his lips move through the telescope.

"How did you know?"

"My Spidey senses. I'm basically Miles Morales, you know this."

I snort-laugh into the line.

"Don't be jealous just because you have a crush on Gwen Stacy," he adds.

For someone who only really hangs out with me outside of school, he knows me too well. I don't know if it's strange to still watch him through the telescope as we're talking, but I think he learned to stop caring. And to shut his curtains more often, even though I try to respect his privacy and only look when he's at the window.

It's harder to spy on people you know and like. Especially when they know about your spying.

"My animated crushes have nothing to do with this."

"It's the shadows. You block the light when you're standing in the window, even if I can't really see you." As he speaks, he adjusts the glasses he only wears at home.

"Why didn't you tell me that before?" I ask. Nobody else would have noticed, I hope. At the very least, maybe they'll assume I'm chilling by my window. Or birdwatching, like I sometimes am and should be doing.

Anderson's sigh is heavy through my cell phone. "Because friends don't enable their friends' creepy habits, Bianca."

"Whatever," I say. "We still watching the new episode of *One Piece* on Sunday?"

Through the telescope, he points at his Monkey D. Luffy T-shirt and gives a thumbs-up. "Of course we are. I am so ready for this next battle."

"I can't wait."

"For sure, we'll talk soon." He makes a face at me before hanging up and closing the curtains behind him.

Anime is the reason that someone like Anderson is friends

7

with me in the first place. We don't really talk at school, where he's popular and has friends in basically every social circle, and I am considerably . . . not and don't.

But our freshman year, we were the only two students to walk home to this area, so we'd see each other a lot. One day I wore a shirt with a subtle reference to *Haikyuu!!*, and he practically ran up to start a conversation.

No one else knows it outside his family, but Anderson is a total weeb. Worse than me. Like his room is covered in anime figures, and not just mainstream Goku and Naruto kinds of figures. He's got, like, super sexy Boa Hancock figures from *One Piece* that I have to look away from when I visit or I start blushing profusely.

I wouldn't be surprised if he has a secret body pillow of his waifu (either Boa or Nami, because he can't decide) and just refuses to admit it. But one thing is for sure: I'm probably the only girl from school who's been in his room, and I'm a socially awkward lesbian.

"Hey, you stalking people again?"

Kate pushes my door open enough to see me. I can't keep it fully closed because Mom assumes if our door is shut, she's going to suddenly become one of those white moms on TV that doesn't understand how their kid went wrong and tried to make a bomb in their closet. It's overkill, because she'd murder me in cold blood for doing anything that'd make her look bad. As for Dad, he'd cuss us out at the mere thought of deviant behavior and ship us to our very Catholic nonna in Bologna.

But having to step into a church and not burst into flames would only be second in torment, right after my cousins constantly teasing me for only knowing a solid fifteen words of Italian, and half of those just being flavors of gelato.

Regardless of Kate and me being the hopeless Valley girls of our family, the doors always stay open. It allows Puck free rein, which she enjoys. You can't even use the toilet with the door closed or she'll freak out, pawing at the wood and meowing like she hasn't eaten in years.

"Bianca, you're in your head again," Kate says. "And as much as I love your overthinking little self, it's awkward when you stare off and say nothing."

"Sorry." Now I'm blushing. I really do get lost in my thoughts too much. "But I'm not stalking people, I'm *birdwatching*." I gesture to the bookshelves on either side of my large window. Encyclopedias, field guides—nearly every text you can easily get on ornithology is in my collection. "So, if you mean stalking this lesser goldfinch, then sure, yeah. I'm stalking."

Like Anderson, my whole family knows about my weird habit of people-watching, but I get by using the excellent cover of birding. It helps that this accidental hobby actually became a big part of my life. With the help of my birding group and Mr. Conspiracy's drawings, birding really grew on me.

My people-watching is like my sexuality. Mom and Dad must have picked up on some clues that I'm gay, like my childhood obsession with Angelina Jolie's *Maleficent* and the fact that I can't even say hello to the hot bookseller girl at the local Barnes

& Noble without tearing up and trembling. I don't know. Since I never came out officially, we don't talk about it. To my parents, I am a raging homosexual stalker and just an awkward straight birder at the same time.

I'm like Schrödinger's queer. Or Schrödinger's creep.

Maybe both.

For being so close, my family is *really* great at not talking about things.

"Sure, kid," Kate says.

She raises her newly waxed eyebrows, a little red around the edges. She's even whiter than I am, which is saying something. I can at least get a color in the sun that isn't red. Kate's hair is that light brown that's basically blond. I'm more halfway between Mom and Dad: her light brown eyes, his dark and wavy hair.

"Seriously," I say. "Birding."

"Whatever, you can save the *birding* for later. Dinner's ready, and since I got dish duty today, you're setting the table. Lucked out."

I tilt my telescope back up to the sky as Puck makes that weird *I see a bird* chatter at the sight of a feathered friend that is not even remotely close to a lesser goldfinch. At least Kate doesn't know the difference.

"Well," I say as I stand. "Did you ever hear of that lesbian sheep thing?"

TWO

ORNITHOLOGISTS HAVE A THING FOR BOOBS

Even though it's early on a Saturday morning, my entire family is already awake. Dad has to start a shift at the urgent care he works at, Mom has rehearsal for her all-female production of *Hamlet*, and Kate agreed to take me to my birding group hike, since I seem to be one of the five sixteen-year-olds in Los Angeles without a license.

Dad wants me to learn to drive, but I can't even imagine myself behind the wheel. I'd have an actual heart attack if the slightest thing went wrong. Not to mention, my reaction time is so bad, I nearly cried trying to play a first-person shooter. How am I supposed to brake in time? It's like everyone else has some sixth sense that I missed out on.

And with our giant freeways and careless drivers that actually seem to have a death wish?

I'm not sure trusting my sister's driving is much better. But Mom and Dad are busy, and I don't think Anderson and I have reached the level of friendship for me to ask for rides or anything. Maybe if a new anime movie was out, he'd ask me to come so I could be his geeky excuse if we ran into anyone from school. But my birding club is a different beast altogether—a geekier kind of geeky—so I'm stuck with my sister.

She looks half asleep. Her light hair's barely combed as Dad pours her a cup of espresso to match his own. I don't know how they drink it black, especially not with the way Dad packs the ground coffee into the bottom of the silver pot.

"Why can't we get one of those nice automatic machines?" I ask. "To make cappuccinos?"

"Waste of money," Dad says.

It was worth a try.

I take my piece of toast after it pops up, a little too burnt for my liking, but good enough. As I spread some Nutella over it, I can't help but glance out the window above the sink. It gives a view into the yard of our other neighbors, who have a small, weathered house and a huge American flag that kind of makes me think they're racist.

The guy who lives there is outside, watering the grass in the front lawn. Guess they don't care much about wasting water either. His farmer's tan is severe, the line clearly visible with the tank top he currently wears. He has something in his hand, the one without the hose, but I can't quite make it out. He moves behind a bush, and I rise to my tiptoes to get a better view.

"Bianca, you want tea?" Mom asks.

I snap my head toward her, trying to hide the fact that I'm watching people again. "No," I say a little too slow. "I'm good."

She shrugs, putting a cup of water into the microwave and pressing one of the buttons to start it. "Kate, did you get an update on the musical?"

Kate's supposed to be starring as Audrey in our school's winter show, *Little Shop of Horrors*. But apparently the PTA has some issue with the content. Not the abusive boyfriend dentist character. Or the multiple murders that happen.

They think the lead, Seymour, taking care of a plant is going to make kids want to grow their own weed.

I wish I was joking.

"We're doing that preview show on the eighteenth." Kate sighs. "If that goes well, we can do the full run next month before break."

"Good, we'll be there, of course." Mom then turns to me. Her mouth opens but she doesn't speak, like she's trying to think of what she can ask me about. "How's the . . . bird group going?"

"It's good."

"School?"

"Good."

"You know, dear, what I really admire about you is your way with words."

She breezes past me to flick my shoulder before grabbing a banana off the counter. Mom's a theater professor at a few community colleges in the area, so everything she says is projected and overenunciated. It's a little weird, but I still love her.

"I'm a regular Chekhov," I say, earning a proud smile from both her and Kate.

For someone who would rather take a venomous snake to the tit like Willy Shakes's Cleopatra than step onto a stage, I know a little too much about theater from living with them.

And that's saying something, because

FEAR #25: SNAKES

Which is nothing compared to

FEAR #1: PUBLIC SPEAKING/HUMILIATION

Dad sits with his espresso, trying to enjoy a small moment of peace before his long shift. "I'm glad you have fun."

"Yeah," I say.

"You know . . ." The microwave beeps, only momentarily stopping Mom as she grabs the mug and adds her tea bag. "You should have some of your bird group over, you never have anyone over besides Anderson, and all you two do is watch those Japanese cartoons."

He's the only person I have to invite over. So. "You know it's called anime," I say, like that's a good comeback.

As if Mom's voice could summon her, I get a text from Jillian, who is in charge of my birding club.

Jillian: You're able to make it today, right?

Yep, will be there.

Her response is almost immediate.

Jillian: Awesome! I have good news!

I feel like her good news is probably just a bird sighting, but I don't mind. I really like Jillian. Aside from running the one thing that gets me out of the house on weekends, she's a cool person.

She's also like, thirty, so I'm not exactly going to invite her over to dinner.

"If I'm off, I can make food for your bird pals," Dad suggests after swallowing his shot of espresso. They just can't let the whole Bianca Has Basically No Friends thing go.

And bird pals? Really?

"Because my cooking's bad?" Mom asks, voice light.

Dad laughs. "Does anyone go to Ireland for the food?"

"*Italians.*" She makes a show of pointing to his espresso.

"Grazie, mi amore. Posso fare il mio Bolognese?"

"We get it, Dad," Kate says, head against the table. "You're Italian. You can do spaghetti whenever, leave Bianca alone."

Dad actually clears his throat. "*Spaghetti* Bolognese non è vero. Te l'ho detto tante volte! Tagliatelle, Catarina, *tagliatelle.*"

Kate rolls her eyes. "Sì, lo so, lo so."

"You're so sexy when you're heated over pasta," Mom says to Dad.

With a smile, she puts her mug down to hug him from behind. He turns to kiss her, then places a light touch on her chin to kiss her again. Kate gives an annoyed groan, but I think it's kind of nice. I can't imagine finding anyone who would like me that much for so long. They're such different people, it gives me hope.

"No one has to cook anything," I say. "It'd be weird to invite them over. They're old."

"Not that one . . ." Kate starts before catching herself. "No, wait. Yeah, Mom, they're all like, sixty. Who is Bianca supposed to invite over?"

The tension in my chest releases. Kate not only knows that I'm a lesbian, but she knows about Elaine Yee. Not even Anderson knows about her, because we don't really talk about girls of the 3D variety. Elaine's the only other person in the Greater Los Angeles Ornithological Enthusiasts group below the age of twenty.

And, also, basically my dream girl.

So, of course, I could never invite her over. I'm a damn sheep. I can barely say hello to her.

In fact, the mere thought of it terrifies me.

FEAR #13: BEAUTIFUL WOMEN

Not that I deal with many, obviously. I'm certainly not going to find them in my bedroom, no matter how many computer ads promise that Sexy Women Nearby Want Me.

"Well, I don't know," Mom replies, defeated. "I'm not saying you should stop birding, but perhaps you should do something where you can meet some people your age." She gets a look in her eyes. Here it comes. "A boy, maybe."

FEAR #11: TELLING MY PARENTS I'M A RAGING LESBIAN

"You sure it won't work out with Anderson?" she asks.

"Yes, I'm sure. We're not really each other's types, and we're just friends."

"I just think you're old enough to date a nice boy. We don't mind."

Dad looks up, grinning. "Or don't date. Focus on school."

Not exactly where I'm going with this either, but okay.

"Yeah, Mom, I don't think I need to worry about meeting a boy right now, and school's fine, Dad, but thanks." I can barely stomach the rest of my toast. I take a bite and swallow the lump along with it. Maybe I should tell them. Kate and Anderson accepted me when I came out to them.

Sure, Kate has gay friends from theater and Anderson's brother is trans, so they have queer people they love, but my parents would accept me too.

Probably. I think.

"I'm only saying," Mom says. "Kate needs to focus on her career, but I would love for one of my daughters to bring a boy home." She brightens. "Maybe you should take one of my improv classes." She eyes my outfit. "And it wouldn't hurt to wear clothes that look like they're for girls."

FEAR #52: IMPROV

There is a lot to unpack there and really all of it makes me want to throw up. "Mom, I love you, but I would rather stab both my eyes out Oedipus style than take a single improv class." I cross my arms. "And I'm not exactly going to wear a dress and heels on a *hike*."

Or . . . ever. But still. I could probably tell them today. Now. *No, Mom, I'll never bring a boy home like that.* So easy.

Say *well, I'm a lesbian so* and be done with it. Simple.

"Mom? Dad?"

They both look at me. Waiting.

My palms sweat.

"I'll see you later, I have to go," I say quickly. "Kate?"

She downs her own espresso shot and stands up to join me.

"Ciao, ciao," Dad says.

"Have fun," Mom adds.

Kate grabs her keys and walks with me outside.

She has her backpack high on both shoulders and a separate rehearsal bag in hand as she gives me a look. "I think I know what you meant by that lesbian sheep thing."

I adjust the binoculars around my neck before applying sunscreen to my arms for the second time today. Despite it being so early, the temperature is fairly high, especially for early November. Most of the group is already gathered. Clutching their cameras and field guides. I stand among them, not talking to anyone.

"Bianca, there you are!"

Jillian Kingfisher, president of the Greater Los Angeles Ornithological Enthusiasts (GLAOE), and leader of the bird tours, smiles warmly at me. She really is a textbook bird enthusiast, down to her last name. She knows everything there is to know about the birds of California—and probably even the rest of the world, if she were tested on it. Currently dressed for the hike in a shocking amount of khaki, her red-framed glasses fall down her nose. She's not unattractive, but definitely the quirky type.

She reached out to me after I submitted a nervous contact

form to the GLAOE when I came across their website last year. It's super outdated, and kind of looks like the page you'd find when typing *.net* instead of *.com* by accident, but the passion for birds was clear in the description.

Jillian reached out and immediately invited me to chat more and go on a hike. It was nice, and Mom and Dad were glad I got out of the house for once, even if they made Kate go with me the first time. What a nightmare that was. Kate is the theater kid who doesn't understand that stage whispers aren't meant for normal life, and probably scared away half the nearby birds. And maybe even other hikers.

I was welcomed into the group and Kate was politely asked not to come back.

But Jillian and I got close enough, and she doesn't mind if I message her with random birding questions. A person like that can't be easy to find.

"Hi, Jillian," I say. "How are you?"

"I'm doing all right," she says, pushing her glasses up. "Hoping that we have some great finds today."

"Me too," I reply because it's something to say.

"I'm so glad you're able to come weekly; I know junior year can get busy. It gives me hope, you know, to see such a promising young ornithologist."

I blush. "Thanks."

"So, onto my good news. We are doing some spring internships at the museum," Jillian says. "I'll definitely recommend you, if you're interested. I can't imagine you won't get accepted even without me, but it would be great to have you!"

The museum exhibit where Jillian works is mostly taxidermy birds, but they do a lot of research. Plus, there wouldn't be contact with many people, and I already know her. Excitement builds in my chest. "That'd be great," I say.

Jillian holds the binoculars around her neck. "The deadline is mid-December, so there's only a few weeks, but I'll send you the application info. I'll also write you a letter of recommendation, you can send that in as well."

"Yeah," I say quickly, "thank you."

"Don't worry at all, I'm just so glad you've been coming. I know it took some getting used to."

Yes, meeting with a group of strangers from the internet in nature was not exactly the most comfortable experience.

"It did," I admit. "But I'm glad I'm here."

"Me too." Jillian chuckles lightly. "Maybe that's why I'm so drawn to birds. They're never really alone. Most of them are with their flocks. It's kind of beautiful, huh?"

I feel like that's a callout for me being too shy and awkward to talk to people, but she's pulled aside by another member before I can question it.

She has a point. At least this group is something. And now there's the possibility of the internship too. Jillian really is the coolest. Without her, I'd be holed up in my bedroom with nothing to do. Now, I might even get to look forward to next semester. I don't know what the hours of the internship are, but it's not like I have any after-school conflicts anyway.

I check the time on my phone to distract myself from smiling alone like a strange person. It's 7:28.

We never start late, so everyone else will have to get here in two minutes. Of course, our group maxes at maybe fifteen people, so it's not like there will be many more coming.

And who am I kidding? I'm waiting on one person.

It's exactly 7:30 when she arrives, parking her blue Subaru in the lot at the bottom of the trail. The dented car stands out in the crowd of Porsches, BMWs, and Teslas the rest of the group drives. But I can't help but stare as she gets out of the car, looking incredible in her hiking gear. Elaine Yee gets my heart fluttering like you wouldn't believe, and her large Nikon and birdwatching field guide only add to the overall hotness of her demeanor.

She could be a model. Or an actress. Or probably, like, end world hunger with an OnlyFans.

But she's a sweet and intelligent badass who spends her Saturdays on birding hikes.

She gives a soft smile that isn't quite directed at anyone, but not *not* directed at me, as she joins the group. Her hair is tied back in a low ponytail. Stray strands flutter in the light breeze as she stands and waits for our birding adventure to begin.

It would be easy enough in theory to say something.

Just a hello. Not like a full question or anything.

My arms itch and my stomach turns like I had too much iced coffee.

FEAR #6: INITIATING CONVERSATION

Jillian saves me from making a fool out of myself.

"Welcome, everyone," she says. "I hope you had a wonderful week, and it is so lovely to be here with you all. Every walk is a new opportunity for sightings! Last week, Terrance and Margaret spotted a chestnut-sided warbler. An excellent find from our newest members." She gestures to Terrance and Margaret, a retired couple who consistently arrive at least fifteen minutes early and hold on to their cameras proudly. Aside from Elaine and Jillian, they're probably the nicest to me in the whole group, and they've only been coming for like two months now.

Jillian smiles like a satisfied mother, giving a moment for congratulations before continuing. "Who knows what incredible species we may spot on the trail."

There's a very small murmur of excitement. Jillian lives for this.

"Now, we can't forget our safety reminders," she says. "We know there is no smoking of any kind from our organization, as wildfires are a constant threat. Also be wary of mountain lions and snakes—don't be too quiet as we go to keep those predators away. Stay on the trail to ensure we don't disturb the wildlife. And go at your own pace, but try not to get too far behind."

It's the same speech every week, and it's virtually impossible to get left behind on a birdwatching hike. It's not really about the exercise.

I take a step closer to the warning signs the park has posted and try to cement the advice into my mind. *Stay on the trail be alert fire danger medium oh dear God in heaven.* I rub in more of my sunscreen.

FEAR #9: WILDFIRES

FEAR #25: SNAKES

FEAR #33: MOUNTAIN LIONS

FEAR #48: SKIN CANCER

It's kind of a wonder that I come out here every week in the first place.

"Let's get started!" Jillian claps her hands together without being too loud about it.

She gets the least enthusiastic response ever, given nobody talks with raised voices for fear of scaring off possible sightings.

My feet crunch over the dirt path as we start up the trail. Trees sprout up from the ground, some greenery visible from the few rainy mornings we had recently. There's hardly a cloud out today. A few wisps of white spread across the sky, but not nearly enough to shade from the huge sun that quickly warms any visible skin. I pull down the baseball cap I'm wearing over my eyebrows. Sunglasses can obstruct birding views, but it's too bright to go without something.

Although there are a few whispers and breaths of excitement at any wing flutters, the group itself stays quiet. Our steps and movements are louder than our voices. I keep my field guide open, occasionally flipping pages like I'm trying to find something in it. But I'm really hiding behind it. Watching the people around me more than the surroundings.

I've gotten so used to everyone here, they're practically like a second family.

Jeffrey Mayfield, a white casual birder in his early thirties or so, looks a bit too put together. Like he's an influencer or something. He scans the sky for birds but also keeps checking his phone every so often. I found his social media account once, and he manages a vegan bakery his dad owns, which kind of fits his vibe.

Mr. Wattson, my least favorite member of the group because of the homophobic things he posts on his Facebook, walks ahead, and I make a point to not even bother him. His exterior fits his horrible personality—I thought he was like seventy until he posted about having his newest kid at fifty-three.

Terrance and Margaret look at the photos in their camera a lot, probably reliving the glory of last week. Terrance is a tall Black man and Margaret is a tiny Vietnamese woman, but they have the same mannerisms. Behavior learned from years and years of marriage.

It even shows up in the way they dress, with matching short-sleeve button-ups dotted with little songbird silhouettes that look great on both of them.

They also avoid Mr. Wattson as he passes by. He's asked if Elaine was Margaret's daughter on multiple occasions, despite the fact that he knows Elaine is Chinese and they arrive separately.

I hope he quits. Or gets pecked in the ass by a goose daily.

Terrance looks back at me, making eye contact. My face heats.

"Bianca, you didn't get to see the picture, did you?" He holds the screen of the camera so I can take a look. "A real beauty, isn't he?"

The clear rust-colored streak on the side of the bird indicates it's a male, and the shot highlights his head capped in yellow.

The photography itself is impressive. "Yes. Such a great find. Congratulations."

They seem to find the sincerity in my robotic tone, which makes me happy. Some people assume my overthinking and fear is standoffishness. I mean, I guess I am kind of standoffish, but it isn't because I don't like people. It's because I'm always ninety-nine percent sure people wouldn't like me. At the very least, Jillian, Terrance, and Margaret seem to understand that.

"Thank you." He scratches his beard and smiles. "It would be nice to get some interesting shots today, but if not, I'm happy for the fresh air. Are you going to the holiday party next month?"

"I'll try to make it," I say. "If I can get up to Malibu . . ."

"We can give you a ride," Terrance says. "I'm shocked it's at such a fancy place though."

"In June, they had a summer event on a yacht," I say. "Not exactly good for birdwatching. I think these are more for socializing."

My least favorite thing, but I don't tell them that.

Terrance whistles. I don't think he and Margaret do bad for themselves, but they don't flaunt their LA wealth like the other members of the group do. I didn't think birdwatching was considered a rich-people activity, but who knows?

"Oh, Bianca, we did get an excellent picture of an Allen's hummingbird this morning," Margaret adds. "The flowers you said to plant are perfect!"

They are the kind of couple that is always optimistic, but so genuine about it you have to trust them anyway. I've got a reputation as someone who knows a lot about birds, even among this group, so a few weeks ago, Margaret asked me how to increase hummingbird turnout in their backyard. I didn't do much—only suggested a sugar feeder and planting some penstemon and scarlet sage.

A flash of Mr. Conspiracy's hummingbird drawing crosses my mind, as if I'm anticipating the picture.

"Oh. Great," I say.

That probably sounded sarcastic. Or like I don't care. Or don't believe them. Why can't I sound the way I want? I force my closed lips into a smile for some hopeful damage control. I actually am glad that it worked, that I was able to help.

"Here it is," Terrance continues on excitedly, putting the image screen back into my view.

"Another great one." I nod like three times. Who does that? And why do I keep saying great?

Neither of them seems to notice what a failure at conversation I am. But Terrance's eyes drop to my arm.

"Oh, you got a little spider there," he says.

A WHAT?

I glance down at the monstrosity on my arm. Hairy and black. About the size of a quarter.

FEAR #2: SPIDERS

AHHHHHHHHNOOHNODEARGODOHNOWHY.

"Oh," I say. "Great."

OF ALL THE THINGS. IT MOVES UP MY ARM. I NOW FEEL THE LEGS MOVING. I WANT TO DIE.

"Let me grab that for you," Terrance says, before cupping his hand to capture the spider.

THANK GOD DEAR GOD MY SKIN IS CRAWLING. IT'S LIKE PINPRICKS INTO MY FLESH.

"Thanks," I say. "Let me know if you take more great pictures. Thanks."

Keeping up my awkward smile and suppressing a shudder and the urge to flail around until my skin stops jumping at every tickle, I walk away quickly and put my binoculars over my eyes like I found something exciting.

At the very least, it covers the few tears that spring up.

When I'm able to calm down enough to actually focus on the environment around me, and not take a constant mental inventory of unidentified bug-like sensations, I look at a few birds and snap some pictures when they let me.

I manage to grab a decent one of an American bushtit.

"Nice shot," a voice says from next to me.

I turn. To Elaine Yee. Talking to me. My palms sweat, staining the sides of my camera. I grip it tighter to keep it from falling.

"Thanks," I say.

Okay, that's a normal response. Good job.

"It was a nice bushtit," I say.

She tilts her head slightly, and I pray the bird will fly back to poke both my eyes out.

"I love birds," she says and smiles. "But it's so awkward saying half the names to people who aren't avid watchers." She starts to turn. "When I was trying to explain how cool it was to my brother, the first picture I showed him on this Insta account was a tufted titmouse. You can imagine how he took that."

A bit of my tenseness fades at the story. My smile splits to show my teeth.

"I guess ornithologists really have a thing for boobs," I say.

It's a joke, but she might not take it well. Maybe my tone was a bit too dry?

Elaine meets my eyes. "I guess they do."

She walks off to look at another spot down the trail.

I stand. Frozen.

Sure, on one hand, even the thought of being naked in front of someone makes me want to dry heave. I'm awkward and not comfortable with any part of my body.

On the other hand . . . if she's agreeing . . .

Could she have meant—? Did that imply—?

I maintain composure over my internal screaming and lift my binoculars once more. The bushtit may as well have shaken his head at me before flying away.

THREE

A TWIST OF EVENTS

What else is there to do on a Saturday night besides creep on the neighbors?

I scratch Puck. She's biting the hell out of a stuffed mouse, using her back claws and everything to really ensure it's dead. So, needless to say, she ignores me to gnaw on it some more.

I've been reading *The Catcher in the Rye* because God stopped answering my prayers long ago. It's required reading for English, so I'm stuck with it. Even though I don't want to fail another pop quiz, I think three chapters is enough for one sitting.

Unfortunately, I can't get Mom excited enough to spoil the whole plot in detail like with the plays.

Tossing aside Holden Caulfield and his critique of the phonies, I roll off my bed and step toward the window. I position my telescope, lens pointing across the street, and do the usual inventory.

Anderson's usually out on Saturdays, which is why our anime-watching day is Sunday, and I resort to my alone-time hobby at my window. Queen Elizabeth, however, is having a night in with the windows wide open. She watches television with one cat draped across her silk-covered lap and the other jumping onto the arm of the chair.

"Why don't you cuddle me?" I ask Puck.

She growls, slightly muffled from the mouse pressed in her small jaw.

As Queen Elizabeth sips a glass of red wine, I turn my telescope to Mr. Conspiracy. His drawings come every week, but there should be a few days left before he hangs a new one, so I only graze by the open curtains and move down to Romeo and—

Wait.

Open curtains?

I tilt the telescope back to his window and focus in. The inside of his apartment is dark. Even though it isn't that late, the sun's been gone for hours, so it's hard to make things out with only the small glow of one lamp.

But why would Mr. Conspiracy have his curtains open? Even when the manhunt happened, he barely peeked through one of them. Now, anyone who wanted to could easily look into his apartment. It feels wrong.

Like coming home to see your bed on the opposite side of the room wrong.

This goes beyond my strange curiosity. I can't help but watch.

For a good while, there's no movement. Nothing. Aside from

the lamp illuminating a warm orange onto the carpet below.

"What's going on, Mr. Conspiracy?" I ask, twisting the focus until the image is crisp.

I get no response aside from Puck jumping off the bed to attack another toy mouse.

Maybe I should let it go. I tilt the telescope when I catch a glimpse of movement and immediately slide it back.

Mr. Conspiracy is there. Standing at the window.

Staring right at me.

Part of me wants to immediately look away. I mean

FEAR #44: PROLONGED EYE CONTACT

But I can't. Because to begin with, I never actually had the chance to get a good look at him. He's so white he's practically luminescent in the moonlight, and it's clear he hasn't gotten any sun in a long time. His brown hair is cut short, buzzed almost to the scalp. For never leaving his apartment, he's dressed fairly nicely, in a button-up shirt and slacks.

He looks like a ghost.

But what is most noticeable, and even most alarming, is the harsh look of fear playing on his face. His eyes are huge, glassy, and he's practically trembling.

His lips move. It's hard to read them, but it's one word.

It looks a lot like *help*.

FEAR #28: BEING NEEDED IN A CRISIS

Oh no. What's going on? Is he okay? I mean, he's obviously not *okay*, but how not-okay? My hands shake around the cool surface of my scope, palms leaving sweat marks again. I can't look away. I can't communicate with him either. I definitely can't go over there. I only know him through bird drawings. It's not like I can run over and knock down his door. We've never even said an actual word to each other.

But what if he really is in danger?

He lifts one finger up, pointing toward the top of the window, around where the bird drawings usually are. The humming-bird is gone. I don't know what that means. I can't exactly ask him—he doesn't have any binoculars out to see me. He must know I'm watching. Should I give him some kind of sign? I lean over to the lamp next to me and turn it off before turning it right back on.

You have my attention, Mr. Conspiracy, now what are you trying to tell me?

I focus in on him, and it almost looks like he smiles. Maybe he just wanted to say hi in the creepiest way possible? Then through the eyepiece, I see him jump as if there was a loud noise, and turn away from the window.

Is someone there? He never struck me as the type to have guests over, let alone have a roommate. Not that I could tell, with his curtains always closed. But still.

Who would be in Mr. Conspiracy's apartment?

And why?

It seems like some exchange is happening. Although he no longer faces me, his body moves as if he is speaking. He steps forward, completely out of view.

My heart is in my throat. I reach up without moving my eyes

to put one sweaty palm against it, like that alone will slow the beating.

Maybe it's nothing. Maybe it's, like, his mom, telling him to get a better job, or to leave the house once in a while because vitamin D boosts your immune system.

Then Mr. Conspiracy falls back into sight.

With a large, bloodied slit across his neck, ruby streams spilling onto the carpet and sliding across the hardwood into the darkness beyond his small lamp. A shadowed figure kneels at the side of his body and places a blood-stained knife in his hand, carefully closing Mr. Conspiracy's fingers around the handle.

FEAR #10: BLOOD

FEAR #5: DEAD BODIES

FEAR #3: MURDER

Oh shit oh God oh no oh shit oh God.

My mouth is open, but my throat goes dry. I jump back from the telescope like it bit me in the nose.

HOLY JESUS WHAT THE HELL.

No, I probably didn't see that. I probably imagined that. Very vividly. Hence, my fast breathing. Too fast. *Deep breaths, Bianca Torre, deep breaths, there was no murder. No sir, my odd kind-of friend across the street did not just get his throat slit open.*

There was no murder. It was in my head.

I can prove it.

I slowly return my eye to the eyepiece, where a bloodied Mr. Conspiracy stares up at the ceiling, empty.

FUCK MURDER THERE WAS A MURDER.

My breathing hikes even higher as my vision starts to go white. For it being nighttime, everything is too bright, too blurry. My ears ring. I'm having a heart attack.

And Mr. Conspiracy is dead.

Immediately, my stomach aching and a cough erupting, I dry heave onto the floor next to me. Spit hangs from my lip, and the blurred sight of it has me coughing up more. Puck pads over and starts sniffing it, so I carefully push her away. "No, Puck, that's gross." I let out a shaky breath. I clutch my chest, willing my heart to stop, and try to blink away my crazed vision. I'm not dying. But Mr. Conspiracy is. Or did. Or . . .

Jesus goddamn Christ.

I have to call the cops. Or something. Someone has to be alerted. That's how this works. When a person is murdered, someone has to handle it.

My hands shake wildly, and between that and the sweat, I can barely pick up my phone.

My fingers hover over the keypad.

Will I get in trouble if I admit what I was doing? It's definitely against the law.

No. No. Mr. Conspiracy saw me. He asked for help. I have to do something.

It takes me three tries to dial 911.

"911, what's your emergency?" the voice says.

I freeze.

FEAR #20: PHONE CALLS

"Well, um, I . . ." I squeeze my eyes shut to block the tears.

34

"I think something happened to my neighbor. I, uh, heard a s-scream. He's a white male, I believe. Lives alone. I'm pretty sure. At 5424 Coral Ave, North Hollywood. I'm not sure of the apartment number, but it's on the second floor. Please hurry."

Before they can ask any questions, I immediately hang up.

Although I think my mind is short-circuiting, I shoot a quick text to Anderson.

> Be careful coming home there will be lots of police, Mr. C was murdered I think??

He doesn't respond, but hopefully he'll get it before he leaves.

Guilt sits in my stomach, but what else am I supposed to do? I'm not equipped to deal with this kind of thing. I called, at least. The police can handle it. Once Mr. Conspiracy doesn't open the door, they'll probably need to investigate the place. And they really can't miss the body laid out on the floor.

My chest hurts. I'm definitely having a heart attack. It may not be likely for a sixteen-year-old to have a heart attack, but witnessing a murder is probably enough to create one.

Oh God.

Mr. Conspiracy is dead. I saw him dead.

And I'm having a heart attack.

Tears add to my already waning vision. But I have to do something—right?

I go back to my window and, without the aid of my telescope, look at the building.

Mr. Conspiracy's window slides open. Which shouldn't happen. Because he's dead.

My heart stops.

The lamp was turned off, and without the telescope, all I can see is the figure, wearing one of those plague masks with the long beak. Layers of clothing are wrapped around their body. They crawl out the window and onto the fire escape.

Can I do something to stop them?

Yell? Scream? Say the police are already on their way? Maybe I can take a picture?

I open the camera app and point the lens at them. With my trembling hand, I quickly take a flurry of photos as they jump down from where the fire escape ends, hit the ground, and disappear into the night.

I open my gallery to check the photos. Between the camera quality at night and my shaking, it's hard to even tell there's a person there.

"Shit," I tell Puck, and bend over to add more into the puddle of bile on the floor.

She laps it up. This time, I don't stop her.

FOUR

AUTHORITY FIGURES CAN'T BE TRUSTED

Fortunately, by the next morning, I'm able to regain myself and play it cool. Anderson spent the night at his friend's house, and we decided to skip today's watch session because I don't think I'll be super fun to be around after the events of last night. Besides, Anderson also has a weird connection to Mr. Conspiracy. He'd pay Anderson to buy and deliver groceries to him.

Or, he *had* a strange connection to him, I guess.

So, the news affected him too. We didn't really talk about it much yet, but based on the quick call we had at, like, four in the morning, he clearly wasn't feeling good about the situation either.

But I'm not thinking about that now. I'm calm. I'm somewhat hydrated and doing fine. By the time I head into the kitchen, I'm entirely relaxed. Everything that happened yesterday may as well have been a nightmare. I'm fine now. I'm great now.

"Morning," Kate says, spreading strawberry jam on a piece of toast.

The red globs on the butter knife are reminiscent of the blood-stained blade, chunks of Mr. Conspiracy's matter coating the silver.

I rush over to the trash can and throw up into it. My throat burns, the acid coating my teeth.

"Jesus Christ, what happened to you?" Kate drops the toast to walk over to me as I hang, open-mouthed, over the trash can.

She hands me a paper towel.

I wipe off the excess spit. "I'm good."

Still fine. Still doing great. Still totally not thinking about the murder I witnessed.

I hold the paper towel against my lips tightly, like that will keep anything else from spilling out. It works well enough for the moment.

Kate gives me a look. She crosses her arms and tilts her head. "Bianca. I know you're not pregnant for a variety of reasons, so throwing up first thing in the morning definitely means something is up."

I lower the paper towel to speak. "It's anxiety vomit."

I can't say it doesn't happen from time to time.

Kate narrows her eyes as she studies me. "Anxiety vomit, huh?"

"Huh indeed." I go to the fridge to look for anything that will get the taste of throw-up off my tongue. I'm not sure I want ginger ale first thing in the morning, even if it does settle the stomach, so I go with apple juice.

"Don't you think you should go to a doctor for that?"

I almost overfill my cup even though I'm staring right at it. "Dad's a doctor."

"He's not a therapist."

I sigh. It's not like Dad hasn't brought up the idea before, but the thought of having to talk to a stranger about everything that's wrong with me isn't really appealing. I'm pretty sure you can't just get meds without an official diagnosis, and . . . I don't know.

How do I really know I need help? And if I did get it, how do I not mention the borderline stalking and witnessing a murder?

"I'm just saying, you look tired," Kate says, watching me as I pour my drink. "Are you sure you aren't sick?"

I try to casually take a sip. "Do I really look tired?"

"Full-on zombie."

I can't exactly explain that I couldn't sleep because I was staring out the window and waiting for the police to arrive and feeling some kind of relief as an ambulance showed even though I knew they wouldn't be able to do much. Plus, I didn't want to sleep without making sure Anderson got my message. And it's not exactly easy to get rest after witnessing a murder.

Maybe I saw it wrong.

Even if they did have a body bag zipped closed. My crime scene knowledge is completely from ancient episodes of *Criminal Minds*—what the hell do I know?

"Interesting," I say, the condensation of the glass already dampening my grip.

"Zombie?" Mom says, breezing into the room in her flowy floral dress. "That's no way to talk about your mother." She shakes off her teasing smile. "But I couldn't sleep at all. Police lights went straight into our bedroom window."

If Mom is a zombie then I must be a half-rotted corpse. A fiery burp shoves up at the thought, and I swallow some more juice to force it down. Mom looks as put together as she normally does. Although I suppose she has a few more flyaway hairs than usual, and it seems like she already put on her makeup, so it's possible the grayed skin around her eyes is covered, unlike mine.

I keep drinking to push down anything else that threatens to rise up.

"Police lights?" Kate asks. "Something happen?"

"It's a good thing you're not religious, Kate, because you'd sleep right through the second coming, I swear to God." Mom puts her hand up, like she has to actually do it.

Kate rolls her eyes. "So, what happened?"

"Apparently someone died," Mom says, holding her hand to her chest. "In a tragic way too. He was only in his thirties, can you imagine?"

Yes. Vividly.

Kate takes a seat but leans forward. "Oh. How tragic?"

Mom shakes her head. "Not many details were released, but they're saying it was suicide."

"What?" I snap, before I can stop myself.

Mom and Kate both turn to look at me and my face heats. I can't exactly explain that I saw him killed, but I definitely wasn't expecting to hear anything other than that.

"I know, dear. I wish I could have known someone so close to us needed help." She wipes at her face, and I can't tell if there's an actual tear there or not. "Right before the holidays, too. They really need to take these things more seriously."

"Are they sure?" I ask. "That it was suicide?"

Now Mom's expression shifts a bit more toward worry for me. "I don't think they'd say that if they weren't sure."

I quickly search for the news in the only way I know how, typing in some keywords on Twitter and pulling up the results by the latest tweets. Sure enough, I manage to find some reports matching the time and clearly listing the cause of death. It's all with his real name: Steven Lebedev. It's weird to think of him as anything more than Mr. Conspiracy. He went by Steven with Anderson, but we weren't sure it was his real name, and Mr. Conspiracy always felt more fitting. Especially with how I saw him last.

But suicide?

Why would they assume that? Because the knife was in his hand?

I saw someone leave it there. It was murder.

Probably one of the most obviously murder ways to kill someone. How can they think Mr. Conspiracy did that to himself?

"Terrible, isn't it?" Mom says. "And so close to home."

"Yeah," Kate adds. "That sucks."

Neither of them can figure out what to say. It is awful and

they never met Mr. Conspiracy. I hardly know him, but we had some connection—not that I could explain that to either Mom or Kate right now.

Oh, that thirtysomething grown man who offed himself across the street? Yeah, I feel terrible because he knew I was creeping on everyone and still decided to cheer me up with weekly bird drawings.

I squeeze my eyes shut, but his expression won't clear from my mind.

The fear. The blood. The slice across his throat.

My breathing gets heavier as I place my hand over my neck, feeling uncomfortable in my own skin and cringing like I'll suddenly split open.

I can't do this. I can't keep this to myself.

"Can someone take me to the police station?" I ask, voice shaky. "I think I saw something last night."

FEAR #22: PEOPLE IN POSITIONS THAT GROSSLY ABUSE POWER

Which basically includes anyone in a position of power.

Especially ones that carry around guns.

At least I'm a minor, so Mom had to come into the room with me to talk to the detective. I'm not sure what I would do alone. Probably be unable to speak at all.

This detective is an old white guy with a scruffy beard and a beer belly. He looks like he'd be friends with my American-flag-toting neighbor. The kind of person who gets mad about gender-neutral bathrooms and content warnings.

I want to leave.

"So," he says slowly. "You have some information you'd like to report?"

I mash my sweaty fingers together.

"Yes. Um, sir."

He doesn't say anything, just waits for me to continue. The moment that passes is too long as I try to formulate my thoughts.

"I'm an avid birdwatcher," I say. "I use binoculars and stuff to look at birds out my window. I also like stargazing, so I have a telescope. I guess I really like to look at things outside from the in . . . side."

It's like I have two settings: barely able to utter two coherent words, or words falling out of my mouth in long chains.

"Great, why should I care?" the detective asks.

I gulp. Mom narrows her eyes.

"My teenage daughter is trying to assist in a case of yours," she says. "Let her talk."

It kind of bothers me that she says it like that. I can't really put my finger on why, though. I almost wish she would've stayed silent, but Mom's not like that. I keep my eyes down on my pants. The jeans I'm wearing suddenly feel too tight. I wish I had put on something else.

"Well, through my telescope, uh, I can see the apartment building across the street. Where the um . . . where there was a death last night." I can't look up to gauge his expression. It takes too much of my focus not to squeeze my eyes shut. "I didn't mean to look, but the windows were open. I, I—uh, saw the body and called for help."

He doesn't say anything.

"I also saw someone leave. A figure. They left from that apartment down the fire escape."

I hear the detective shift in his seat. Maybe this was enough to intrigue him.

"Yeah? What did he look like?"

"I couldn't really tell . . ." I say. "They had dark clothes and one of those pointy beak masks that, like, cosplayers use from the black plague, you know, uh . . ."

The detective leans back again. "So a plague doctor killed him, you're saying."

"Not, uh, not a plague doctor. But he had the mask, yeah."

Sure, it's a little weird. But his expression makes it seem like my statement is a complete waste of time. It's not like strange things never happened in the valley before.

"I have a picture." I pull out my phone and open to the series of photos, sliding it toward the detective. He scrolls through them, but it is clear from his expression that there's not anything he can work with. "If you squint, you can kind of make out the beak," I add weakly.

The detective sighs. "Look, kid. I believe that you called in the location, which was the right thing to do. You saw the body, it was messed up, shook you up. Of course it would. I didn't like the sight of that, and I've seen a lot." He shakes his head and holds up his hands. "So, in your shock, you think you see some villain, some way to make sense of it. It happens."

I open my mouth and close it again. Sure, I haven't faced a lot of shocks like this one, but I haven't heard of hallucinating an entire person because of it. And that doesn't explain Mr. Conspiracy's weird behavior beforehand. It's like he knew someone was coming and was trying to get help wherever he could.

And I failed him.

"No, no, I didn't invent it, I saw them."

Mom reaches out to put a hand on my shoulder. I didn't explain the whole story to her, so for once, she's probably at a loss for words.

His look is a weird mixture of pity and annoyance.

"Whether you saw him or not, it doesn't matter. I'll admit, I don't see a lot of suicides like that, but there was a note, okay?" His hands fall back down onto his desk like that's the end of it. "It explained everything. He was a lonely, messed-up guy. I'm sorry you saw what you did, but this is a real open-and-shut case."

Mom leans forward. "You can at least look into—"

"No, Mom, it's okay," I say. My voice is hollow. "The detective is right. I was seeing things."

She twists to me. "Bianca."

"It's fine." I stand up from the chair and give the detective a nod without any eye contact. "Thanks for your time."

I make a beeline for the office door and keep walking quickly until I'm out of the police station. Mom has no choice but to follow me back to the car.

"What was that?" she asks, finally getting ahold of my arm to pause me. "Do you truly believe there was someone else involved?

I'll go back in there and demand—"

"Mom." My voice actually comes out forceful. I pull back a little. "It's fine. There was a note. It . . . it was a lot to see."

Her expression softens, and she pulls me into a tight hug. "Oh, honey, I'm so sorry. I'm always available to talk if you need it. Or your father. I'm sure he's seen everything in medical school, he probably has ways to deal with it."

I nod. Dad is more like me, and not the most open about experiences and emotions, but I'm sure Mom will call him regardless of what I say, so maybe he can help.

"Thanks, Mom," I say, awkwardly trying to return the hug.

But despite everything, I know I'm right.

I know what I saw.

Mr. Conspiracy was definitely murdered.

FIVE

ASKING FOR HELP

I don't leave my room for the rest of the day. I don't even attempt to look at *The Catcher in the Rye*, even though I have the second half of the book left to read before class. It seems bad enough that I have to go to school tomorrow as if I didn't have the worst possible weekend. I stay at the window, in front of my telescope, looking at the now drawn curtains of Mr. Conspiracy's apartment.

What happened last night? Who was in the room with him? Why would they kill him?

I can't imagine Mr. Conspiracy doing anything to be added to someone's hit list. He was the kind of guy to draw birds for a weird teenager across the street. Really detailed, good drawings too. And based solely on the glimpses of his apartment that I did get, it seems he didn't get out much. He was probably the type of person who wouldn't even use a computer for fear of being tracked.

At the very least, he definitely has his laptop camera covered like I do.

FEAR #27: BEING WATCHED THROUGH MY LAPTOP CAMERA

Sure, it may also apply to my phone, but I have to try not to think about that one too much. I at least turn it facedown when changing—I hate seeing my naked body, no way in hell I'm subjecting my FBI agent or whatever to it.

I keep watching the window curtains of Mr. Conspiracy's apartment like they will suddenly open.

What is Mr. Conspiracy hiding in there that would lead to his death?

I mean, it's really none of my business.

The police determined it was a suicide, and that's literally their job, so I should accept it. Maybe it was a suicide, and the person I saw didn't actually exist. It's not like I witness murders daily and know how it will affect me.

Help.

I'm pretty sure that's what he said.

He knew I was watching. His only hope.

And I did nothing. I let him die.

My breathing grows faster again, a sickness nestling into the pit of my stomach. I don't know a lot about Mr. Conspiracy, but he was a part of my life. And I was part of his. Don't I owe it to him to figure out what really happened that led to his death?

Even though I know they won't shift on their own, I take another look through the telescope at those curtains. Does he have any family or friends to go through his place? It didn't seem like he had either, but maybe distant relatives? What are they going to do with his things?

Maybe he left a message for me. He was pointing to where he leaves the drawings. Was that his way of just saying he's the one who did them?

No, he wouldn't do that with his dying breath. He had to know he was in trouble. He was freaked out. He had the curtains open, so he wanted to tell me something.

But what?

Maybe he left something in his apartment. Something that I would notice that the murderer wouldn't.

I back my face away. No. That's absurd. I cannot break into a dead guy's apartment.

FEAR #16: GETTING CAUGHT DOING SOMETHING BAD

And that's definitely criminal activity. I'm not bold enough for criminal activity. I'm a little weird and casually invade the privacy of others, sure—and okay, maybe that's criminal. But criminal from the comfort of your own home is different. What kind of lesbian sheep could sneak into someone else's apartment and dig around for clues? I'm no Nancy Drew. What would I be able to uncover that the actual investigators didn't anyway?

Unless, like the bird drawings, only I would know the location.

The thought is a little out there, but what about this isn't?

To distract myself from the unwanted internal dilemma, I look for anything interesting and nonmurderous in the other windows. Romeo is actually alone, it looks like, talking to someone on the phone. He has a huge smile on his face as he speaks, looking more relaxed than I've ever seen him.

It's kind of nice, even if I can't hear what he's saying.

He had to have gotten news someone in the apartment building died. I wonder if he knows it was right above him.

Today, Queen Elizabeth isn't at her window, but the cats are. They're both perched on the sill and watching the world outside.

A knock sounds on the other side of my open door.

"Come in," I say, pulling away from my telescope.

Dad's standing there. I already knew it was him, because neither Mom nor Kate are the type to wait after knocking. Or to knock at all. He looks tired, getting back from a long shift, but his eyes don't droop. If I didn't know him so well, I probably wouldn't be able to tell how exhausted he is.

"Ciao, cara," he says. "Come stai?"

His expression shows that he already basically knows the answer, so I don't give it to him.

"Did Mom make you come talk to me?" I ask instead.

"Yes," he says. "But I still want to know how you are."

I'm assuming Mom told him the whole story in great theatrics. She probably portrayed me with a more dramatic reaction than I actually had.

I don't really know how to start.

"Do you ever stop seeing it?" I ask.

Dad walks into my room to delicately sit at the edge of the bed. He looks like he's trying to hold himself off the comforter as much as possible.

"Seeing what?"

I open my mouth a few times before I'm able to answer. "What people are like. When they've just died."

"Nothing ever leaves you," he says carefully. "But it gets easier."

I nod. I'm not sure what to say to that.

"The good things in life, they're not easy. Leaving my family back in Italy, marrying your mom, becoming a physician, having you and your sister." He smiles. "It's not easy, but I wouldn't change anything." Dad looks over at me, awkwardly standing by the window. "Helping people isn't easy. But it's something I feel I need to do."

I swallow. "Even if nobody helps you?"

He gives a weak smile. "Especially then."

In the small silence, my guilt rises. Mr. Conspiracy was alone. I could have been all he had, and I did nothing.

"Thanks," I say.

Dad nods, standing slowly and heading back for the door. "You need anything, I'm here." That's like his version of "I love you."

"Thanks," I say again. "Me too." That's mine.

He gives a quick nod, kind of looking past me, and exits the room, closing the door to the point where only a sliver of light comes through.

How can I help Mr. Conspiracy? What can I do from my bedroom?

Then again, maybe I don't have to do it completely alone.

I pull out my phone to shoot a quick text to Anderson.

51

Hey can we talk?

His response comes quickly.

Anderson: Sure B, is it about Mr. Conspiracy?

Yeah. How are you doing?

It takes a moment for his message to come through.

Anderson: I don't know, it's weird. Like we didn't know him
well but we still kind of did? Not really sure how to feel?

I get that

Anderson: Are YOU okay? You actually saw it

I bite my lip as I start trying to think of ways to compose this
message. Maybe it isn't something I should just text him about?
He's right, it is a strange situation, but actually talking about it
could help. Especially because I can't seem to let it go.

I'm okay, more or less the same. Can we talk more tomorrow? In person

If that's okay

I rush to add the second message. It isn't like we don't hang
out in person, but it is usually manga- or anime-related.

Anderson: Yeah ofc, just let me know

I can't help but smile. Anderson's smart and good with people.
I'm sure he doesn't have a list of fears so extensive and unwieldy
that it gets a little hard to keep track of.

Maybe, with his encouragement, I can do something to make
a difference and figure out what actually happened to Mr. Conspiracy.

SIX

THERE'S A METAPHOR HERE SOMEWHERE

I stare at the paper in front of me and really regret not reading the second half of *The Catcher in the Rye*. Keeping my eyes on the pop quiz question until the letters blur together, I will them to reform into a new sentence.

But as the shapes return to their crisp state, I am at a loss.

What, or who, is the catcher in the rye?

That's definitely something I should know. It's the title of the book, it had to be addressed at some point.

Can I make up an answer? Eighty percent of English class is confidence and bullshit. And I have one of those things.

Holden's belief that . . .

No. Cross that out. *His* fear *in which . . .*

Um.

Well.

FEAR #19: GETTING BAD GRADES

My pencil practically slides in my sweaty palm as my chest clenches and I give up. I rub graphite over the previous attempts and jot down my new answer.

A metaphor.

Maybe Ms. Richards will take mercy on my soul and do some partial credit. Although that leaves nine other questions I have no clue how to answer. Still feeling sick, I take the quiz up to the front of the room to add to the pile on her desk.

I usually wait until half the class turns in their quizzes, even if I'm the first to finish, because it draws too much attention otherwise. Today, it doesn't matter. Any attention is better than someone accidentally catching a glimpse of my embarrassing answers.

Ms. Richards has a nice blazer and dark jeans on, with a chunky red necklace that seems like it would be heavy.

"Do you need to see the nurse, Bianca?" she asks. "You look a little sick."

Maybe this is my excuse to get to leave school. Seeing a dead guy on Saturday night has to be grounds for going home.

But I'll probably have to do the work anyway and be forced to talk to someone on a weekly basis.

FEAR #37: OPENING UP TO STRANGERS

"I think it's just my face," I say, before heading back to my seat.

Quite a few people are still working on their quizzes, so I try to sit quietly and stare at the wood of my desk. Of course, my eyes can't help but creep around the room. Toward Beatrice

Hernandez, who casually tilts her quiz in clear view of Max Hanford next to her. At Kyle Kowalski, the brother of my sister's theater nemesis, doodling a small dragon onto the wood of his desk in pencil. To Faye Reyes, directly in front of me, her forehead practically pressed against the table as she reads a book that is definitely not assigned for class under the desk.

To Anderson, sitting in the front row, seeming to be working on an assignment for another subject. At school, he looks different from the Anderson I'm used to. He wears contacts instead of glasses, his usual baggy anime shirts are replaced with stylish sportswear. When not in class, he's surrounded by groups of people.

It makes me feel like our friendship almost pauses with the morning bell, because here, I blend into the crowds. I'm basically a no one.

And even though he agreed to talk to me, would it be okay to approach him in the hall after English?

I glance down at my outfit. I'm not wearing anything anime-related, so at least there's that.

"All right," Ms. Richards says, right as the bell rings. "Turn in your quizzes if you haven't, and remember, your data sheets on this book are due tomorrow. If you're going to say you didn't work together, at least insert some synonyms or something to change up the answers." She watches as everyone starts shifting, grabbing their books and turning in the remaining quizzes. "Oh, and Anderson and Bianca? Can I talk to you both really quickly?"

My chest squeezes. Ms. Richards never speaks to me aside from a few greetings here and there. I've definitely never been called up after class. Am I really doing that badly? There's no way Anderson isn't doing well. I've seen his essays and Ms. Richards practically writes a love letter to his brain after every A-plus.

Anderson casually scoops up his things and approaches the desk as the rest of the class files out. I try to collect everything and join them, standing a respectable distance away, but still close enough.

"Mrs. Torre called to alert us that both of you are neighbors to someone who died by suicide over the weekend," Ms. Richards says carefully. "I just want to make sure you're okay."

Of course Mom had to say something. I'm almost surprised none of my other teachers brought it up. I wouldn't put it past her to have emailed all of them.

"I'm good, thanks," Anderson says. "Nice of you to check in with us."

Ms. Richards turns to me. "And you, Bianca? You look rather tired."

I blink. Right. I should answer. In a totally normal way, just like Anderson.

"Yes, I'm good as well. I mean, not good with someone dying. Just as good as you can be after your neighbor dies, I guess. You know."

That was smooth. Anderson and Ms. Richards give me a similar look, like they both know I'm not okay. Anderson's mouth also twitches, like he wants to laugh at my response. He'll probably save that for later. I want to disappear into the floor.

"All right . . ." Ms. Richards drags out the word. "Well. I'm here if either of you need me."

"Cool," Anderson says.

"So cool. Thanks," I add.

Anderson stifles a laugh and I awkwardly nod as we step out of the classroom together. Even though his pace matches mine, it feels like there's more distance between us than usual.

"Hey," I say. It's probably even more awkward. When am I uncomfortable around Anderson, the one guy who I can talk to about how *One Piece*'s Doflamingo is a top-tier villain (and potential queer icon) and not be judged for it? "Sorry, it's almost weird to talk to you without Crunchyroll on in the background."

I say the Crunchyroll part quietly, just in case.

"It is kind of weird?" he admits. "Like seeing a teacher at a restaurant or something." He scratches the top of his head. "Not that you're like a teacher. You know what I mean."

"Should we wait until after school to talk?" I squeeze my bag.

"It's fine, we're good," Anderson says. "I don't want you to think you can't talk to me at school. I mean, not about . . . the obvious stuff. But normal things, yeah."

I'm not really sure our murdered neighbor falls under normal things, but I know he's referring to manga and anime.

I feel my face heating. "I wouldn't be mad if you didn't want me to. I get it. Because you're cool and I am . . . well. You know how I am."

I don't want Anderson to have to feel embarrassed of me,

and I can be pretty embarrassing. Plus, he already goes through enough effort to hide his geekier side. I guess I'm worried people might start to think of him as weird for hanging out with me.

"You're cool." He puts a hand on my shoulder. "Strange? Yes. Absolutely. But still cool. You just need to open up to more people. Like some of the other queer kids, maybe."

I snort. "And where I am supposed to meet queer kids? It's not like there's a club."

Anderson gives me a look. "I mean, the Queer Student Alliance?"

Well, all right, there is a club.

"Ronan's in it," Anderson continues. "He can totally introduce you. And you don't even have to feel pressured to come out. You can just be an ally."

That kind of sounds nice. Not that I'd be able to do it.

FEAR #6: INITIATING CONVERSATION

"You sort of have to talk to people to be in a club," I say.

We keep walking down the hallway. I don't think anyone is giving Anderson a what-the-hell look for talking to me. Everyone is probably too focused on getting to their next class, and if anything, they know he's nice.

"I'm in the Black Student Union, and not everyone talks all the time," he says. "And what about your bird club?"

"It's easier not to talk there. We look at birds. Being quiet is basically a bonus."

"And I think *I'm* a geek," he teases quietly.

"You definitely are, but at least anime's cool now."

The hallways have basically cleared out. We can afford to be late since we both have fourth period study hall in the cafeteria. The teacher in charge never pays any attention and instead leaves a sign-in sheet on a table as she reads romance novels.

"Oh, please." Anderson gives me a look. "*Dragon Ball Z* is cool. *Fullmetal Alchemist: Brotherhood* is cool. What's my favorite anime?" His eyebrows are raised, waiting for my response.

"*Fruits Basket*—"

"*Fruits Basket*," he says pointedly, "is not cool."

I shake my head. "You sound like those girls that make fun of anime but have literal Studio Ghibli stickers on their laptops."

"Because there are layers to this thing." Anderson reaches up to adjust his glasses before realizing he has his contacts on.

"Okay, I'm just saying that you are great not in spite of being a weeb, but because you are one."

He rolls his eyes but smiles. "Yeah, you too."

As much as I enjoy talking to Anderson about this kind of thing, my mind keeps drifting back to the murder. I have to bring it up to him, but now probably isn't the best time to do it.

I meet Anderson's eyes. "Wanna come over after school?"

"Anime watch?" he asks.

"Not exactly." I scratch my wrist and put on a smile. "How would you feel about discussing a murder?"

SEVEN

EXTRACURRICULAR CRIME SOLVING

Anderson sits on the edge of my bed so he can pet Puck, who traitorously likes him better than me. She even rests her head on his leg. "All right," he says. "So, what about murder?"

"Everyone's saying Mr. Conspiracy died due to suicide, but I saw him get killed. That means we're literally the only people who know that he was murdered." I lean against the wall, trying not to bring the more visceral memories to light. "I'm almost positive he was asking for help and pointing to the roof. Like he wanted me to do something, and I didn't."

Anderson holds up a hand to stop me. "What were you supposed to do? Fight the murderer? I don't even think you know how to throw a punch."

"Of course I don't."

"It might not be bad to learn. My MMA gym is super nice."

A little over a year ago, Anderson started training at an MMA gym, where he learns Muay Thai and Jiu-Jitsu for self-defense. According to him, the number of Shonen anime fans that later decide to go into martial arts is not insignificant. I've seen his Vegeta and Akatsuki rash guards, so I have to believe it.

While I like the idea of a sport where you don't *have* to be giant and strong, since neither of us are and he always talks about how Brazilian Jiu-Jitsu is technique and leverage, I don't know if I can stomach being that close to people and having an audience see me fail every day.

"That's not the point, although I appreciate it. The point is I have to do something *now*. And I think I should figure out what actually happened. Who killed him."

Anderson rubs both his eyes under his glasses before looking back at me. "You're telling me you want to investigate his murder?"

I suck in my lips and then answer. "Yes."

"That's a terrible idea."

"It is, but I'm going to do it, and I wanted to know if you'd be down to help." I squeeze my fingers together. "I'm not saying you have to jump in completely, but maybe, like, I can consult and talk to you on what I find? I mean, you're the smartest person I know, and you've seen like every episode of *Case Closed* and there are so many."

That's rich coming from a fellow *One Piece* fan like myself, but he lets it slide.

He lets out a short sigh. "That doesn't mean I'm good at solving mysteries."

"We can be like Detective Conan and Rachel."

61

"You've never even watched that show."

"True, but . . . I can't do it alone."

I can't. I'm too scared, and I can barely picture myself talking to people I don't know. It would be nice to have any kind of support from Anderson.

"Look . . ." He leans his head back. "It sucks that Mr. Conspiracy died. Steven. I cared about him. Like as much as you'd care about a boss you never met, I guess. He was nice in letters, and he paid well. Plus, it was right next door, and I don't want whoever did this to start targeting other people in the building. But . . . do you really think we should get involved?"

It's a valid question. I'm clearly not experienced in solving murders, and it's not like Anderson goes around chasing killers in his free time. But I don't know what else to do. I failed Mr. Conspiracy, and it seems like this is the only way to make it right.

Even if it feels a little impossible.

"We're basically all he has left," I say. "I think we have to try."

Anderson drops his head into his hands for a moment, but then looks up over his crossed arms, glasses slightly askew. "I want to help you, because we're friends. And I can't say I'm not interested in knowing what happened. But . . . considering I'm doing this for you, it might be nice if you finally agreed to go to Anime Expo with me next summer."

He's been casually bringing it up during every *One Piece* watch-in, and I've been pushing off committing to it. The Artist Alley seems amazing, and I'd do pretty much anything for Anderson, but it's hard to psych myself up about the huge crowds.

This investigation is a major ask of him though, so it's time for me to offer the same commitment in return.

After all, I'm scared of convention crowds, but getting involved in a murder case is way scarier when it comes down to it.

"We don't have to cosplay?"

"Absolutely not." He shrugs. "You could pull off Edward Elric though."

I don't know why that makes me incredibly happy, but it does. "That's the best compliment I have ever received, but no cosplay. We have a deal."

Anderson grins, but it falters slightly. "Well, then. Let's talk murder. What happened again? No detail is too small." He opens his notes app to take down ideas. Keeping his phone in one hand, Anderson stands from the floor to take a look through my telescope, aiming it toward Mr. Conspiracy's window like it would help to envision the crime. His expression is serious.

"Like I told you, Mr. Conspiracy was at his window and he looked freaked. I think he said 'help,' but I could only read his lips. Then he was talking to someone I didn't see before his bloody corpse dropped to the carpet. I saw them put the weapon in his hand, then they left out the window. The murderer was dressed in black and one of those plague masks with the beaks. I don't think they saw me. I hope not. But, come on, Mr. Conspiracy wasn't even holding the weapon when he died. They definitely killed him."

He takes a few notes on his phone, then returns his gaze to the building, toward Mr. Conspiracy's window. "Yeah, that sure screams murder."

"So . . . what next?" I ask.

He blinks. "I have no idea."

I shrug. "I really don't either."

"No How to Solve a Murder guides in here?" he asks, jokingly gesturing to the shelves.

"Not really." I pick up the nearest one: *Encyclopedia of Warblers*. "Just the bird stuff."

"Guess birds don't really plot elaborate murders, huh?"

"Not nearly enough."

Anderson returns to the telescope, looking directly at Mr. Conspiracy's window. "Well, we have to start somewhere, maybe we can talk to my other neighbors? I'm not sure he was close to anyone else in the building, but we can try." He looks back at me. "Didn't you say he was pointing somewhere?"

"Yeah. Toward the top of the window, in the center. That's where he would tape up drawings for me. But there wasn't anything there the night he died."

"Wait . . ." Anderson mutters. "There is something there."

My head snaps over to him. "What?"

"His window looks different from the other apartments. There's a lump at the top where the indent is before the glass," Anderson says. "It's like he left something there. Maybe that's why he was pointing up?"

He moves aside and I take a look at where he left the focus.

He's right. Really looking at it, I can make out a bulge, like

64

something was taped to the top of the window, right behind the glass. It's stuck up there, wedged enough so that the killer probably wouldn't have noticed it in the dark. It blends in, so I'm not sure anyone would spot it without knowing to look for something.

"Do you think he left that for me?" I ask.

"We can't know unless we take a look. But how are we supposed to get it?" He scans the outside of the building. "You can't do a pull-up to get up the fire escape, huh?"

"No chance." Almost embarrassed, I hold my scrawny upper arms. I wish I had more muscle definition, but I am severely lacking. "Does that mean we have to break into the place?"

"Uh, no. Not we. First of all, my mom would never be okay with that. Second, what do you think would happen if they found a Black boy breaking into a dead white man's apartment?" He gestures to himself.

I didn't immediately think of that, which is on me.

"You're right, I'm sorry. This is my thing. If Mr. Conspiracy left it for me, I should go and get it."

Anderson sighs as he sits down on the carpet. "Do you really think you can do that?"

"No. Yes. Probably?" I shift on my feet. "Maybe you can help me by keeping watch? From a safe distance."

Anderson doesn't look put off by the idea, but he seems confused. "How?"

I point to my telescope, and he smiles.

EIGHT

ANOTHER SMALL FELONY

FEAR #16: GETTING CAUGHT DOING SOMETHING BAD

FEAR #26: DANGEROUS SITUATIONS IN GENERAL

And perhaps, since those two are a little vague, I can now add

FEAR #55: BREAKING INTO A DEAD GUY'S APARTMENT

My heart thumps wildly in my chest and my stomach squeezes. The idea of it was one thing, but now that I'm actually walking into Anderson and Mr. Conspiracy's apartment building, I feel I'm on the verge of puking again.

There's not a muscle in my body that isn't tense as I step into the elevator, which only worsens the shaking of my hands. My cell phone practically smacks the side of my head.

FEAR #35: ELEVATORS

I should have taken the stairs.

On the bright side, I'm alone for the moment. I'm not sure if that makes the elevator situation better or worse. Hopefully the call doesn't drop. "Do you really think this will work?" I ask.

"I guess we'll find out," Anderson says on the line.

"I watched a good fifteen minutes of lockpicking videos, so I'm practically an expert." I press the button to the second floor and the doors slowly close.

"That confidence sounds good on you."

I don't know whether to take that as a compliment or sarcasm, but my focus is pulled by the elevator slowing to a stop.

The doors open with a ding. I let out a breath and thank Jesus.

Ronan, Anderson's younger brother, is in the hallway, heading toward the elevators, and spots me coming through the doors. He's in a loose Lebron James Lakers jersey and sweatpants. He looks a lot like Anderson, but a little shorter and with his hair dyed a bright red.

"You don't want to be seen with me," I blurt.

Ronan blinks a few times. "Are you okay, Bianca? You seem weird. Well, weirder."

It's a fair point.

"What are you talking about?" Anderson asks over the phone.

"Ronan's here," I say.

"Is that Anderson?" Ronan asks. "Can you tell him to grab some tampons? It's shark week, and Mom used all of them. I was going to go now, but I'd rather not."

"We're gonna buy your brother some tampons after this," I tell Anderson. I lower the phone a bit to look back to Ronan and keep my voice low. "We got you. But I'm trying to look in Mr. Conspiracy's apartment, so it might be a minute."

"I didn't see or hear you," Ronan says, "and I'm not asking questions."

He's the best. "Thanks, I'll see you later. If this goes well. If it doesn't, I've never met anyone else in this building in my entire life."

Ronan winks before turning on his heel and heading back into his apartment.

"Okay," I tell Anderson. "I'm approaching the door."

"You probably haven't even moved yet."

"I'm about to." I take a deep breath, and then start forward. I just stare at the door of Mr. Conspiracy's apartment. "Here. I'm putting the phone down while I try to get this open."

"Go for it," Anderson says.

Placing my phone in my jeans pocket so my hands are free, I pull out the bobby pin that I stole from Kate. Apparently I'm taking the "Be Gay, Do Crime" meme incredibly far. I think back to the instructional videos I watched on YouTube and carefully go through the steps.

But there's no click.

Okay. It's fine. I look both ways down the hall, but no one else is around. It's quiet. This is good.

I insert the bobby pin again. This feels better. I think I got it.

A snap!

Oh, wait. That was the bobby pin. I pull out the broken piece sticking from the lock. This isn't going to work, of course it isn't going to work. What was I thinking? A few videos and suddenly I'm a locksmith?

It's not like I can just walk right in.

I twist the doorknob and it opens. My jaw drops.

I fumble inside as quickly as possible, taking the phone out of my pocket and holding it to my face to give Anderson an update. "The door was unlocked. I'm just walking right in."

"Wow," he says. "Seriously?"

"Yeah."

"Good thing you didn't even have to try to pick it."

My face flushes. "Totally."

I quietly close the door all the way. There are some remnants of the police going through and likely taking pictures of the crime scene, like they didn't seem to remove many items after ruling it a suicide. I peer into the living room, which is where the whole thing happened. It looks like the building management is already feeling the end-of-year slacking mood, because they didn't even get around to cleaning the bloodstains or ripping out the ruined carpet yet. My head spins as my eyes rake over the red.

Deep breaths. Mr. Conspiracy isn't here. Pretend it's ketchup?

Doesn't work. I try to keep my eyes off the floor, which is made a lot easier due to the sheer amount of papers hanging from every available surface.

He not only has some Post-it notes on the walls, they cover the entire apartment—squares of different colors connected by various strings. There are three different maps of Los Angeles tacked up with circles and markings I can't make out from the doorway.

"How is it?" Anderson asks.

"It's . . . exactly how you'd expect. There's maps and notes everywhere."

I look across the living room to the window where I saw everything.

To where the strange object is taped. I have to do this.

I head toward the window, carefully avoiding the discolored carpet.

"I see you," Anderson says. "Wave a little."

I give a half-hearted one.

"I kind of get why you like doing this," Anderson adds from the phone.

I kind of get why people don't like that I do.

"Don't get any ideas," I tease.

"Yeah, you don't have to worry about that. You should hurry up though."

Anderson's right. Every moment I stay in here is a moment I can get caught.

That's when I see it. Discarded on the floor, the edges a bit torn.

The Anna's hummingbird drawing.

I don't know where Mr. Conspiracy kept the rest of them, but I don't want to leave it on the floor like that. It was the last one he made for me. I pick it up and quickly fold the drawing so it can fit in my pocket.

Then I turn back to the window. I study it and spot a rectangular object taped to the top, just like we saw from the telescope. The tape is nearly the exact color of the wall. "There really is something there," I mutter.

"Well, that's good."

I set down my phone so I can use both hands to peel off the object and yank away the tape. It's a small notebook. I flip through a couple of pages and then press my phone back to my ear. "It looks like his diary."

"You might want to check it later," Anderson says, his words rushed. "Ronan texted me that he can hear the landlord talking from down the hall. He thinks they might be going into Mr. Conspiracy's apartment."

I let out a breath. "Oh, great."

FEAR #16: GETTING CAUGHT DOING SOMETHING BAD

My heart is pounding in my throat. I hate the feeling. I swallow, like that'll help.

"The fire escape," I say. "I can use it to jump down. That's what the killer did."

Anderson sighs. "At least no pull-ups are required."

Now I hear the footsteps. My breathing comes out rapid as my chest squeezes. I'm about to have a heart attack. I rub my fingers over my eyes. My hairline itches. Now's not the time.

"Bianca, are you okay?" Anderson asks.

I open the window, clutching my phone and the diary. I close the curtains as best as I can as I step onto the fire escape. It's creaky and almost sways in the wind.

My heart slams in my chest and now my stomach turns. I feel light-headed and want to keep my eyes squeezed shut.

FEAR #29: FALLING

Behind me, voices echo from the doorway. I have to move.

My legs shake as I look down. A few tears pop up in my eyes.

"I'm not sure I can do this," I whisper into the phone.

"I see you, you're okay," he says. "You can do this."

Still shaking, I make my way across to where it drops off toward the dirt below. I stand on the escape, wondering why in the hell they made the stair part stop on the second floor.

"I can't," I whisper. I'm not even sure if he can hear me. "I can't. I'll get caught, it's fine, it's . . ."

"You can jump, I promise you'll make it. See that bush underneath? That can break your fall." Anderson's voice is urgent on the line. I look down and spot the greenery he's talking about. "What would Roronoa Zoro do?"

This would be nothing for him.

I drop down so I'm sitting on the edge and squeeze my eyes closed.

"You sure I'll make it?"

"I'm sure."

"Promise?"

"Promise."

Keeping my eyes shut, I slide off the edge and into the bush. My stomach lurches, but I land right in the mess of leaves and branches. It hurts, and I think I might have a few cuts and bruises, but I'm okay.

I open my eyes. I'm on the ground. I'm okay. And while my heart rate is fast, it's not overwhelming. I take a deep breath and stand up.

"Nice job, Pirate Hunter," Anderson jokes on the line. "Now, get the hell out of there."

NINE

DEAD MAN'S BOOK OF CONSPIRACIES

We stopped at CVS after my mostly successful break-in to get tampons and Ben & Jerry's, and brought both back to Anderson's apartment. Sometimes you have to celebrate the little things, like breaking into your murdered neighbor's place for his secret journal and getting out alive.

Anderson digs into his pint of ice cream, Strawberry Cheesecake, as I take a bite of Milk & Cookies. He leans back against the edge of his bed, next to me on the floor. "Are we ready to do this?" he asks.

"I mean, I already broke in and stole it. Might as well read what I took." I have to give myself credit for getting the words to come out calmly. On the inside, I'm a bundle of nerves. Are there any clues inside that journal that will hint at the motive behind the murder?

Anderson puts his ice cream down on the floor next to him and opens the diary to the first page. He reads for a moment. "All right, a lot of this is boring, or just random bird sketches, probably for you—cute. I think we should skim . . ." He starts turning pages. "Oh, he writes about feeling like he's being watched. I wonder why." Anderson takes a whole beat to look accusingly at me.

Heat rises to my face. "Okay, sure, that was me."

He flips through the pages like he's shuffling a deck of cards until his eyes widen and he stops on one. "He was being threatened."

I hold my hands up in defense, and a bit of chocolate slides down the end of my ice cream spoon. "Okay, that was definitely not me." I lean forward to try to see some of the writing. It's surprisingly neat. I was expecting a frantic chicken scratch, but I guess if you're going to leave a diary for someone else to read, you should at least make it legible. "I don't have the balls to threaten anyone."

Anderson nods. "I believe that." He eyes the diary. "Especially because they left messages in blood outside his door and sent dead animals. You don't seem the type."

The mere thought of it wrinkles my nose and has me biting hard on my cheek.

FEAR #10: BLOOD

And while I'm not sure I gave it much thought before . . .

FEAR #56: ANIMAL CARCASSES

It's like they say, fear something new every day.

"Yeah, I'm more of an observer than someone who takes action."

Anderson gestures to his window. "Clearly."

I scoot closer to Anderson, so I can get next to him. "What else does it say?"

I reach for the diary and he snaps it to the side, keeping it out of reach. He looks slightly offended. "Well, if you give me a second, Bianca, I'll tell you."

"Sorry," I say, sitting back.

It's almost strange that the TV isn't on with some kind of show, but it's surprisingly comfortable.

Anderson flicks through more of the diary, looking intently at the pages. He bites his bottom lip as he concentrates, glasses drooping on his nose. He's holding the diary on top of his bent knees.

Since he's focused on that, my eyes drift around the room to the various figures carefully displayed. They don't even have dust on them—I know as I've helped him clean the shelves quite a few times. I stop on one of Roronoa Zoro, posed in his three-sword style.

"How do you get muscles like that?" I ask.

The words sort of come out, and my face immediately heats, especially when he looks up from the diary and at me.

"Excuse me?" he asks.

"I'm just . . ." I hold up my own arm, with more jiggling skin than muscle making up my barely there bicep. "I don't know. I might like to build a little strength."

I don't feel comfortable in my body and I certainly don't like it. Maybe a little weight training or whatever would actually help. For some reason, the idea of building up my physique, looking a little more masculine . . . it sends this excited tingle through my chest.

It's like I'm immediately forgiven for the interruption because his lips turn upward and his eyebrows raise. "Well, first of all, Zoro is a fictional character, so maybe lower your standards a little. And, like I said, you should come to the gym with me."

I don't know if I can make any promises. Would it help me feel better? He might have a point about self-defense being helpful. Especially with a murderer on the loose. "You're okay with that?"

He makes a face. "Why wouldn't I be?"

I shrug, leaning back against the bedspread. "I don't know. It's just like, I don't want to overstep. We're anime friends, and while you're basically my only friend, I don't want to intrude into other parts of your life if you don't want that."

He thinks for a moment, like he's trying to pick the right words. "I appreciate that, but I'll let you know if it's overstepping, and this isn't. That's why I invited you. Besides, they kind of know I like anime there."

"The *Naruto* and *DBZ* variety?"

He nods, wincing, and looks up at the dark screen of the television. "I didn't really think about it, but I guess this is the first time we've hung out and not talked about anime."

"Is that bad?"

He shakes his head. "Nah, I mean, there's always going to be parts of us we don't share. It's just different sides that others sometimes bring out of us or we decide to keep hidden."

He's right.

"Yeah, and I guess we don't really owe all of ourselves to anyone," I say.

"Exactly."

I haven't really thought about that before, but it's kind of nice. I've always felt so pressured to tell everyone I'm a lesbian, including my parents, but maybe it's a part of me that people should earn the right to get to know.

"That being said," Anderson continues, "I'm not saying we can only talk about anime and murder. Sure, you happen to be my go-to person when it comes to weeb stuff, but that doesn't mean I only like you because you're a geek." He turns his head toward me. "What's your favorite bird?"

I shake my head. "That's like the hardest get-to-know-you question for me. There are so many. I'd at least need to narrow it down by order or genus."

Anderson laughs. "How is that the most Bianca answer in the world? Moving on. What's something about you that no one else knows that you'd want to share with me?"

I don't have that many secrets since I told Anderson I'm a lesbian and about the whole people-watching thing not long after we started hanging out. Sure, he doesn't know about Elaine, but I don't think I'm ready to share that with anyone yet.

I'd probably die even trying to admit my crush on her.

"I kind of want to buy clothes in the men's department," I blurt. Wait. Why did I say that? I wasn't expecting to say that. "I mean, actual pockets. I think I'd like the cuts better."

Anderson doesn't question or make me explain further. "I can go with you, if that would be more comfortable. Or we can look together online. I have excellent taste."

I gesture to his oversize Frieza tank top with the words *This Isn't Even My Final Form* on it. "Is that right?"

"Please, you've complimented me on this shirt every other time I wore it." He waves me off.

And he's right. I love that shirt.

"Really, though. Thanks."

Anderson pushes up his glasses, looking away from me. "I really want to learn to draw comics."

I wasn't expecting him to confess that, but I actually love the idea. To the left of us, he has two bookshelves filled with manga and graphic novels. It's already a shared love, but to be able to read something Anderson created? That would be incredible.

"That's so cool? Oh my God? You should. I'd read all of them."

He seems slightly embarrassed as he looks back at me. "Yeah? It's not like I'm a real artist. I can draw pretty well, but I feel like everyone already has their things at this point, stuff they've been doing forever. I'm worried that I'd already be behind."

I know what he means. I have no idea what I want to do with myself, and my biggest example is a sister who has been obsessed with theater since entering stage left out of the womb. But while

I talk to myself in negatives, I don't want to do the same for Anderson.

"There's, like, grandmas that start new hobbies and skills and end up mastering them. I think you should try it." I put a hand on his shoulder. "Besides, you're super smart, creative, and very funny. So, worst-case scenario, make the story so entertaining that people no longer care whether or not it's actually good."

He cracks a smile that shows his teeth. "Those are our favorite kind."

"Absolutely." I pull away and shift to sit cross-legged. "We can even look up some classes or something to try together. Or just YouTube our way through it to save money."

"I'll think about it." He lifts the diary. "And as much as I appreciate this conversation, we probably should get back to the murder."

I blush. I was so excited, I sort of completely forgot that we were doing that in the first place.

"Okay, where were we . . . here." Anderson points at the open page. "Before these threats happened, he was investigating this company called VQ. Apparently, his nephew was a part of it but wanted out, and then his nephew went *missing.*"

That's big news. I didn't even know Mr. Conspiracy had a nephew. Not that I would have. It's just still a little weird to think of him as someone with a family.

"That's extreme. Wouldn't he just go to the cops?"

Anderson scans some lines. "He did. They thought his nephew blocked him and he was a paranoid weirdo, so they didn't take him seriously."

I can believe it.

"Well . . . VQ?" I ask. "What else did he say about it?"

"Not much," Anderson says. "I mean, he might have left this book for you if he knew they were coming after him. But would he give you information they killed him for? I'd hope not."

That's fair. Maybe Mr. Conspiracy had no other choice than to reach out to me. Even if it gave the killer a chance to find this diary first. Going on what I know about Mr. Conspiracy, he would probably have backups of information, and spend a lot of energy in hiding the most important evidence. Based on the state of his apartment, he tracked everything. I don't think he'd be careless.

Although it definitely doesn't help my anxiety with getting involved knowing that looking into this group was likely the cause of his death.

"You said his nephew went missing?" I peer over Anderson's shoulder to the book. "We can start there. He must have some information on that."

Anderson nods, flipping through the diary until he seems satisfied with the notes on one of the pages. "Okay, here is a bit of a time line. It was last September that his nephew—I guess his name is Nate?—got involved with this VQ. He disappeared January of this year, and no one seems to know anything."

Anderson reaches up for his laptop on the bed and hands it to me. "See if you can find anything on him."

I type the name into Google, but don't get any promising results. "Nothing on Nate Lebedev. Or Nathan or Nathaniel. He might have had a different last name from Mr. Conspiracy."

Anderson groans. "Why can't anything be easy?"

"Back to the time line, though. Is there anything about why he immediately thought it was these VQ people? What if Nate did just . . . run away?"

Anderson's eyes don't lift from the diary, although he nods when I speak. He must have real skills in speed-reading—he flips through the pages, appearing to absorb the information quickly when I can only get a few sentences.

"Apparently, everyone else seemed to think that was the case," he mutters. "Nate was twenty-four, so it wasn't like he couldn't go off on his own. According to this, he left a note. But Mr. Conspiracy was convinced he didn't actually write it."

My chest tightens. While it is possible that Nate really did write a note and skip town, it feels a little too similar to what happened with Mr. Conspiracy.

After all, he left a note too.

"Okay, okay, let's write what we know so far." I set aside the laptop and pull out a notebook from my bag. Opening it to a clean page, I start to jot down information.

September—Nate joins VQ.

January—Nate goes missing, leaves (possibly fake) note.

Jan-Feb—Mr. Conspiracy starts investigating VQ.

November—Mr. Conspiracy is murdered.

Anderson looks it over and nods. "Cool, so we need to figure out who is behind this VQ, and prove that they killed Mr. Conspiracy, and possibly also his nephew."

I swallow. "And not get killed in the meantime."

"Definitely a major goal, yes." Anderson stretches his arms over his head. "I think we should talk to some of the neighbors. Maybe tomorrow? It's getting late."

"Wait, how late?" I ask.

Before he can even answer, I rush to my phone, where I have ten unread messages, two missed calls, and an Instagram DM from Kate.

"I promised my sister I'd run lines with her. I better go."

"No worries," Anderson says, closing the diary. "Like I said, let's pick this back up tomorrow. I can try to find Nate's actual identity too."

"Cool, text me if you get anything."

"You got it."

I gather my things. "Good night, nerd."

He rolls his eyes. "Night, weeb."

I walk out of the apartment, after giving a quick goodbye and thank you to Ronan, and start to head in the direction of the stairs. I don't look toward Mr. Conspiracy's empty apartment. I've had enough excitement for one day.

TEN

QUEER KIDS LOVE ENGLISH CLASS

I didn't read a single additional word of *The Catcher in the Rye*, but I somehow managed to put together a data sheet using three different YouTube videos and the SparkNotes website. It's not a direct copy-paste, but I'm certainly hoping Ms. Richards doesn't read too closely. I turned it in at the start of class, and I haven't been able to pay attention since. My leg bounces in my chair, hitting the underside of my desk. It's obvious I did everything last night at one thirty a.m., but I had more pressing issues on my mind.

And Kate forcing me to run lines from the show. She's basically word and lyric perfect. I'm starting to think she likes to see me suffer.

I still have the lyrics of "Suddenly Seymour" stuck in my head.

The day's been dragging on, but at the same time, my stomach is tight and I nearly sprinted to the bathroom after first and second period. After school, Anderson and I agreed to talk to some of his neighbors to see if anyone noticed or heard something that night, or if they might know anything about Mr. Conspiracy or his nephew.

And the thought of all that talking really irritates my stomach.

FEAR #6: INITIATING CONVERSATION

Not just initiating in this case—the whole conversation part makes me want to rush home and bury my face into Puck's fur until she bites me.

FEAR #57: HAVING TO TALK TO ANYONE I DON'T ALREADY KNOW WELL

Especially about a murder. That I witnessed. Because I spy on half of the residents.

I place my hand beneath my belly button, where my insides let out a disturbing low groan. Will probably have to run to the bathroom once this class finally ends too.

My phone lights up from where it sits on my lap.

I casually open it to see the message.

Anderson: u good?

Anderson: u look like ur gonna throw up

I try to keep my attention focused on the themes Ms. Richards talks about on the board while typing out a response with one hand.

I'm fine

General anxiety nausea

still on for later?

I'm looking down at my lap way too often, but maybe Ms. Richards doesn't notice.

It's kind of weird. I've never texted anyone in class before. It's nice, even if I feel so guilty, I have to slide my phone into my hoodie pocket with the screen facing in like I'm giving it a time-out.

I press my palms to my jeans because they are basically always clammy—maybe I should ask Dad if that could be a medical issue—and rub them back and forth until the skin burns a little. I keep my blank stare at the board, the dry erase letters going blurry, and try to breathe.

The bell chimes.

Thank God.

"Oh, Bianca," Ms. Richards says, "stay behind for a minute, all right?"

This is why I'm an atheist.

Anderson makes a face at me, teeth clenched like I'm in trouble, before walking out into the hallway.

The room empties as I gather my things and approach Ms. Richards's desk.

She's put together, with a nice blouse and fitted black pants, but wears a blue leather jacket and dark purple lipstick that probably has some of the other teachers talking about her.

"Yes?" I ask.

Is that a bad way to address someone? I mean, it's got to be better than *What do you want?*

"I want to check in," Ms. Richards says. "Your mom had mentioned that you actually witnessed what happened to your neighbor."

My teeth dig into the inside of my lip. Why would Mom tell the school that? Telling them about his death was bad enough, and she should have talked to me first. How do I even respond? I certainly can't go around saying it was a murder before we even have evidence.

Plus, if I do admit what I saw, they'll definitely make me talk to a counselor or something, and that's the last thing I need with everything going on.

"I didn't see much," I say. "My mom can be dramatic. I only saw the ambulance arrive."

I don't know if it's a convincing lie, but I hope my fear of opening up and having to deal with the school's idea of "helping me" can outweigh my trash lying skills.

Ms. Richards's lips are tight. "Hmm. Okay, good. I just wouldn't want this to affect your grades. You've already failed the last three reading quizzes."

I swallow. I didn't think witnessing a murder would be the thing that causes me to get called out for my lack of effort. It isn't like I'm failing my classes. I generally stay in the B or C range. Normally, teachers don't really care what I'm up to, as I stay relatively unnoticed.

"Look, Bianca, I understand you are probably going through a lot," Ms. Richards says. "You experienced something traumatic. But I am here to help you, and I think if you put some effort in, you'll find you can succeed."

I blink.

I don't think a teacher has ever seen me as the kid-who-could-succeed. I've gotten kid-who-is-really-different-from-Kate before fading into the average-enough-to-not-bother zone, but that's about it.

It would almost be nice, if I wasn't itching for the conversation to end.

Ms. Richards continues. "You remind me a lot of my high school self. Just getting by under the radar. But colleges like to see that extra work. Going above and beyond."

"I'm going to community college," I say. "I think my GPA is fine."

Ms. Richards nods.

A long moment passes.

"It would be nice . . ." She chooses the words carefully, picking them like flowers. ". . . To see you have some drive. Passion."

"I have passion," I say automatically, even though it comes out like a question. The look on Ms. Richards's face implies that she catches that, and I go for a desperate recovery. "I like birds."

Her mouth parts slightly, a crease between her eyebrows forming.

"Birdwatching," I say. "I'm part of a club and everything. The Greater Los Angeles Ornithological Enthusiasts. We meet every week and have a group chat now."

"Well, that's a start," Ms. Richards says. "Maybe your admissions essay could delve into your experience in the club? We can probably push it as both community service and an extra-curricular."

I give her a look, even though I kind of appreciate her willingness to help.

"Community college, Ms. Richards."

She forces a smile. "Right. I'm sorry." She sighs. "Like I said, I see a lot of myself in you, so I'm projecting, and that's not fair. I missed my chance to go to a great school on a scholarship because I wanted to follow a girl to Ohio University."

I stare at her. Probably a little too long. "A girl?" I blurt. "Like romantically?"

Ms. Richards looks a little taken aback at first, but she smiles through it. "Yes."

My face goes hot. "Sorry, I didn't mean it like that. I mean, like, I'm super gay and only, like, Anderson and my sister know and to hear you say that is really cool."

Why is it that I come out through rambling?

She lights up a little.

"There's no rush to tell everyone," Ms. Richards says. "I didn't until I was in college. But thank you for confiding in me, Bianca. I'm available if you ever need anyone to talk." She thinks for a second before adding. "Assuming it's appropriate. I am your teacher first."

As if I would be able to ask an adult woman anything inappropriate. When Anderson and I watch an anime episode with a little too much fanservice, I'm a blushing mess.

It's really cool that Ms. Richards is queer though. I've barely talked to any openly queer people about this stuff before, let alone a functioning adult one. That's goals, right there. I get she was just trying to be nice because my mom called about me seeing a dead neighbor, but I appreciate what she's doing.

"Thank you," I say, continuing to rub my palms on my jeans. "Really."

The next group of kids start coming in a little closer to her desk, so Ms. Richards nods. "Well, I won't keep you any longer. Let me know how the birding group on Saturday goes, okay?"

"Thanks," I say with a real smile. "I will."

With one last goodbye, I turn out of the classroom. As much as I'd prefer not to be faced with a murderer on the loose, maybe something good came out of it.

Between Anderson and Ms. Richards, it's like I'm not so alone.

ELEVEN

WATCH YOUR BACK

I stand outside Anderson's apartment door and try to keep my breathing slow. I count the breaths. In . . . there's no need to have a panic attack right now . . . out . . . it's cool don't think about talking to people too much . . . in . . . Anderson will be there with you . . . out . . . so calm down okay?

The last thing I want to do is throw up outside my only friend's doorway.

I lift my shaking hand and knock.

After a few moments, the door opens to reveal Mrs. Coleman. Her brown skin doesn't have a single wrinkle, and she looks great in a soft pink blouse I could never be feminine enough to pull off.

"Hi, Bianca," she says with a smile. "Anderson said you were coming over. It's nice to see you on a weekday."

"You too, Mrs. Coleman." It's nice to see her in general.

She pulls me in for a hug before ushering me in and closing the door. Ronan's on the couch and sticks his hand up to give me a wave.

"Hey, Ronan," I say.

"Want some tea? Water? Soda?" Mrs. Coleman already starts toward the kitchen like my only option is yes.

"I'm okay, thank you."

"Anderson!" Mrs. Coleman yells, pouring a glass of water. "Bianca's here!"

She hands me a glass of water, and I drink it because I guess I did want water. I'm at their house. They could give me a cup of bleach and I'd politely accept. Plus, I probably haven't been hydrating enough; my lips are pretty chapped. "Thank you."

FEAR #31: BEING RUDE

Kind of goes hand in hand with not liking confrontation.

Anderson steps from around the corner. "I was in the bathroom, sorry." He changed into black jeans and a button-up shirt that's nicer than the usual anime tees and school sportswear. Not sure my jeans and baggy T-shirt with a cat on it gives the same effect.

"No worries," I say.

"Ready to go?" he asks.

I nervously glance down at the cup of water. I drink a few more gulps and cautiously walk over to the sink, hoping I can leave it there. As much time as I've spent here, we've never really had dinner or anything that allowed me to learn the rules for dishes.

"See you soon," Mrs. Coleman says. "Be safe and call me if you need anything."

She kisses Anderson's head, and we start toward the door.

"Later," Ronan calls without looking up from his phone.

We exit into the hallway and I go back to regulating my breath. Maybe I should take up Mom and Kate on their offer to do some breathing exercises with me.

"All right, well, let's start with what's close," Anderson says, walking across the hall to another apartment.

Before I can say anything, he knocks on the door.

It's opened by a white woman who looks to be in her forties.

She eyes Anderson and me. "Can I help you?"

"Sorry to bother you, ma'am," Anderson says. "We're friends of Steven Lebedev, who lived right across the hall. We have some questions about the day he passed, looking for some closure."

Smart to use his real name.

"I don't know him." Her expression is pinched.

"If you have a moment, maybe you saw or heard . . ." Anderson adds.

She looks directly at him. "I'm going to call the cops; you're trespassing on private property."

"Excuse me? He lives . . ." I start, but she's already slamming the door in our faces.

"That went well," Anderson jokes, before moving on. "Way to back me up."

I open my mouth, and an acidic burp comes out. I should have brought my Pepto. "You know I'm not good with speaking."

Anderson puts a hand on my shoulder. "You tried. She seems like the kind of woman who doesn't wear masks in pandemics and freaks out at people in customer service." He shakes his head. "On the bright side, I know building management."

"Speaking as a white woman, it's basically a fact that rich white women are the worst," I say. "I worked a summer job at my uncle's gelato shop. This is from experience."

It's true. I cried three times at that job, and all three were caused by rude white women in nice cars coming from their plastic surgeon in Beverly Hills or whatever they do in their free time besides harassing underpaid teenagers.

"You are preaching to the choir," Anderson says. "Hopefully the next one goes better."

There's no one at the next door over, so we cross the hall, past Mr. Conspiracy's apartment to the next door. Apartment 204.

Anderson knocks.

It opens, this time to Queen Elizabeth. Right in front of me.

I freeze. It's so weird. To see her standing right here.

"Sorry to bother you, ma'am," Anderson starts, giving the same excuse for help that he gave to the woman across the hall. He has to speak over the music in the background, which I'm pretty sure is from *West Side Story*.

I'm staring at Queen Elizabeth.

Of course, it makes sense this is her apartment. She's on the opposite side of Mr. Conspiracy from Anderson. I just didn't think it through from this angle.

"I'm not sure how much help I'll be . . . I can try though.

Come on in," she says, practically sweeping her long gown across the wooden floor to make room for us. Anderson steps in first, and I follow. "I like your shirt," she says to me.

"Thanks," I awkwardly mumble.

As if on cue, the two cats walk over to see us. The fluffy white one and the tabby both look directly at me. It's almost like they know.

My heart beats a little faster.

No. They're cats. Even if they do know, it's not like they can say anything.

"These are my boys, Verdi and Puccini," Queen Elizabeth says. "And you can call me Florence."

Florence, Florence, Florence, I repeat in my mind to avoid accidentally using her nickname aloud.

"I'm Anderson, and this is Bianca," Anderson says.

Queen Eliza—Florence shakes our hands. She has a strong grip despite her wrinkled and splotchy skin. "Please, have a seat," she adds.

Anderson and I awkwardly sit on the couch so she can take the chair. The cat I believe is Verdi immediately jumps up onto the couch and sits on my lap. So even if he knows I'm a creep, at least he likes me. I scratch him behind the ears, and he purrs.

It smells like potpourri, which reminds me of my nonna's bathroom in an oddly nice way. Between that and the purring cat, my shoulders relax.

I run my hand across Verdi. Okay. That actually kind of helps with how tense I am, even if pieces of fur stick to my palms.

"It's really a tragedy," Florence starts. "I'm sorry for your loss."

She has a nice voice. It's fairly low, although maybe a bit higher than mine, but richer and resonant. Mom would love her.

"Thank you," Anderson says, sounding more assured than I feel. I'm ready to toss up a cushion and hide myself within the couch.

FEAR #47: BEING CAUGHT IN A LIE

The song changes to something more intense, which I unfortunately recognize as *Les Mis*. Guess Queen Elizabeth is into theater like my mom and Kate.

As if catching my thoughts, Florence moves the needle off the record, pausing the music. "My apologies, I adore musicals." She gives a tight smile. "What would you like to know?"

"Do you remember anything strange happening the night Steven was m . . ." Anderson clears his throat. "The night he died?"

Florence lays a hand out on the armrest. "Well, there was one thing . . ." She leans forward a bit, almost like we're sharing gossip. "I thought I heard a small argument, although I couldn't make out the words. I remember finding that strange, as I *never* heard voices coming from that apartment. I don't think he's ever had a visitor, and I'm not really out that much." She shrugs. "I'm a bit shocked to know he had friends at all, sorry for saying."

"I live next door, on the other side, and delivered his groceries," Anderson says. "He helped us with our computer and math homework."

I guess saying Mr. Conspiracy paid him to pick up groceries

and left bird drawings for me is a lot weirder and might require more follow-up questions.

"Ah, I knew I recognized you. Your brother is such a handsome young man. He helped me find poor Puccini when he ran out into the hall." She smiles. "Tell Ronan dear that me and the boys say hello."

"He's great," Anderson agrees. "And I will."

As adorable as that is, what Queen Elizabeth heard that night matches what I saw. There definitely was someone else in Mr. Conspiracy's apartment.

"But the argument you heard . . . It wasn't like a TV or anything?" Anderson asks.

"It didn't sound like it, at least," Florence says. "And I've never heard him watching anything before. Honestly, not a peep came from that place in all the years I've been here."

I don't even recall seeing a TV in his apartment, and I'm pretty sure he wouldn't be blasting a series off his computer. My family moved in five years ago, and Mr. Conspiracy has lived across the street from us that entire time, and at a distance, his behavior was fairly consistent. Even if I didn't really start my intense people-watching until I was fourteen, it's clear he hasn't had any in-person friends in a long time.

"He had a nephew," I blurt. "Did you ever see him?"

Queen Elizabeth leans back and thinks. "Like I said, he didn't seem to get many visitors. But I know he constantly wrote letters. He asked me to take them to the post office on occasion so he wouldn't have to leave. Perhaps he sent those to his nephew? Or he could have visited during the times that I was out. Maybe he was just very quiet about it." She brightens. "I remember seeing a few envelopes he sent with little drawings on them! Birds and flowers, that kind of thing. Those may have been for family."

It hurts a little when I swallow this time. Did Mr. Conspiracy start making the drawings for me because he missed his nephew? It probably did start earlier this year, now that I think about it.

"We have reason to believe someone was threatening him," Anderson continues, bringing me back to the conversation. "Did you notice anything that seemed, well, threatening?"

He must really have been watching a lot of *Case Closed*, because he's good at this. I'm still sitting with my back too straight, petting the cat that's sitting on my lap in a happy little loaf, and trying to push away anxious thoughts.

"Nothing in particular . . ." Florence starts. "Although when I was taking the kitties to get their claws trimmed last week, I did notice something taped to his door. None of the other apartments had anything taped, but I didn't go over to look."

It's possible that someone left a threat. And if it was a written one, that would definitely mean something, because I doubt Mr. Conspiracy put his address out there often. Anderson had to pick up his deliveries from a different address; it couldn't have been easy to find him.

"That's very helpful," Anderson says. "Thank you."

"Of course." Florence adjusts the skirt of her dress before looking between us. "Do you suspect foul play?"

Anderson opens his mouth to respond, but I interject with a soft "Yes."

Florence doesn't ask for more details, she simply nods. "Well, you know where to find me. Let me know if I can be of any help."

Anderson and I give polite smiles and goodbyes, and I gently lift the cat off me and place him back on the couch. When the apartment door closes behind us, Anderson looks to me. "That wasn't so bad."

"It's at least confirmation that someone else was in the apartment." I glance over to Mr. Conspiracy's door. Even with that confirmation, it seems like we have more questions than answers.

Anderson must notice me staring because he gently gives my arm a pull. "We can probably check with a few more people."

No one else seems to have information. Anderson does most of the talking, but everyone claims they didn't see or hear anything. Neither Romeo nor Juliet was home, which was great, because I'd probably be way too awkward around them. And there was one woman who wanted to help, but both Anderson and I don't really know more than a few phrases of Spanish, so we had to apologize and leave.

Not exactly super successful, but I didn't throw up, which was something.

"I had an idea on how to find Nate," Anderson offers. "Does Mr. Conspiracy have an obituary posted yet?"

"Maybe? We can check." I take out my phone and search Steven Lebedev. There isn't a whole lot. "I don't see an obituary for him anywhere . . ." But on the second page of Google search results, there is an obituary for someone named Kira Lebedev-Ward. I click on the result. "Wait, look at this. Kira Lebedev-Ward is survived by her brother, Steven, and son, Nathaniel James. That's got to be him. Try Nathaniel James Ward."

Anderson does a search on his phone. "I found his Instagram. He hasn't posted since January."

"So either something did happen to him, or he really did just start a new life."

"Bianca?" Anderson's expression is hard to read. "I don't know if this means anything, but look at his account."

Anderson tilts his phone toward me. Nate's Instagram is filled with various pictures of birds. There's one post of him on a trail, decked out with binoculars and a field guide. He has some similarities to Mr. Conspiracy, but he looks like he gets out more, and seems . . . happier.

"I guess I reminded Mr. Conspiracy of his nephew because of the birdwatching," I say. "That's why he made the drawings for me . . . and that might be why he left this to me too."

"Left this to *us*," Anderson corrects. "Don't think you're getting all the credit when we're Twitter famous for solving this."

I roll my eyes. "So that's why you're helping me."

"I'm definitely in it for the money. And Anime Expo."

"I don't think we'd get any money."

He sighs. "At least there's Anime Expo."

I glance back down at my phone. Pretty soon, Mom and Dad will start reaching out if Kate mentions that I'm not home yet. "Well, we can try to find more on Nate tomorrow, but I should probably be getting back."

"Come on, I'll walk you home, it's dark out."

Even though my house is right across the street, I don't argue. It's nice having someone to walk with.

"By the way," Anderson says. "You're caught up on *My Hero Academia*, right?"

"Of course," I say, before we get into a discussion about the anime.

I'm about to go into a theory I have regarding the ending when we approach the front door to my family's town house, and there's something on it.

"What the hell?" I ask.

Anderson walks up to it first, and based on his expression, it's not anything good.

I take a few steps closer.

Taped to my door is one of those cat toy attachments made up of three feathers, each of the feathers speckled with what looks like blood. On a white paper next to it, also possibly written in blood, are the words WATCH YOUR BACK.

"I'm assuming the threat on Mr. Conspiracy's door looked something like this," Anderson says.

My chest tightens and my head spins. I might be in danger of passing out.

"Yeah," I squeak as I make a mental note of

FEAR #58: WHATEVER THE FUCK THIS IS

TWELVE

WHAT THE PUCK?

Coming out to my parents is going to be hard, but having to tell them I've been threatened will probably be a close second. At least Anderson sent his mom a message letting her know he'd be a little late and stayed with me to break the news to my family.

It would be a tense situation, coming clean about being threatened, if not for the smell of capers from Dad's chicken piccata in the kitchen.

Mom and Dad are cuddled on the couch, both with concerned expressions, and Kate has the *Little Shop of Horrors* libretto across her chest as she reclines sideways on the armchair.

"So," Kate says. "If I'm understanding correctly, Bianca was threatened by like an actual serial killer."

She gestures to the bloody feathers and the note now on the coffee table.

Dad turns to me. "Why would anyone threaten you?"

"Really, dear, you don't *do* anything," Mom not-so-helpfully adds.

I gulp, palms sticking to my pants now. This whole situation is so uncomfortable. Maybe it was a bad idea to tell them. I feel bad for Anderson, who has to sit through this with me.

No, it would definitely be wrong not to tell my family. What if someone tries to break in when I'm not home and hurts them? It's smart to tell them.

Sucks it has to be this freaking awkward.

"Anderson and I are investigating the neighbor's murder," I say. "It was all my idea though. So, mostly me."

Mom and Dad both look shocked. Anderson gives me a nod in what I think is encouragement.

"I thought you changed your mind and agreed it was suicide?" Mom winces after she speaks, like she's not sure that's the right thing to say, but none of her plays or acting books prepared her for this scenario.

"Well, if she's being threatened, I think it's safe to say that was a cover-up." Kate slides across the chair to sit a little more normally, libretto placed to the side. "This is like *Unsolved Mysteries.*"

"What you are saying," Dad says slowly, "is that a murderer is after my teenage daughter and her best friend."

My skin is practically crawling. Anderson's fingers dig into the carpet as he responds. "Seems like it."

"Huh," Dad says. "If they do anything to hurt either one of you, I'll kill this person."

Kate sits up. "I don't know. I'm not condoning murder, but if someone is about to kill you and Anderson, I'd also kill them."

"Can we cool it with the talk of killing?"

"That's all I'm saying," Dad adds. "I'll protect you both from anyone."

"I appreciate that, Mr. Torre," Anderson manages to say, although I'll probably have to apologize profusely for my family's behavior.

"Well, you're Bianca's only friend," Dad says. "If anything happens to you, she'll be a shut-in."

Oh my God. There is about to be a murder in this building, too.

"That's a good point though," Mom says. "Not Bianca as a shut-in, but we should talk about this with your family, Anderson." She bites her lip as she looks at him. "They should know since Bianca went and involved you too."

Mom isn't always the best with wording, but she's not wrong.

Within fifteen minutes, Anderson's parents and Ronan are crowded around the table with my family, eating chicken piccata. Because my dad doesn't know how to cook without making mounds of leftovers, there's more than enough for everyone.

What would have normally been an incredibly awkward situation is made slightly less uncomfortable given that the threat to my, and potentially Anderson's, life is at the forefront. Although Anderson wasn't as keen to share with his parents our impromptu murder investigation.

"Bianca broke into the dead man's apartment?" Mr. Coleman

asks. He's a little shorter than Mrs. Coleman and has Anderson's eyes. He's in his work clothes, as he just got home when Anderson called them over. "To see if he was murdered."

"He was definitely murdered," Ronan interjects. "Weird guy." He then looks over at my dad. "Mr. Torre, this chicken is awesome."

"Grazie," Dad says, like one of those college students who studied abroad one semester and suddenly can't say *cappuccino* without an accent. Sure, he was born in Italy, but he moved here when he was like thirteen.

"I second the chicken," Mr. Coleman continues. "But what the hell?"

"I mean, bad decisions aside," Kate starts, because she always wants to be included on the adult side of things, "I think we can agree whoever is behind this is some creepy-ass motherfucker."

"Kate," Mom warns. "Language." She swats her arm. "Even if, yes, they are."

No one seems to disagree with that.

"Can I see the murder note?" Ronan asks.

"Don't call it the murder note," Mrs. Coleman says. "No one's getting murdered."

"Well, someone got murdered, so." Ronan sips his water.

I stand to grab the note, but the feathers are no longer there. I glance around the living room floor but can't find them anywhere. "Mom, did you move the evidence?"

"What?" she calls.

I step back into the kitchen. "The feathers. They aren't there."

Everyone goes quiet at that point, making it easy to hear a low growl from the hallway.

"Jesu, Giuseppe, e Maria, *Puck*!" Kate groans as she pushes her chair back and rushes over.

I hand off the note to Ronan before following my sister. Puck has the bloodied feathers clenched in her teeth, holding tight as Kate tries to gently pull them away.

Not sure what that will do if Mom and I take it to the police as evidence. If they actually decide to take me seriously.

Kate finally gets the feathers free and hands me the cat-spit-coated, chewed-up threat.

"Thanks," I say.

"You doing okay?" Kate asks. "I mean, this is a lot."

It's kind of nice. Between the chaos and figuring out what to do with this, no one else really stopped to check on me.

"I don't know," I say.

And it's the truth. It's like I'm okay and very not okay at the same time.

"Is Anderson all right?" she asks.

"Probably the same."

"They're going to tell you two to stop investigating this," Kate says.

I nod.

Honestly, at this point, we probably should.

Whatever we are getting involved in seems a little too big for us. I've barely discovered anything, and they somehow know where I live?

Maybe it's a little hypocritical but

FEAR #23: BEING WATCHED

Because unlike my creepy pastime, whoever may have been following me has actual bad intentions.

But at the same time, I'm all Mr. Conspiracy has left. Since we don't know what actually happened to Nate, I might be his only hope too.

"Something tells me you won't listen," Kate adds.

I don't answer. It's clear she can understand a lot without me talking anyway.

"You get it from me," Kate says. "They're trying to take away the Audrey II puppet for *Little Shop* and I can't let that happen."

I blink. "I think a puppet in your school show is a little different from a man who was actually killed."

"Close enough. The whole plot of *Little Shop of Horrors* revolves around Seymour growing a man-eating plant that gets out of hand. How are we supposed to do the show without the plant puppet? They are trying to murder our production, but we have a plan. I'll tell you more about the walkout when you aren't dealing with your killer thing."

I force a smile. "These situations are not even remotely the same."

"Regardless, I'm proud of you." She pats me on the shoulder. "And I sincerely hope you don't die."

With her kind-of heartwarming statement and the remaining evidence in hand, Kate and I walk back into the kitchen, and everyone looks over to us.

"Did we come to some sort of agreement?" Kate asks.

"I'm going to report this incident," Mom starts.

"And no one is going inside that dead man's place again," Mrs. Coleman adds. "You got that?"

Her brown eyes look right into mine until I nod, and she does the same to Anderson, Kate, and Ronan, just in case.

Mr. Coleman nods. "And if anything happens, we better hear about it."

"Got it," I say.

Technically, no one said anything about not investigating. They said not to go back to Mr. Conspiracy's place. Given that Anderson already has the diary, we should be able to keep looking into it but not be quite so obvious and put ourselves in danger.

Besides, these VQ people, the murderers, they already know where I live at this point. Who knows if staying out of it will actually help?

"Also, Bianca, I had an idea . . ." Anderson starts with a smile. "If you're free tomorrow after school."

I'm free and he knows it.

"Okay," I say.

"Don't worry," Mr. Coleman says. "It's a good idea."

"A great one," Anderson adds.

FEAR #58.5: ANDERSON'S "GREAT IDEAS"

THIRTEEN

A ROSE BY ANY OTHER GENDER WOULD SMELL JUST AS SWEET

This time, on my way over to Anderson's apartment, I look over my shoulder every three seconds. It's so close to Mr. Conspiracy's place—I don't want to give the potential murderer-stalker the wrong idea.

After one more check down the hall both ways, I knock on Anderson's door.

He opens it and looks me up and down. "What the hell are you wearing?"

I glance at my own jeans and oversize purple T-shirt. "This is what I always wear."

"You need clothes you can move in," he says.

What the hell does that mean? Did my mom pay him to trick me into one of her acting classes or something? "You never said what we're doing."

"Come on, we can see if Ronan has something."

I don't argue, because he's the one who invited me, and I'm still the sheep. I follow him into his apartment and over to Ronan's door without another word.

"Ronan? You have any workout clothes that might fit Bianca?" Anderson calls through the door.

"Workout clothes?" I ask.

Ronan opens the door. He has on a button-down shirt with a floral print and shorts. "Hey, Bianca. And yeah, sure."

Ronan walks over to his dresser and pulls out a few things. He hands them to me. "Let me know if these don't work."

"Thanks," I say.

Although I'm questioning what Anderson has planned and trying to come up with potential excuses to get out of it, I head into the bathroom and change into Ronan's clothes. We're fairly close in height, so the fit isn't bad. I pull down the green shirt over the loose basketball shorts.

I was basically wearing the equivalent of a sports bra anyway, so I still look like I barely have boobs at all. But there's something different about this look. It's boyish, almost. I kind of like it. How masculine I look. I have a sharp jaw. I hold my hair back behind my shoulders, so it seems like I cut most of the brown strands off.

I smile. I'm not really used to liking my reflection. Even my normal brown eyes seem a little more sparkly, like I'm more myself than I've ever been.

I quickly tie my hair back and exit the bathroom, my clothes balled up in the crook of my arm.

"You look good," Anderson says. "Ready?"

Absolutely not.

"Sure," I say.

"We'll be back," Anderson calls to Ronan.

"Thanks for the clothes," I add.

"No problem," Ronan says. "Try not to get murdered."

It's actually kind of a valid concern.

Anderson throws a large gym bag around his shoulder and leads me back out of the apartment. We start down the sidewalk, heading down Victory Boulevard. He immediately starts to talk about anime, and about ten minutes pass before I'm actually able to interject the subject change.

"Are you going to tell me where we're going?" I ask.

"You asked about getting some muscle, right?" Anderson taps his gym bag. "What better way to do that than also showing you how to punch creeps in the face?"

He points ahead to an MMA gym.

"What." I look at him. "You were serious about this?"

Anderson smiles and walks me inside. It's bigger than it looked from the outside. There's a huge floor of mats to the right, where people are grappling in tight clothes. I watch UFC fights with my dad when the neighbors aren't home for me to watch instead, but just because I've seen people fight doesn't mean I know how they do it.

In the back, there's a full-ass octagon, and over to the right, a whole array of punching bags.

And while I've never really thought about it much before:

FEAR #59: GETTING MY ASS KICKED

111

FEAR #60: ALSO . . . RINGWORM

"I don't know about this . . ." I start.

"I'm not going to throw you in the ring with someone," Anderson says. "I'll only show you a few things."

I really doubt Anderson is going to actually punch me, so I guess being shown a few things can't hurt.

"Okay," I say, although it doesn't sound that sure.

Before we step in, I have to sign two waivers I really should read through but don't.

"We don't mess around," Anderson says.

"Fair," I say. After signing the waivers, I squeeze hand sanitizer from the bottle at the front desk. The idea of injuries are bad enough, but getting sick might be even worse.

FEAR #4: PANDEMICS

It used to be #41, but that changed. Everything else shifted and now

FEAR #41: RABBITS

Once both Anderson and I are cleared to enter, he leads me over to the punching bags where there aren't many other people. He starts taking things out of his bag. "I have an old pair of gloves for you, because rental gloves are gross as hell. Also, these wraps are unopened, so don't worry about that."

"Okay," I say.

"I'm assuming you don't know how to wrap your hands." Anderson holds up the pack of two black rolls.

"Good assumption."

"Hold your hands out and spread your fingers."

I follow his instructions. He unravels one of the wraps and

puts the loop around my thumb. Then he keeps winding around my knuckles, my wrist, and between my fingers in some order I can't follow, until the Velcro closes around my forearm.

"This looks badass," I say, squeezing and opening my fist.

"Right?"

Imagine. Me, a lesbian sheep, looking badass. Wild.

Anderson wraps my other hand and both of his before turning to me. "Before we even put the gloves on, let's work on your stance. How do you think you'd stand if you're about to fight?"

I put my hands up like they do in *Megalobox* because that's really all I got.

"Jesus," Anderson says. "Is it okay if I touch you?"

"Sure."

"You right- or left-handed?"

"Left."

Anderson grins. "Nice, a southpaw."

He adjusts my legs so they are more spread out, my left foot in the back. Then squares up my torso and lifts my hands higher. "You want to defend your face, so keep your hands up." He moves into a fighting position. "I learned more of a Muay Thai stance, so my front heel is off the ground."

I copy Anderson well enough, and he shows me the difference between a jab, cross, hook, and uppercut.

"It's in the hips," he adds after a few attempts. "That's where the power is, even if you aren't huge."

We keep going through the motions until my stance is good enough, and then I get the gloves on and practice with the heavy bag. Anderson calls out combinations for me to follow and starts to go into some of the head movements to avoid punches.

We continue on until Ronan's shirt is sticking to me.

"Nice work," Anderson says. "You're a natural."

"Shut up," I say, but I feel super flattered anyway.

I catch a glimpse of myself in the mirror, and I'm almost unrecognizable. No one would mistake me for a lesbian sheep looking like this.

I won't ever be a lion, like queen Amanda Nunes, but maybe I'm on my way to a little kitten.

A tiny weak kitten practically straight from the womb and scared of everything, but one with claws, nonetheless.

It's also kind of weird because I feel . . . hot. A little masculine and tough. I like it. I want to live in it.

As we take off our wraps and reroll them, Anderson keeps watching me.

"What?" I ask.

"Nothing," he says. "I never saw you smile like you are right now."

I didn't even realize it, really. Once the words sink in, it's like my cheeks practically hurt. I guess I enjoyed that more than I thought I would.

"You should come back with me," Anderson says.

"Yeah," I say.

And it's about as much of a promise as I've ever made.

Puck curls up next to me, purring, as I randomly scroll through Twitter on my phone. It's a way to pass the time. I mostly retweet birds and cat memes. The only things I actually tweet myself are pictures of Puck. Not that my Instagram account is more than birds, my cat, and anime memes, but I use it to follow the GLAOE account, Kate, and Anderson.

And Elaine Yee.

At the thought, I quickly switch over to her newest selfie, which I didn't double-tap earlier, because I saw it the same minute she posted it and I don't want her to know how desperate and thirsty I am.

But Twitter is different. When I reopen the app, my time line is flooded with queer content. I keep it on private, and I can follow whoever I want, since it's not like anyone besides my sister knows about it. I don't use my full name; my handle is Bianca-Birder06. Jeffrey from the GLAOE somehow found me and tried to follow me there, but I didn't accept it. Twitter is my space where I don't have to worry about liking posts from other lesbians or way too much *One Piece* content.

As I scroll, a meme pops up that is along the lines of "my only gender is tired," and it kind of hits me different.

Dealing with creepy threats from a murderer is tiring enough, but . . . what if my gender identity has something to do with how I've been feeling? I'm a little familiar with some of the terms but didn't make a connection.

Since it's only the cat and me in my room now, I go to the search bar and type in *nonbinary*.

I mean, just in case. It's like the thought has been there for a while, but I've never allowed myself to really explore and consider it.

I don't know. Today has me feeling some kind of way.

While there's things I enjoy about femininity, I never quite connected to it. Like I'm not actually a woman, I'm some kind of anxious void in a femme bodysuit. I'm attracted to girls, but I guess I don't necessarily consider myself one. Words like "sister," "daughter," and "woman," feel like masks I've worn, but the masculine counterparts don't quite work either.

The idea of looking into my identity—my gender as something more complex than the letters *F* or *XX*—sends a thrill through me, an excited little flutter of the chest, like hummingbird wings.

But it's confusing too, because if I'm not a woman, or not only a woman, does that make me not a lesbian? Or if I'm interested in women and other nonbinary people, should I consider myself bisexual? That doesn't seem right. I can probably still use lesbian because I'm attracted to women and maybe I still have some connection to femininity. I think. Is the doubt I'm feeling ridiculous and a product of my overthinking and exposure to label gatekeeping?

Probably. Nonbinary lesbian pops up a few times, and that feels nice at least.

I take a breath and scroll through the tweets. There's a lot of people posting selfies and claiming the nonbinary label with LGBTQ+ hashtags. I hate that a little jealousy rises up in me. I have no right. I should be able to come out.

Well, coming out as lesbian alone is one thing. I'm not sure how my parents would feel about me possibly-most-likely-perhaps-definitely not being cis. We've never really talked about other genders, so I don't know how they'd react. Dad might be okay with it. He was raised Catholic, but he's not remotely religious now and is open-minded when it comes to sexuality and gender issues. That doesn't mean he'll be one hundred percent supportive of me, but there's a good chance. Mom . . . well, she's another story.

Her all-female productions don't exactly scream nonbinary inclusion. She's already made comments about me not being feminine enough, not wearing the right clothes or doing the right things. It's almost like she knows I somehow missed the necessary components to be a girl and overcompensates to get me to make up for it. If I had a dollar for every time I heard her say she's so happy to have daughters and not sons, I'd be able to buy myself an entirely new wardrobe, just to try it out. She acts more like the kind of feminist that puts down men to hold up women.

If I'm not a man or a woman, I don't really know what she'd think of me.

I come across a chart that shows the 3D-spectrum nature of gender and how it goes beyond a simple understanding of solely two genders, and nonbinary isn't some midpoint between male and female. The more I read into these types of genderqueer identities, the more they fit. I move from Twitter to Google and look up some additional points and terms.

Like, for example, my gender expression can differ from my gender identity, and presenting as female wouldn't make me less nonbinary. Even if I'm gender fluid, my masculinity doesn't have to fit the textbook definition—however I look and feel is non-binary because I'm nonbinary.

Just thinking that makes me giggle.

I'm nonbinary.

It's kind of wild that I assumed there is a right and wrong way to have a specific identity.

And there are some labels that resonate with me. If I primarily identity as female but also as nonbinary, I could be demigirl. But I don't think I like the *girl* at all, as I take comfort in the masc side of me. Demiboy seems maybe a little too far in that direction. It's not a linear scale though. Maybe genderflux would fit?

I scan the description. I'm not sure I really connect to a female identity much at all, so maybe nonbinary alone is fine to say. It's hard to grasp what I'm feeling, but this strange excitement continues to build within me.

It kind of feels like, no matter what terms I may settle on, for the first time, I'm not leaving a major part of myself behind. I can include all of me into my identity, even if for now, no one else knows. Even if I'm not exactly sure how to name it or define it.

It's like I'm allowing myself to know what it feels like, at least.

I'm both tearing up and smiling. A laugh escapes me. It's so silly. I feel like I'm meeting myself for the first time.

I come across a link for a Los Angeles nonbinary and transgender support group. I enter the address into my maps app. It's close. Maybe I could go?

Just to see.

My phone buzzes, breaking me away from my thoughts.

It buzzes again, with another text delivered. I quickly bookmark the page; I can sit on this for a little and figure it out. I doubt I'd be able to go alone anyway, if at all.

FEAR #37: OPENING UP TO STRANGERS

One more buzz from my phone. Everyone in my family is already home and can just come talk to me directly, which means it is definitely . . .

> **Anderson:** I'll bring the diary to school tomorrow—we can look into it more during lunch

> **Anderson:** we can try to get more info on this VQ and Nate

A part of me instantly wants to make some excuse to meet him after school instead, but he's the one who brought it up. Maybe it's fine if we hang out in school. It's not like I'm *Naruto*-running through the halls. Just being friends with me wouldn't make Anderson seem uncool.

I sigh. I shouldn't be worried about it if he isn't.

We're friends, and I don't have to think beyond that.

> Sounds good

I feel like I always sound angry through text messages. I don't want Anderson to think I'm being moody or anything, so I quickly type out a

> :)

> **Anderson:** see you then, striker

> Shut up

Another text quickly comes in. This time from Jillian. I can't help but smile at it. I'm sure she wouldn't think differently of me if I told her about my gender feelings. The only binary in her head when it comes to people is birders and nonbirders.

Jillian: I have the internship recommendation done for you! Would you be able to stop by tomorrow to pick it up? The museum will only take physical letters to make sure they aren't altered, so I want to give it to you properly, and just check in!

Jillian texts exactly how she speaks, all songbird energy and proper grammar.

I've never been over to Jillian's place before, but I know she doesn't live that far. I can probably get Kate to drive me over.

Sure, thank you so much

:)

She texts me the address and I confirm I'll meet her there at five thirty. I am kind of curious as to what her house looks like. Maybe she actually has a really cool birdwatching setup.

"Bianca!" my mom calls from downstairs. "I'm doing laundry—get your dirty clothes."

I slide out of bed and force myself to start picking up things. Maybe I should tell Mom I want to start doing my own laundry. I'll need to if I want to get masculine clothes like I was able to borrow from Ronan today. Most of what I have now is from the women's section, even if it doesn't pass for what Mom accepts as feminine.

I don't really want to deal with what she'll say.

I grab a pair of jeans I left discarded on the floor next to my bed. As I throw them over my arm, a piece of paper flutters out of the pocket. I pick it up and unfold it.

Anna's hummingbird.

I completely forgot that I took this from Mr. Conspiracy's apartment.

Now that I'm holding it up close, I can make out the breath-taking detail. The way he blended the colors together, strokes delicate to give the appearance of real feathers.

I can also make out a pencil marking in the upper left corner. I definitely didn't notice that before.

I slide the paper onto my nightstand so it's right under the lamp and I can read the message.

VQ EX-MEMBER. 11.18. 7:15AM. 5753 PICCOLO STREET

My heart pounds in my chest. It looks like Mr. Conspiracy had a meeting planned with someone who was involved in VQ.

I have to tell Anderson about this.

Closing out of my open internet tabs, I snap a picture of the message and text it to Anderson.

I don't really have time to focus on keeping more queer secrets from my family, or to look for places where I can start to buy masculine clothes. Not with Nate missing, Mr. Conspiracy dead, and this new development.

Still.

No time to question your gender identity like the middle of a murder investigation.

FOURTEEN

THE ANSWER LIES IN DESTRUCTION

It's a nice day, sunny, but cool enough to wear a sweater, so Anderson and I take our lunches outside to study Mr. Conspiracy's diary. While it's definitely a lot better than it would be in the crowded cafeteria, there are curious eyes peering in our direction. It makes my sweater ten times itchier around my neck, and I keep pulling on it and wishing I wore a hoodie or flannel like normal.

People are definitely making comments. Talking about us.

FEAR #18: HAVING RUMORS SPREAD ABOUT ME

It was never an issue. Most people don't really know me, at least, not as more than Kate's sibling. Not enough to have a strong opinion.

And honestly, I'm good with that.

But everybody knows Anderson.

What they don't know is why he'd bother hanging out with me.

"Have people been asking about us?" I tug at the ends of my sleeves. "Or, not us. Why you're hanging out with me?"

"Maybe," Anderson says. "I just tell them you're cool."

I don't really know how that's a believable response.

"I'm sorry," I say. I don't really know what I'm apologizing for.

Anderson's eyebrows lift. "You don't have to be sorry. I don't care about people talking."

I wish I didn't. "Sure . . . but I know you don't want all the anime stuff coming out, so I don't want people to make connections or anything."

"It'll be fine, it's not like you come to school in cosplay." Anderson shrugs. "And I care about you and what we're doing more than any rumors or anything. It's all good."

He doesn't really give me a chance to respond, just goes right back to the book.

I try to ignore any intrusive thoughts and focus on other things. The grass beneath my feet, legs dangling slightly off the edge of the ledge we sit on. The palm trees towering to the left of us. The fact that, at least for this fifty-minute period, we get to be in outside air and away from the barely windowed classrooms.

We're not really finding anything, though.

Keeping my voice low, I read one of the entries involving VQ.

"'I know what they are doing. VQ is a cover. It's widespread in the city. Hollywood connections? Unsure. This is big. This is what Nate was trying to get away from' . . . Who are they, though?" I ask the diary like it will tell me.

"He also refers to a whole section on Hollywood executive conspiracies," Anderson says, peering at the book.

"Given the way I've been threatened, I'm going to assume we should focus on the conspiracy at hand."

Anderson looks up excitedly. "We could totally have a crime-solving show."

"We should probably solve a crime first . . ."

"A, B, Conspiracies?" Anderson frowns. "Name's a work in progress."

I laugh despite myself. "Come on. Focus." I smack him with the diary. "Although an animated series would be cool."

Anderson widens his eyes, probably ready to procrastinate more by going into that, when a voice interrupts.

"Hey, Anderson," Ryan Pérez says, passing with an obvious pipe in his hand. "And . . . hey . . . Anderson's friend," he adds to me.

Ryan's one of the popular types, and not the kind to have shared common ground of a love for anime.

"Hi," I say softly.

"What's up?" Anderson asks.

"Nothing much." He eyes our books. "You two studying?"

"Yeah, I'm tutoring Bianca," Anderson says.

"Dude, you should help me in chem."

"Sure, just let me know when."

"We can do group study sessions!" Ryan smiles. "Is it cool if I chill out here with you both?"

Anderson looks to me. I was sort of just watching the conversation play out and not expecting to be involved. But I should answer. It would be weird and probably rude to say no, but talking about a dead guy's diary isn't exactly normal either.

"Sure," I say, voice high. "Maybe you can also help me with this . . . extra credit thing Ms. Richards gave me. It's like . . . a mystery."

For some reason, Ryan takes a seat right next to me on the ledge. I'm surprised he doesn't sit on Anderson's side, but I guess it makes sense since I'm currently holding the diary.

"I'm not going to lie, I'm incredibly high right now, but sure," Ryan says.

I mean, maybe you need to be high to understand Mr. Conspiracy's thoughts. Figuring I may as well take the chance, I hand over the diary. I have pictures of every page saved to a Google Drive folder anyway.

"Be careful with that," Anderson says.

"Relax." Ryan flips through the pages. "I'm, like, so careful." He slowly looks through the pages. "This is wild."

"Right?" Anderson bites into his sandwich, hovering close as he looks over my shoulder. I playfully shove him back to avoid sauce dripping on me.

I hate to admit it, but I'm trying to look closely too. See if there's anything I missed in the style of the handwriting, or some kind of important information Anderson and I both overlooked. But despite mentions of VQ, Mr. Conspiracy never seems to go into what they're actually doing or who they are.

I'm kind of awkwardly close to Ryan, to the point where I can tell his eyelashes are long and I spot a small freckle to the side of his nose over his golden-brown skin.

"Wait a minute," Ryan says. He holds the diary up to the sun before closing it and setting it on his lap. He squeezes the cover between two fingers. "I either have a great idea, or a not-great idea," Ryan says. "But I'm going to go for it."

"Okay . . ." I say slowly.

He rips off the corner of the cover, and before either Anderson or I can protest, he tears it open into what looks like two pages.

"What the hell?" Anderson snaps and snatches back the diary, reaching over me to grab it from Ryan.

"There was a drawing on the inside," Ryan says.

Anderson drops his gaze to the diary, and my eyes follow. Where the cover was ripped open, there is a sketch of a symbol. It's a small bird silhouette—it looks like a shorebird, but it's not clear which one—with a sword above and below it.

"What the hell?" Anderson repeats, but this time, it's sprinkled with awe.

"You're welcome," Ryan says. "And that's on me. See you." He gives me a smile and does like a little bow. "Nice speaking with you, Bianca. You seem cool. Let me know if you wanna smoke or study sometime."

It's really flattering. Like maybe people don't actually think I'm all that weird and just don't really have an opinion of me. That would be nice—then it'd be easier for people like Ryan to consider me another one of the guys.

Which is . . . exciting?

"Sure, Ryan, you too."

Wait, did that come across as a yes? Was he actually asking me or was it an I'm Only Saying This to Be Polite invitation? I need to focus on the weird symbol we uncovered before my thoughts derail and I question this interaction for the rest of the day.

With one last wave, Ryan heads off, and a part of me is almost sad to see him go.

"Does this help us?" Anderson asks, holding up the new clue.

"Not sure," I admit. "It's something, though."

"Definitely something." Anderson rubs his left temple. "This keeps getting weirder."

"You can say that again," I mumble, looking back down at the symbol.

It's not detailed enough to really tell the species, it's more of an outline, but still, effort was put into this drawing. Like Mr. Conspiracy needed to capture the symbol exactly right. The shading is delicate, the edges crisp.

I take a picture of it with my phone.

Anderson looks like he wants to say something but then looks past me. "Is that your sister?"

I twist my body to catch a glimpse of the growing scene. Kate stands on the steps that lead to the school with a microphone, a whole mess of students around, listening in. Cory Kowalski stands near her, the breeze no match for his perfectly styled hair.

I toss my things in my backpack, the diary included, and

walk closer. I can hear Anderson following, but I don't really look back—I'm too busy trying to figure out what's happening.

Kate must have said something interesting, because the crowd has their phones out, recording and livestreaming. There are a lot of cheers and whoops. Then Yoneta Ocana, one of Kate's best friends and fellow theater geek, steps up in front of Kate and Cory. Yoneta ties her curls back and then immediately launches into "Over the Moon" from *Rent*.

And she can really sing.

I still have no idea what this gathering is.

Creeping around the crowd and trying to avoid getting in too many livestreams, Anderson and I walk over to Kate, and I pull her aside.

"What is all this?" I ask.

More students keep coming outside, pouring from the front doors of the school and adding to the already large crowd. I know Kate doesn't have fifth-period lunch. Maybe this is some weird drama club event?

"I told you, the walkout. Well, like a walkout-strike-concert mash-up," Kate says, like that makes perfect sense. "We've been planning it since the PTA decided we need the preview performance of *Little Shop of Horrors*. We're also selling tickets for that."

Anderson looks as clueless as I do.

"Why?" he asks.

"The treatment of the arts at this school," Kate says, voice raised so we can hear her but not too loud to distract from the performance. "First, the school literary magazine is straight-up shut down due to reallocation of budget, and now they officially killed Audrey II."

For a second, I don't think I hear her correctly. That's when I notice the #BringBackAudreyII and #NoPuppetNoPerformance banners.

Anderson and I share a look before I respond.

"As in the man-eating plant puppet? From the musical?"

She nods. "Yep. They keep saying the actual plant is too close to marijuana." She points to the right of us. "That is what they want to do instead."

I follow her finger to the senior who I believe is cast as Audrey II in the show, literally wearing a green morph suit with fake plant leaves glued to it.

It's bad. Like ruin-the-show bad.

"How is *that* any better?" I ask, unable to sugarcoat my tone and expression.

"Also . . . didn't they do a show last year that literally took place in a strip club?" Anderson asks. "That seems worse."

"Basically. It was *Cabaret* and they even used iced tea to pass as whiskey."

"And that's more acceptable than a sentient plant?" Anderson asks. "That makes no sense."

Kate looks put together, but I can tell she's disappointed. "I didn't want to ask either of you to get involved, you have a lot going on already." Even her gaze is a little glassy as she meets Anderson's eyes. "But you're right, it doesn't make sense. There are rumors that there's been some issues with the budget and that's what this is really about. Like, come on! My character in the show literally has an abusive dentist boyfriend, and later *dies*, and the PTA is upset because one of the characters is a plant? It doesn't even look like weed!"

"I'm sorry, Kate." I don't know what else to say, but something does seem off about the situation. "Do you really think there's some issue with the budget?"

She wipes at her eyes now, finally showing a bit of her feelings. "I mean, probably. First they went after the writers, and now the actors. They always take money from the arts and give it to athletics and make some ridiculous excuse. They just redid the entire soccer field and tennis courts! Who even watches tennis?"

Anderson looks at the people gathered and my sister on the brink of tears.

"If there is something weird with the budget . . ." he starts, seeming to pick up on what I was implying with my earlier question, "I have an idea on how we can find out."

FIFTEEN

LESBIAN SHEEP MEETS VALLEY QUAIL

"Why am I always the one that has to save you?" Ronan says, his arms crossed as he stands in front of Anderson.

"Because you're the best brother ever," Anderson says. "And you love me."

"True on the first part, jury's out on the second."

"Come on, Ronan," Anderson says. "I'll owe you one."

Ronan mumbles something along the lines of Anderson already owing him ten, but his brown eyes shift across the computer lab to Kate and me.

"Okay, what's going on?" Ronan asks.

Anderson takes a seat at one of the computers. "There's something weird going on with the musical."

"Oh, yeah, I heard the puppet died," Ronan says. "Someone in my D&D campaign is in the show."

"It didn't exactly die," Kate interjects. "It was brutally murdered by moms with too much time."

"Maybe take it easy on the brutal murder mentions?" I ask.

"She's right," Anderson says to Kate. "Mr. Conspiracy died like five days ago."

I flinch at *she*. I don't even really mean to. It's not like I one hundred percent know if I use other pronouns. It's something I want to figure out, and until I do, I kind of wish people wouldn't use any pronouns at all.

Just Bianca. I'm okay with my name. That's about the only thing I do have figured out related to my identity.

Of course, Anderson doesn't know.

I should tell him, but with everything going on, it hardly seems like the time.

It's so dark and quiet in here compared to everything happening outside. Technically, I'm supposed to be in math, but with the walkout, basically no one went to class anyway. I'm not sure if teachers generally use the labs, but I barely go in this section of the school at all. It's pretty much only used for the embarrassingly outdated computer science class everyone has to take freshman year.

"Bianca?" Ronan asks. "You okay?"

"She does this a lot," Kate says. "Gets lost in her thoughts."

She. Her. Goddammit. Now it's all I can notice. It shouldn't affect me this much. I *just* started thinking about it seriously last night.

I swallow the bile that rises. "Sorry." Another breath. "They can't pay the puppet rental fees," I say. "People think it might be a budgeting issue, and Anderson said you could get access to the school records."

"Is that true?" Kate presses. "Can you?"

"It's a possibility," Ronan says.

"How?" she asks, perking up.

"I am a man of many talents," Ronan says, getting into the whole cryptic-but-cool hacker thing. "Anderson and Kate, you two keep watch outside." He turns to me, and there's almost something knowing in his expression. "Bianca, can you stay in here and help?"

I nod and sit. I don't know why Ronan would want me here rather than Kate or Anderson. Sure, he doesn't really know Kate, but she's definitely the more interesting Torre. Still, she and Anderson are already outside the computer lab, gently shutting the door behind them.

Ronan starts to log in to the computer.

"How do you have an admin login?" I ask.

"Secrets of coding club," he responds. "And student council. I also volunteer in the main office."

"Wow, that's impressive."

"I'm really just nosy and like to have access to things." He gives me a big grin. "How do you think I got my name and gender changed in the system so easily?"

Ronan is the smartest person I've ever met, and that's saying something with Anderson already being near the top of our class ranking.

A moment passes as Ronan waits for the home screen to load. He looks over at me. "Speaking of . . . this is personal, and I'm sorry to bring it up like this—Bianca, have we been misgendering you?"

I don't know what I was expecting, but it wasn't that. It feels like a light punch, how I'm stricken by the question. Am I that obvious? How could I possibly be that obvious? If it's so clear that Ronan can see my discomfort with my pronouns, will everyone else notice too?

In another sense, a bigger one, relief runs through me.

"Sorry," Ronan adds. "This could be totally off base, but for some reason . . . you kind of remind me of . . . well, me, like a few years ago."

I bite my lip. I didn't necessarily want to talk about it with anyone at the moment, but this is Ronan. Out of everyone I know, he'd probably be the most understanding.

FEAR #37: OPENING UP TO STRANGERS

I know Ronan isn't a stranger, but that doesn't make it any easier. In fact, I might have to make a tiny change and revise

FEAR #36: GETTING MY HAND CAUGHT IN THE SINK GARBAGE DISPOSAL
to

FEAR #36: OPENING UP TO FRIENDS

My palms sweat again, shaking slightly, so I stick them under my thighs. My chest flutters instead. I bounce my leg to get some of the energy out.

"I don't really know," I admit. "I don't think I'm a man, but I know I'm not a woman either." I try to formulate the words into something that makes sense and hope that I don't say anything wrong. "I don't necessarily hate she/her pronouns. But I don't feel any attachment to being female really, and while I don't necessarily feel male, I'm most comfortable when I'm more masculine, even if I don't present that way. I don't know. Like the idea of being able to . . . like to encompass all of me into a *they* . . ." Now my eyes are tearing up again, and I force my gaze onto the carpeted floor. Gray, with tiny red and green squares every few centimeters. "It feels like a relief, and I get so excited."

Ronan's brown eyes are steady on me. He's listening.

"I don't want to say the wrong thing, and it's like every step of the way, I'm not sure I'm doing this right." My eyes are really watering now—I'm so embarrassed. "I think I'm a lesbian because I definitely like women, and then I read things saying I can't be? Because of some weird label gatekeeping? I like the idea of just saying I'm a nonbinary lesbian, but I shouldn't be second-guessing myself this much, right? I know I definitely don't like men, so maybe that's fine and I'm overthinking?" I brush away at my eyes because they sting a little. It makes it worse, and I'm rambling. "But that's the problem too. I'm too afraid. I can't stand up for myself, I hardly even know myself because I'm too afraid to even be me. To do anything! I'm a lesbian sheep. Or a nonbinary lesbian mess of a human equivalent to a lesbian sheep."

Ronan cracks a little smile before recovering, but lets me continue without really questioning the lesbian sheep thing. And the words keep tumbling out, like I've kept too much in for too long and my mind is overstuffed.

"So many people think of gender like . . . if being a man is blue and a woman is red, then you are one of those, or at best, you're purple. But sometimes I'm teal, sometimes I'm yellow, sometimes I'm a mix of colors or no color, but never only one or the other." That probably doesn't make sense. I close my eyes. "I just . . . I want to stop hiding parts of me," I say quietly. "Even if I don't really like most of them."

It's hard to tell Ronan's expression through my lowered eyelids that are already filled with tears. Something's wrong with me. Ronan is probably so uncomfortable. He's definitely wishing that he had Kate or Anderson stay with him in here instead.

"Want to try something?" Ronan asks.

My face heats, skin awkwardly buzzing, as I force myself to keep looking at him through my tears. "Okay."

"Bianca's awesome," Ronan starts carefully. "They were my brother's friend first, but I've always thought they're really nice."

For some reason, another tear leaks out. I can no longer bring myself to keep Ronan's gaze, so I look back down at the floor and listen.

"They went through a lot lately, but they're really trying to make things right." Ronan's voice is soft, but strong. "Not because they have to, but because they are a good person. Not to mention, my brother says they have a strong left hook."

I chuckle a bit. While my eyes keep watering, I can't stop my smile.

"They are kind of weird, to be honest, but that's why I like them," Ronan says. "And I hope they consider me a friend."

I'm at a loss for words. Strangely enough, I have the over-whelming desire to start giggling. I try to swallow the urge, but a few giggles escape. Ronan cracks another smile. I kick my legs on the chair and he directs some of his attention back to the computer, starting to go through files.

"Let me know what pronouns you want me to use," Ronan says. "And if it changes, no problem, please correct me if I'm wrong."

Maybe opening up to friends isn't that bad. Thirty-six is way too high on my list for this, so I'll push that down and make another slight revision.

FEAR #61: OPENING UP TO FRIENDS

FEAR #36: OPENING UP TO FAMILY

Because that will likely still suck.

"Maybe you can use they/them for now," I say quietly. "At least, with me. I'll use she/her around everyone else until I'm ready."

Ronan nods, but he's a little distracted with what's on-screen. "Sorry," he says. "Of course. But I got the budget."

"You, like, hacked the computer?"

Ronan gives me a look. "No, that's not how it works. I already have the admin login. I just searched 'budgets' in the files."

"Oh," I say, blushing. I try to go for a quick recovery. "Notice anything weird about it?"

"First off, our school has a big budget, so it's easy to hide stuff, but doing a quick search . . . there might be one thing."

I peer at the screen. Ronan has a folder open that seems

to hold the budget for this school year. It's a little depressing when you see what goes into the arts compared to the rest of the departments and extracurriculars. But it doesn't necessarily look weird. "What?"

"This money that's allocated to Valley Quail, Inc. The category is listed as education, but I haven't really seen any mention of them when helping in the office?" Ronan organizes the spreadsheet so the educational supply tags are lined up. "Okay, those numbers are huge compared to other educational supply sources. What are we buying from them?"

I look at the tab. It's definitely a lot of money compared to the rest of the entries within the category, but not so much it would make a huge dent in the total budget.

Valley Quail, Inc.

Wait.

"Valley Quail. Ronan, this has to be the company that Mr. Conspiracy was looking into! He was calling it VQ, and we didn't find much on it, but that's probably because we didn't have the full name."

"This is big," Ronan says. "Maybe we can find something on it now?"

Ronan opens an incognito internet tab and types the name into a browser called DuckDuckGo. Pretty much nothing comes up, except for a bird breeding supplier and information on California quails and the egg incubation period. Which I already knew is a little over twenty days.

Ronan clears the browser history and goes back to the Excel sheet.

"Okay, that's weird. They should at least have some basic online presence."

Ronan goes to an earlier saved version of this year's budget. "Whoa," he says, eyes scanning over it.

"What?"

Ronan points to the row where Valley Quail was located. It's not in this earlier version. "The theater budget was a lot higher in this draft. And the literary magazine had a whole separate line that's not in the final copy—that money was shifted to Valley Quail, Inc."

Well, at least we know where a good chunk of the musical's budget went.

"So someone suddenly added it . . ." I swallow. "Does that mean it wasn't supposed to be part of the budget initially?"

"That'd make sense. I can't imagine why they would change it later on, and no one would likely notice unless they were specifically looking for it."

"Like us. But what the hell is Valley Quail, Inc., actually?" I ask.

Ronan prints out a copy of the original and the revised budgets before exiting out.

"Who knows?" He shrugs. "It seems like Mr. Conspiracy was trying to find out. And he got killed for it."

While my stomach feels heavy, and I make a mental note to stop at my locker for a Pepto tablet, I have the feeling he's right.

SIXTEEN

REASONS TO ACTUALLY BE AFRAID

"Are you sure you'll be okay if I just drop you off?" Kate asks in the car after school. "I don't want masked murderers to kill you on your way home."

Kate had a break before her rehearsal at six and was able to take me to Jillian's house in time for our meeting. I didn't want to be rude and just rush in for the letter, so I offered to request a rideshare back. Besides, a part of me is kind of hoping I'll get to talk with Jillian about birds. I've been so caught up in the murder investigation, an evening of ornithology talk would be a welcome break.

"I'll text a picture of the Uber's license plate to you, Anderson, Mom, and Dad. That way, we're totally covered." I tap my phone. "Besides, Jillian will be there, it's not like I'm alone."

"Okay . . ." Kate expands the vowels so the one word feels like an entire sentence. "If anything happens, or seems a little weird, just call me. I don't care if I have to miss rehearsal."

There isn't anything she could've said that would prove she cares for me more. Kate Torre offering to miss rehearsal is basically like her offering to put her own life on the line. I glance at the maps app on her phone, attached to the dashboard. We're only a few minutes away.

"What does Jillian do again?" Kate quickly glances at the houses on the street around us. "I mean, this is a really nice area."

"She works at a museum," I say. "It's probably family money."

"Remind me to marry rich," Kate mutters.

I can't really blame her. I'm not super familiar with the Glendale area, but Kate's right. This is a nice neighborhood. It's much more suburban looking than where we live, and the houses are five times the size.

That doesn't mean that Jillian's house is huge.

Kate slows in front of a house that has the right numbers painted on the curb and listed on the mailbox—if *house* is even the correct term for it. It's a full-blown modern-style mansion with property that clearly stretches back beyond what is visible to us from the car.

"Wow," Kate says. "Now that yacht party makes a lot of sense."

"No kidding." I'm a little in awe of the property. It's not like I haven't seen nice places before, and I kind of figured that Jillian came from money, I just didn't realize how much.

"I'll wait until you walk in, at least." Kate shuts off the car.

I nod and shoot a quick text to Jillian.

Here

After a moment, I add a little bird emoji, because I don't want to sound mean. Within a minute or two, she steps out from between the two front doors and gives a wave. She looks different from how she usually does on hikes, wearing a colorful dress that stops at her knees, but it suits her.

"You sure you're okay?" Kate asks.

"Promise. If anything happens, I'll call right away."

Kate nods. "And you better send that Uber info."

"Of course." I unbuckle my seat belt and open the car door. "Drive safe."

Kate stays until I walk up the driveway and meet Jillian at her front door. Jillian knows I'm not the comfortable-with-contact type, so she waves as I approach.

"Your sister can come in too, if she'd like," Jillian says.

"She has to get to rehearsal, it's all right."

"Got it, well, come on in." Jillian steps aside so I can enter.

The inside of the house is even more impressive than the outside. The area we step into is huge, with two curled staircases leading up to the second floor, and between them, a large walkway that seems to go into the kitchen. A giant chandelier hangs above us, and I immediately get the desire to step out of the way.

FEAR #53: LARGE OBJECTS FALLING UNEXPECTEDLY ON ME

"I just made some muffins, if you want one," Jillian says. "Pumpkin spice. I get really into it during the fall."

"Sounds great, thanks."

It's hard to pass up free food, and I know Jillian's a good baker because she's brought treats to quite a few of our bird hikes.

Jillian starts walking in the direction of the kitchen and I follow. The house is so big, I'll get lost if I don't stay within a few feet of her. The kitchen itself would be enough to make my dad cry. She has two ovens and an island with a standing mixer!

And an espresso machine.

Wow, Jillian is living the life.

Immediately, I'm greeted with a smell that's like pumpkin pie, but even more warm and sugary. Jillian has the muffins cooling on a wire rack. She takes one of them and puts it on a small plate for me.

"Did you get to take a look at the application?" Jillian asks.

She hands me the plate and I take it. I definitely did not look at the internship application yet. I've been a little preoccupied with Mr. Conspiracy and Valley Quail, but I can't exactly get into that now.

"School's been busy this week, but I'm hoping to do it this weekend."

Jillian smiles. "Perfect. If you have any questions, you can text me. Plus, I'll see you at the hike on Saturday."

It will be nice to go. At the very least, I can get some fresh air and also maybe say, like, three sentences to Elaine Yee.

I bite into the muffin. It's delicious.

"You have a nice place." I'm not good at small talk, but I feel like I can't not address how cool Jillian's house is. Toward the dining room, there are sliding glass doors that lead into the backyard, which has a large pool and a firepit. A few bird feeders are set outside by a flower garden.

Jillian's cheeks redden. "It is, but I'm not really one for this . . . showiness. It's more my partner who is used to a particular kind of lifestyle."

It's interesting that she says partner. I can't assume that she's queer just from the word choice alone. I mean, she could be straight and just says partner to be more hip and inclusive. I feel like she would be that kind of person.

I gesture toward two large sculptures in the walkway back to the front of the house: one a belted kingfisher and one a red-winged blackbird.

"Come on, Jillian, those statues are totally you."

She laughs. "Okay, agreed, but in my defense, it was an anniversary gift!"

"Your partner has some taste then," I say. "Giant bird sculptures are way cooler than jewelry."

"It's weird that not everyone thinks so." She looks around the house, almost like she's seeing it for the first time. "Neither of us really had families that saw us for who we were or believed in us . . . so I guess we go a little overboard in proving them wrong." She rubs her hand over the side of her neck.

I'm not quite sure how an abundance of overpriced home decor achieves that. I can respect it, though.

"I understand." The words slip out of me. "I don't think my mom sees me for who I am. Or much at all, really."

144

Especially not in regard to my sexuality and gender identity. She won't be able to accept that right away.

Jillian is silent for a moment. "I'm sorry, Bianca. But that's why we just have to find people who do understand us. Our pasts don't have to influence our futures. Tomorrow will be so much better."

It's nice to hear it like that.

"Well, I don't want to get too serious, you're here to talk about the internship!" She practically shakes away any residual sadness as she heads to the large touch-screen fridge. "Can I get you anything to drink? Water? Tea? Pop?"

I raise an eyebrow. "Pop?"

"I went to school in Ohio, some habits die hard. So, what'll it be?"

"Water would be great, thank you."

"Any preference on the kind of ice?"

I blink. There are multiple options for ice? Rich people are really a different breed.

"Um, any is fine," I say.

I'm still taking in the appliances and interior design as she fills a glass. With this kind of money, I'm sure she has a cleaner coming in, because every room looks like it could be straight out of a magazine.

Aside from the bird art pieces, but they still look nice and had to be expensive.

Jillian sets the glass of water down on the counter in front of me. "I do think it would be great to have you at the museum.

Ever since you reached out to me about the GLAOE, I could see your passion for ornithology." Her smile isn't huge, but it's sincere. "I'm so happy you stuck with us over the past year."

"Thanks for having me," I say. "It's been great. You made it super comfortable for me, too—I appreciate that so much."

From the beginning, Jillian didn't force me to make conversation or immediately push me to get to know everyone. She let me go at my own pace. Even when it felt like I was just with the group and not a part of it, she was there when I needed her without ever pressing.

Plus, she literally knows everything there is to know about birds. I've texted her for some identification tips, especially on my weak points of nests and calls, and she never made me feel like I was overstepping. If anything, she was too excited to help.

"I'm glad." She takes a muffin for herself. "We might actually accept two candidates for the internship, and I was thinking of inviting Elaine to also apply. You would work well together."

I practically spit out my water.

The possibility of doing the internship with Elaine? I can't tell if that would be a complete dream come true or a nightmare— I'd probably be only half functional as a human being in her presence.

But as much as I love Jillian, I'm not ready to admit that Elaine has been my crush since she joined three months ago.

"That would be cool," I say.

My phone buzzes loudly from where it sits on the counter. I glance over at it.

My stomach leaps. This could be important. After all, Nate could still be alive somewhere. If he is, he might have the information we need on Valley Quail.

"I'm so sorry, Jillian, I have to get going." I turn my phone upside down. "Family emergency."

Her expression shows real concern. "Is everything okay?"

"Yeah, my family can be a little dramatic in what an emergency is, but I still should head out."

"No problem, let me just grab that letter for you!" Jillian walks off into another section of the house.

While she's gone, I request an Uber. Luckily, there's one only a few minutes away. I screenshot the car's details and send it to Anderson and Kate as promised. I add Mom and Dad to the message to keep them in the loop, even though they probably aren't home.

Jillian returns with the envelope. "Just make sure to include this when you send your application in."

"Of course, thank you so much, it really means a lot." I take another sip of water, since she went through the effort of pouring it, and then get my things together. I glance down at my phone. "My ride's here."

"Let me walk you out."

I'm glad she does, because even though it should be a straight shot to the front door, I can hardly trust myself in this house. They should have maps to use once you enter.

Jillian waves me off as I get into the Uber and give an awkward greeting to the driver. He doesn't really seem in the mood to talk, which is perfect, so I text Anderson instead.

I'm on my way back. Should I go straight to your place?

Anderson: yeah I'm home!

What did you find?

Anderson: you want to ruin the surprise?

He knows I'm not the type of person who likes surprises.

Since I'm by myself, I don't love the idea of the driver knowing where I live, so I put my destination as the CVS a few blocks away. After he drops me off there, I watch the car drive away and then start down the street.

My phone rings. It's an unknown number, but sometimes Mom's office line comes up like that.

"Hello?"

There's breathing on the other end. But the person doesn't speak. My skin crawls. This is like textbook creepy behavior and exactly what I mean when I say

FEAR #20: PHONE CALLS

"Um . . . can I help you?" I ask.

There's another pause, and I'm about to hang up when the voice on the other line speaks.

"Watch your back," it teases.

The same phrase that came with the bloody feather threat. My neck tingles with the feeling that someone is watching me.

FEAR #23: BEING WATCHED

The call disconnects.

I turn around to check behind me. There's not a lot of people on the sidewalk, although there are plenty of cars bustling by. Maybe I'm overreacting. It's not like I never overreact to things.

But something isn't right.

Then I see them.

A person in black, with a plague mask over their face.

At the same time as I start walking in the direction of my house and Anderson's apartment, I press the icon next to his name to call him. I try to present as calm as possible while I'm anything but.

They're here.

They're here and I'm alone.

"Bianca, what's up?" Anderson sounds a little concerned, like he knows I wouldn't call for no reason.

"By CVS. I'm being followed. It's the killer. I think. I got a threatening call, I . . ." My voice is low and rushed. "Can you start coming toward me? It might be safer to be together."

His own voice does a whole one-eighty shift into complete worry. "Stay on the line, I'm coming. I'm going to run, but keep talking."

I start babbling about my visit to Jillian's house, mentioning every little detail. I barely know what I'm saying as my heart pounds in my throat. I glance back. The masked figure is at the CVS, standing where I just was a few minutes ago.

They must be testing me, seeing if I'm going home alone.

Or waiting for the opportunity to strike.

I blink back tears and continue on with my story, keeping my face straight ahead. On the line, I hear Anderson's breath.

Unlike the killer's call, the repetition of his air flow hitting the speaker brings comfort.

He's on his way.

I won't be alone.

It'll be okay.

I have to repeat the last part over and over in my head so many times I stop talking for a minute, and then quickly recover by saying how good Jillian's pumpkin muffins were.

"Bianca!"

I see Anderson's figure up ahead, wearing mix-matched socks, and his glasses are slightly fogged. I don't care if anyone watching me sees. I run. I run as fast as I can and don't stop until I practically barrel into him. He catches me and holds me as I bury my face into his shirt. "Thank you," I mumble into the fabric.

"It's okay," he says. "We're okay."

It sounds even better in his voice.

I pull away from him long enough to look back in the direction of the CVS.

But the person in the mask is already gone.

SEVENTEEN

THE WEIRD-ASS BIRD SYMBOL

Anderson and I weighed the pros and cons of me going back to the police, but without any evidence someone was following me, we decided against it. They didn't believe me last time, so I doubt they will now. Mom got basically laughed at for the cat-toy threat. She was assured it was a prank, but they'd make note of it. This would only be worse. I have no proof. I'll get my parents and the authorities involved if anything else happens, but in the meantime, Anderson and I promised each other not to walk places alone.

For now, I feel like we just have to be more careful and figure out something on Valley Quail, Inc. that we can actually use against them.

We didn't get a chance to talk about Nate last night, since I was too busy having multiple panic attacks and Anderson helped calm me down by distracting me with one of his favorite comfort anime series, *Monthly Girls' Nozaki-kun*, before we started a YouTube instructional series on the basics of learning how to draw comics. (Anderson started to pick up on details quickly, while I was pretty hopeless at it.) Still, it was a much-needed break. But to get back on the investigative track today, we decided to meet up in one of the library's study rooms during our lunch period. We made sure to close the glass door and sit on the side of the table that isn't as easily seen from the window. We spread out notebooks to keep up the appearance of working on a school project and not an extracurricular murder investigation, just in case.

"How are you holding up?" Anderson asks.

"I'm fine." I rub my hands over my arms. "I mean, it's almost the weekend, that's nice."

"Which means next week is our meeting with Mr. Conspiracy's inside guy." Anderson pulls up the picture I sent him. "I don't know why it has to be so early. Who's up at seven on a Saturday?"

I don't know if this is the time to admit that I am up at seven every Saturday because of my birding group. I'm sure Jillian won't mind if I miss the hike next week. I can always say that I'm sick—I don't have to say I'm meeting up with some questionable person who might know something about a murder I'm investigating.

"Anyway, back to what we can do now. What did you get on Nate?"

Anderson pulls the sleeves of his shirt up above his elbows and then opens a page on his phone. "I found the LinkedIn page for Nate, and he was last active in January—right before he went missing. Someone with his same job title started at his company, not VQ, in early February, so I'm thinking they replaced him." Despite the dark nature of the topic, his voice is excited with this development. "I found a company number to double-check. They were closed last night, but I thought we could call today."

"Do you think they'll tell us anything?"

Anderson gives me a look. "He worked in an office, Bianca. All they have to do is gossip."

I feel like they also have work to do, but I want to know more about Nate, so I go with it. "Okay, you talk though. I can't speak well on phones."

Anderson puts a hand on my shoulder. "You can't speak well in general." I give him a light shove, even though he's not wrong. He chuckles and dials the number in his phone.

I glance around us—since the door is closed, no one should be able to hear us from outside. I'm not sure if we're allowed to make phone calls here, but the librarian isn't in sight, so maybe she doesn't care.

"Hi, my name is Marc Ward, and I'm calling because my brother used to work with you." Anderson really is great under pressure. It would've taken me five minutes alone to come up with a fake name. "Uh-huh, his name is Nate. Nathaniel Ward . . . Um, short hair, bright blue eyes . . . really into birds? Great, yes, that's him. Yeah, so, I haven't heard from him in a while, and I wanted to know if he had mentioned anything before he left . . ."

This probably won't work. They might not even know Nate well, and even if they did, who just gives out an ex-coworker's information to a random person over the phone?

"Great guy . . . Oh, really? Huh . . . No, totally. He owes me money, that's why I'm calling. What a snake . . . I hated him too. Uh-huh, well, thank you for your time, ma'am . . . No, you have a blessed day." Anderson hangs up the call. "So, Nate didn't quit his job."

"He didn't?"

"Not exactly. Apparently, they thought he was stealing money from the business, but before they could investigate further, they think Nate caught wind of it, cleared out everything, and skipped town. No one has heard from him since. The company has no idea where the money went, and they can't find him for questioning."

I sit with that for a second. "If he was stealing money and got caught, that could be reason to skip town."

"Or, he could have been stealing money for Valley Quail, and they killed him for being sloppy." Anderson crosses his arms. "Which is seeming more likely."

Either way, we're right back to needing more information on Valley Quail, Inc.

"Okay. What about the symbol Ryan found?" I double-check the window of the study room for any strange plague-masked figures out in the library before I pull Mr. Conspiracy's book from my bag. "We can try to look into this—it might have something to do with Valley Quail." I check over my shoulders again, even though we're alone in the room. I guess I'm a little paranoid after yesterday. "If someone from the school is involved, should we come up with a code name or something to discuss this?"

"Good call." Anderson thinks for a moment. "Aren't big conspiracies always like something-gate?"

"That sounds right."

"Code name: Feathergate." He expands his hands like an explosion and accompanies it with a sound effect.

I sigh. "Are you making it bird-related to tease me?"

"What can I say?" He leans his head on one hand, expression smiling but serious. "If we're not talking anime, everything seems to be bird-related with you."

Even the murders. Feathergate it is.

"So, how are we going to look this up?" I ask. "Google weird-ass bird symbols?"

I was being sarcastic, but Anderson shrugs and does it. The search results in a lack of symbols and an awkward amount of creepy birds with big eyes.

"Well, it was worth a shot." Anderson sighs.

Really anything would be remotely helpful at this point. We've been grasping at straws since the beginning.

"Maybe we can take a picture of it and do a reverse image search?" I point to the symbol inside the book. "You know, like *Catfish*."

Anderson gives me a look. "You realize most people know

about reverse image searching without watching *Catfish*."

"I honestly don't believe you."

I snap a picture of the symbol, trying to make it as clear as possible, and email it to Anderson. He saves the photo and inputs it. We can't find a clear answer as to what it may be, and most of the related images aren't helpful.

Except for one, which is an exact copy of the symbol from the diary.

"There," I say, tapping Anderson's shoulder quickly.

"Yes, Bianca, I am here experiencing this with you." He clicks it. "So impatient."

I roll my eyes but smile as the page loads.

It's from a Reddit post, under r/AmItheAsshole. A user, ancientlake0514, posted the picture included in the post. It was from a while ago, but the image likeness is uncanny. I quickly scan the text.

AITA for trying to get my husband fired from his job?

I (32F) and my husband (36M) have only been married for about a year, and I thought things were going great. Now, some backstory, he has a really nice job, well paid, but often has to travel. For this reason, he's been given a company credit card. Outside of his job and me, he doesn't really have much of a life. I was excited when he found this club that related to a passion of his. I don't know much about it. They would meet twice a week—I think it was something science-related? Like people who are into chemistry or something? Honestly, I didn't care, I was glad to see him happy.

But then he started putting all his time into the club. Like outside the regular meetings. And when he did go to those meetings, he'd come back super late. I was convinced he was having an affair with someone else in the club. I'm not exactly smart, so of course I'm going to be self-conscious if he's around glamorous science women, right?

Anyway, I know he's too clever to leave a paper trail with our joint bank account, so I wait until he's sleeping and get the info for his company credit card. I'm expecting to see the usual signs—hotel or motel rooms, convenience store purchases, sex toys, jewelry—I don't know—whatever would be obvious for an affair.

Instead, there are various payments to this company called Valley Quail, Inc., which apparently handles office supplies, but seems kind of odd because after some research, I couldn't find anything else about Valley Quail online.

I then became convinced that he was stealing from his job to give money to this fake account, which has to be some excuse to screw some science-loving slut. Like I'm pretty sure anyone can make a corporation to funnel money. So, long story short, I get in contact with his workplace and straight-up get him fired—they didn't investigate his fake company for sexy time, but they found enough to confirm they aren't the paper supplier. So.

Of course, after this happens, and I get the papers to file for divorce, I go through his phone and don't see any suspicious contacts or correspondence. I'm now wondering if he was actually cheating on me, or if he was using the extra money to help us out? Do I tell him it's my fault he was fired? AITA?

(Side note: He had this weird kind of book with this symbol on it. Anyone know what this is? If it's a sex cult thing I definitely need to know!)

I can tell Anderson finished reading first, because he watches me, waiting for a reaction.

"Based on the time line, this isn't about Nate, but it definitely seems like Valley Quail stealing money," I say.

"From multiple places, it looks like."

Anderson scrolls down to the comments, but most of them are yelling at OP to divorce the guy or making fun of her—none of the comments seem to address the picture she attached.

"Well, we know this symbol has something to do with Feathergate. And that these people are stealing from their jobs and throwing money into this weird-ass sham company." While I try to keep my voice quiet, I can't exactly hide the excitement in it.

"So, we have to figure out who is doing this, and what the money is being used for," Anderson says. He sighs. "Well, at least it's something." He clears his browser history.

Probably a smart move. I can't help but feel like someone is always watching now.

The bell rings to signify the end of lunch, but this is a good breakthrough.

"We on for training at four thirty?" Anderson asks, closing his laptop and sliding it into his backpack.

I nod. He seems ready to head out of the room, but I stop him.

"Hey, Anderson?"

He looks at me, waiting, because I clearly have his full attention. I squeeze my hands into fists. "I want to tell you something."

"Sure . . . as a murder investigation partner or as a friend?"

"Friend. I'm nonbinary," I say quickly before I can bitch out. "Can you use they/them pronouns for me? Just . . . not around my family or people at school?"

Part of me expects him to have a lot of questions or need follow-up explanation, but Anderson hugs me.

I kind of stand there, frozen, before I hug him back.

"I'm so glad you told me." He grins. "Let me try it out: I'm happy for my friend Bianca. They are the coolest no matter what their gender is." He hugs me again, like this is a big moment or something. Half of me kind of appreciates it, even if the other half is embarrassed. His expression falls a bit. "I'm sorry for using the wrong pronouns before."

"It's okay," I say. "I mean, I kind of figured it out recently. You had no way of knowing."

"Correct me every time I mess up. You even have permission to *lightly* punch me. That's what Ronan did, and I learned real quick."

I laugh. "You got it."

And it's like that. So easy. Everything is easier with Anderson around. From a gender identity crisis to a goddamn murder.

This next part shouldn't be hard either. Not even if my hands shake and my chest is tight.

I take a deep breath. "Can you maybe do me a favor?"

Right after lunch ended and Anderson agreed to go with me to the nonbinary and transgender support group on Sunday, the news spread that Audrey II was resurrected from the dead, complete with memes of the plant's face photoshopped onto Jesus paintings.

Kate found me in the hallway and practically knocked me over, saying that some anonymous benefactor donated the money when they saw the protest broadcast on the news, putting the donation in honor of Verdi and Poochie. She doesn't seem to care who it is, only that they get to use an actual puppet.

At least, if the PTA doesn't cancel the show immediately after the preview.

Now I'm standing outside the English and history office. Ms. Richards was just being nice to me because I saw someone die, but I figured I could milk that and ask her for help with my essay for the museum internship application. She seemed to care about me putting in effort, so this is something. She was busy after class and asked me to come back at the end of the day.

Which is unfortunate. Since other teachers are here.

I step inside. Mr. Rodney, the APUSH teacher, looks up at me. His desk is one of the ones by the door.

"Hi, um . . . I'm looking for Ms. Richards."

He points to the back before returning to the papers he's grading.

Even though I'm wearing my backpack, I have a few books clutched to my chest. It gives me something to do with my hands, at the very least. Ms. Richards sits at her desk, and she looks to be grading the *Catcher in the Rye* data sheets.

Yikes.

"Um, Ms. Richards," I say, causing her to look over. "Hi. Just had a quick question. For you."

Clearly I'm not great at this. Ms. Richards smiles. "Sure, Bianca. How can I help?"

"I'm applying for a birding internship." I pull out the printed paper of the essay I mostly wrote during today's history class when we got to use laptops. "Part of the application is an essay, and I was wondering if you could look at it."

Ms. Richards takes the paper. "Absolutely. I can have it back to you next week, if that works?"

"That's perfect, thanks."

The natural flow of conversation is paused now, and I'm not really sure where to go from here. Can I just leave?

"Is there anything else you wanted to talk about?" Ms. Richards asks, like she can sense my absolute weirdness.

"Maybe," I say.

After coming out to Anderson, I feel like I could use another person at school on my side. Ms. Richards is queer, so she might be accepting of my gender identity. She doesn't seem like a person who would judge.

"I have time," Ms. Richards says.

I squeeze my books tighter, so the edges practically cut into the skin right above my inner elbow. I look around the room and make sure the other teachers are far enough away that they won't overhear. I step right up to the desk and keep my voice low. "I, um . . . I'd like to use they/them pronouns now." I look to the left, toward a shared bookshelf placed against the wall between different desks. "I'm not out to everyone, so I guess not in class . . . but when you can."

My face is red, I know it because my cheeks are so hot, they'd practically burn my fingers if I touched them.

Ms. Richards keeps her voice careful. "I'm so sorry I've used the incorrect pronouns, but thank you so much for trusting me with this, Bianca."

I nod. I'm not really sure why she's thanking me.

"No, thank you," I say, even though it sounds ridiculous with my awkward tone.

I shift on my feet. I'm not sure if I have anything else to say.

"You know, I have a book you might like on gender and sexuality," Ms. Richards says. Her eyes do the same sweep of the other faculty across the room. "I know you might not be able to get something like that yourself if you're not out, so I can lend it to you."

At first, words escape me. Technically, she's right. I don't drive, and there's not really any bookstores within walking distance. Plus, something tells me the school library probably won't have anything that detailed.

She could've ended the conversation too, but no, she's trying to help me.

Ms. Richards is so cool.

"Yeah," I say finally. "That'd be awesome."

"I have a small library in the trunk of my car, so it should be there." She laughs and adjusts her leather jacket. "If you wait here, I can run and grab it?"

"Sure. Seriously, thanks."

"No worries, I'll only be a minute." She practically skips out the office.

I'm so glad I have her as my English teacher and not someone like Mr. Foyer, who literally calls on people off the seating chart. Thankfully he's not sitting at the nearby desk. There is a special place in hell for people who force participation instead of asking for volunteers, especially when it comes to making people read aloud.

And don't get me started on the assholes who seek out the distracted and quiet kids to call them out on purpose.

No, the world needs more teachers like Ms. Richards.

I don't want to keep standing this close to her desk, or one of the other teachers might think I'm trying to look at the grades or something. I step across the office toward a bookshelf next to some of the history teachers' desks and browse the titles. Oddly enough, there is a strange book placed directly on the top, spine right at eye level.

The Rules of Flight?

I've never heard of that one. But it kind of sounds ornithology adjacent. It doesn't have an author though, which is weird. Maybe it was like a collaboration? Or some local ornithologist who doesn't really know how covers work? Either way, it could be something to mention if I get an interview for the internship. I open the cover to the title page.

And immediately see the weird-ass bird symbol from the diary. My stomach drops.

Why would a teacher have something with this bird symbol? I guess it makes sense, because money from the school is being laundered, but it's hard to believe that someone in this office is related to VQ. And why would they leave it out? Is it some kind of trap?

I want to look through it, though. If it has answers, it could be invaluable. I glance back toward Mr. Rodney, who is engrossed in an essay, and some younger teacher I've never had who's on their phone.

Despite my head swimming, my chest squeezing, and

FEAR #16: GETTING CAUGHT DOING SOMETHING BAD

I quickly shove everything I'm holding, the strange book included, into my backpack.

I'm barely thinking. The heart attack I narrowly evaded while being followed yesterday is now back with a vengeance. My chest is going to explode.

I stumble back around the desk. Does Ms. Richards know about this? Would she be able to tell me who owns it?

With impeccable timing, Ms. Richards walks back into the office, her red lips curled upward. "Here it is." She holds out a book to me. My vision is too blurry to make out the cover well, but I take it. "Are you all right?"

I force myself to breathe, even if my heart is nearing its demise.

"Great," I say, putting on a smile. "I'll read it this weekend, thanks so much!"

It must be convincing enough. She actually laughs.

"Of course, see you Monday."

"Yes, then, bye, thanks, bye!" I say, heading out the door. The hallway has cleared enough with the time that passed since final bell, so once I turn the corner, I start running.

I can't think or stop moving until I make it home, the backpack burning against me with the weight of the strange book.

EIGHTEEN

JOIN THE FLOCK

It took all my willpower to not immediately tell Anderson about the *Rules of Flight* book, but we agreed to meet at the gym, and he was already warming up when I got here. I don't want to interrupt the session, and it seems weird talking about it in public.

Sure, it's very unlikely that anyone at the gym is involved. But I didn't think one of my teachers would be involved either and look where that got me.

So I spend the next hour biting my tongue and going along with Anderson's instruction.

I really twist on my hip to sink a right hook into the punching bag, and while hitting things doesn't necessarily solve my problems, it does make me feel slightly better about them.

"Nice one," Anderson says. "We good for today?"

"Yeah," I say weakly.

With it being only my second time training, my muscles are

not used to the movement. The soreness made today's session that much harder.

I am tired enough as it is. More than that, I want to get out of here so we can talk.

"I still think you should try some grappling," Anderson says. "Jiu-Jitsu is technique, not just strength."

I've seen enough of the grappling to know that it involves tons of

FEAR #38: CLOSE CONTACT

FEAR #46: SWEAT AND OTHER BODILY FLUIDS

And despite the fact that I like this gym, everyone sweats on the same mats, which makes me have to once again bring up

FEAR #60: RINGWORM

"I think I'm good," I say.

"So, maybe someday," Anderson adds, always the optimist.

I shake my head but don't bother arguing. To be fair, I never would've imagined myself going anywhere near this place just a week ago. I can barely believe I know how to throw a punch, even if Anderson makes me repeat daily that if anyone were to attack me, the goal isn't to fight them, the goal is to get away.

One of the professors, Rafael, who is Anderson's favorite, catches us on the way out. Anderson talks about him so much I know that Rafael is originally from Nicaragua, a black belt in Jiu-Jitsu and judo, and an Aquarius sun, Gemini moon, and Leo rising.

To think Anderson called me a stalker.

The two of them bump fists and give like a half-hug, half-back-slap thing. Rafael smiles and does the same to me, and I kind of feel like I'm part of the club.

Like whatever the nonbinary equivalent of "bro" is. Not that I mind "bro" that much because personally I'm okay with masculinity. I don't really have a connection to being a man, so another option might help. I saw that some people say "sib" when it comes to their actual siblings, which would work with Kate, but I'm not sure if that applies to gym settings.

I'll have to look that up later.

"You enjoying it so far?" Rafael asks me. "For a beginner, you have good form."

"Thank you," I say. "Yes."

"They're a natural," Anderson says. He states it so easily, so automatically, and it fills my chest.

Rafael doesn't seem to notice, but for some reason, it's not as big of a deal for strangers to know. This is a place where I can one hundred percent be myself, especially with Anderson, and I don't have a lot of places like that.

I'm not sure if I have *any* other place like that.

It's as exciting as it is a little sad.

"You have to take my class," Rafael says. "If you can make it at night."

"I'll try," I lie.

I'm not sure I would do as well in a class setting.

FEAR #23: BEING WATCHED

That entry was definitely made to include being watched in a group setting or activity where I make a fool of myself. But it's nice that he offered.

"See you both soon," he says, giving one last wave.

Oddly enough, for people who literally fight for fun, everyone at the gym seems nice and welcoming.

Anderson and I both use hand sanitizer on the way out and head back in the direction of our places.

"Okay, are you ready to tell me what's up?" Anderson asks. "Are you nervous about the group on Sunday or is this something else?"

"I've been waiting to tell you. I found something," I say. "At school . . . I think it might relate to the case."

Anderson's eyes go wide. "Why didn't you tell me right away? And where?"

"You were already training, I felt bad." I look at the sidewalk in front of us as we walk back home. "I found it in the teachers' office. The English and history one."

"One of the teachers has something to do with it?" He whistles. "I bet it's Mr. Rodney. I could totally see him killing someone."

"I mean, I don't know, it could be any of them, really." I shrug. "We've known someone at the school is involved, though. And it has to be someone with power to influence the budget, so probably not a student."

"Well, what did you find?" Anderson asks.

"A book," I answer. "It had the symbol inside. From Mr. Conspiracy's diary."

We're almost back home by now, but Anderson stops in his tracks and meets my eyes.

"Bianca. Be honest. Did you look at it without me?"

I don't have to lie. I've been so stressed since finding it that

I haven't so much as opened my backpack since coming from school. "No. I wouldn't do that without you."

Anderson loosens his expression into a smile. "Good. I would've actually been mad. Let's shower really quick, then meet at your place?"

I do need a shower. Plus, it gives me time to mentally prepare for whatever is in this book. "Sounds good."

I'm glad I don't take a long shower because barely two minutes after I throw on sweatpants and an oversize Queen T-shirt, there's a knock on the door.

Since both Mom and Dad are working and Kate is at rehearsal, I check through the peephole. It's Anderson, but given the weird threat, I promised my parents I wouldn't let anyone in without making sure.

Puck meows from next to me.

"Hey, my sweet sunshine girl," Anderson says from the other side of the door.

I'd say she's actually *my* sweet sunshine girl, but Puck meows back, pawing at the wood. She really is a traitor.

I open the door, and she immediately rushes to Anderson, brushing against his leg. He picks her up like a baby and looks at me. "So, the book?"

"I'll get it."

He heads to the kitchen, and I close and lock the door behind him.

Even though my hands shake as I do it, I pull the book from my backpack and bring it to the kitchen table, where Anderson plays with Puck. There's this odd feeling that settles in the pit of my stomach. Like, despite being in my house, we're in danger as long as we have this.

"*The Rules of Flight*," he reads, Puck now settled in his lap. He gently opens the book and starts turning the pages. "It's a bunch of poems."

"What?" I ask.

Anderson hands me the book. The first page has the same symbol as the title page, no names of authors or anything like that. I flip to the next page, which has a printed poem that spans two pages.

I. Join the Flock

In every single story ever told
When freedom was a concept to be heard
In days of new or even days of old
What better symbol used than of a bird?

Creatures of such majesty and grace
So high up in the sky they know to soar
Inspiring the dreamers below to chase
Those left on land wishing and wanting more

For who alive feels freedom like in flight
When we remain chained by the broken earth
But shed all of your doubts and you just might
Find a way with us to break this curse

Ignore doubters who only say never
Just join the Flock, and all else you must sever

While it's weird, it doesn't give away any conspiracy. I turn the page to another poem in the same format: kind of unsettling and also has to do with birds but doesn't reveal any additional information.

I skim through the book. More poems in the same format, each one having to do with birds.

Is this some strange coincidence?

"How many poems are there?" Anderson asks. "Does that mean anything?"

Since they're numbered, I flip to the last one. "Forty-seven."

"Forty-seven . . ." Anderson sits back, stroking Puck as he thinks. "No idea. It probably means nothing."

"It means it was probably someone in the English department," I say. "Either that, or a history teacher who is really into poetry."

"Kind of bad poetry for someone who majored in English." Anderson makes a face. "And would a regular teacher have that much control over the budget?"

I shrug. "Maybe more than one person at our school is involved?"

Anderson rereads the first poem. He continues to look through some of the other ones. "There's a lot of mentions of this Flock. That could be what the Feathergate people call themselves. Because it one hundred percent feels like some weird-rich-person cult."

I hate to admit it, but he's right.

Anderson puts the book down on the table, and it falls so the inside back cover is visible. Both of us look down at the Post-it note stuck there. Only one thing is written on it.

11.18.

"Wait . . ." Anderson looks up. "Isn't that the same date Mr. Conspiracy noted? Do you think the "Flock" or whatever have something planned that day too?"

"They have to, I mean, it can't be related to Mr. Conspiracy's meeting, unless it's a setup?" It's certainly not related to the preview performance of *Little Shop of Horrors*. "I mean, Mr. Conspiracy's informant could be a trap, and this was a reminder."

"But it wouldn't exactly be bad for us to go, right? If it was a trap for him, it's probably canceled, considering he's dead. Can't exactly make it."

That makes sense. I bite my lip. "Okay, but if it is something else . . . what if it's something bad?"

He grimaces. "Maybe that's why Mr. Conspiracy planned the meeting so early in the morning—Valley Quail's next evil plan debuts that day."

I don't really know what we can do about it except try to stop them first. "Okay. Great. November eighteenth. We have a deadline."

"This Flock, Valley Quail . . . it has to be related."

"That's true . . ." I start. "But how do we know where to look?"

The small line between Anderson's eyebrows deepens. "Bianca, you are in a birding club."

"One birding club. Of how many?" I counter. "Besides, just because it's bird-related doesn't mean any groups are involved."

"I don't know." He shrugs. "We can look into it. The birding community here can't be that widespread."

I guess he has a point. Jillian works at the museum, so maybe she'll know of other birders? It'd be kind of weird to ask, though. I wouldn't want her to think I'm leaving GLAOE or something.

It can't hurt to give Anderson a chance to see it for himself and possibly do a little recon.

"Okay," I say, voice small, "we have a bird hike tomorrow morning. Why don't you come?"

NINETEEN

SHALL I COMPARE THEE TO A BIRDING GAY?

Anderson is able to borrow his mom's car to take us to the hike, which is a bit of a drive, since we're meeting in Pasadena this week. He seems to be doing surprisingly well with the early start, although the half-empty energy drink in the cup holder probably has something to do with it.

The 134 is pretty, for a freeway. I like the mountain view, especially right now, when the traffic isn't so heavy. Where Anderson and I live, the mountains are in the distance, and the only real views we have are of a bunch of auto and liquor shops. It's kind of nice to get out, especially because I don't have the ability to do it myself.

FEAR #50: DRIVING (AND INEVITABLY FAILING AT IT)

"You just meet up and look at birds?" Anderson asks. "That's it?"

"Yeah," I say. "It's a birding group. That's it."

"No, that's cool, no worries." Anderson keeps his eyes on the road, but looks over slightly, like I'd actually be offended. "I'm excited."

"I'm not sure exciting would be a word I'd use for this," I warn.

"I mean, it's like a hike, right?" He shrugs. "I've been on a hike. Once."

I'd bet the hike he went on wasn't with a bunch of people only obsessed with birds. Still, if Kate can survive a birding hike, Anderson will be fine. And at least he doesn't have the natural embarrassing quality of a sibling in theater.

"If it's that bad, I'll let you teach me takedowns," I say. "And buy you Ben & Jerry's."

"Well, now it's going to be that bad no matter what."

I flip him off, in case he can catch it in his peripheral vision. Which he does, based on a quick eye roll.

"You played yourself," he adds.

"If you get that bored, we can work on our sketches." I cringe as I remember my failed attempt at drawing a green heron. "Or, you can. And I will support you."

He smiles. "Sounds good."

I open the drawstring bag on my seat to make sure I have everything. Bird field guide, binoculars, camera, sunscreen, bug spray, water bottle, and the *Rules of Flight* book with a cover placed over it.

The poems have to mean something. If only either of us

actually cared about poetry. Why couldn't the book have been written as a comic instead?

"Do you want to study birds?" Anderson asks. "Like after graduation? We never really talked about it."

I shrug. "I guess. I'm not really sure what else to do."

"I know that feeling." Anderson grips the wheel while keeping a steady speed on the freeway. "I still don't know what the hell I want to do with my life."

It's kind of weird to hear that coming from him. I always feel like I'm the one who is confused and unsure of what they're doing. "Really?" I ask. "What about the comics thing?"

"Well, yeah." His jaw looks a little tight. "Maybe, but I wonder if that would be better as just a hobby? Like it's fun starting to learn, and I've always liked drawing, but once it becomes something I want to pursue, there's like all this pressure not to fail. It's the same with Jiu-Jitsu, I'm not some prodigy or training consistently every day. I'm not even sure I'd want to make a career out of it. I like it as something I can get better at only because I want to."

I never really thought of it that way, but he's right. There is a difference in allowing yourself to do something because you enjoy it and then being pressured to study it in college and feel like it has to be your whole life.

"And it's hard," Anderson continues, "because no one in my family has ever really been that successful. Like my parents do all right, but they aren't doing what they're passionate about. They tell me and Ronan to keep pushing. We will have to work twice as hard, Ronan maybe even four times, but to never stop pursuing what we love." He lets out a long breath. "But what if I don't have any one thing I love? What do I do then?"

I wish I had an answer to that, but like most things, I don't.

Because I'm in a similar boat.

And Anderson might actually have another big thing in common with me.

FEAR #12: THE FUTURE

"I'm jealous of people like my mom and sister," I say. "They knew they liked acting since they were kids. It's part of them, especially Kate. She's an actor: that's what she loves, that's what she does. It doesn't matter that it's hard, she has that dream. She has something to come back to. I don't have anything either. Not really. And without any real dreams, I feel kind of lost."

"Yeah," Anderson says. He smiles softly. "Maybe that's why we get along so well, Bianca T. The one thing lost people are good at is finding each other."

He has a point. If it's possible for the platonic version of a soul mate to exist, that might be what Anderson is to me. One of the best decisions in my life was wearing a shirt from a volleyball anime, because it started my friendship with him.

"I hope you find your dream," I say. It's kind of a heavy moment. I add, "Whether it's comics or something boring like accounting I'll have to judge you for, I'll support you."

"Even if it is boring, it won't be nearly as boring as bird-watching."

"Shots fired, *Coleman*."

He laughs, a real laugh, and I can't help but join in.

"But thanks," he says. "You know I got you, too."

The GPS tells Anderson to get off at the next exit, and he does. It's only about another five minutes before we're at the park that's the meeting point of the group. It's a really pretty area. I never have a reason to go out to Pasadena, but I know it's fancy and suburban. Similar to where Jillian lives.

"Anything I should know?" Anderson asks. "Like club rules?"

"Not really," I say. "They'll do an introduction speech of stuff."

He nods. "Is literally everyone there white?"

"Like ninety percent, yes," I say. "And like ninety-five percent are middle-aged or older."

"My favorite kind of people," he deadpans.

"Birding could definitely use improvements in diversity," I admit. "Especially our group. Luckily, you can kind of keep to yourself here, but it's what you'd expect."

No one is overtly terrible in the group, aside from the total dick that is Mr. Wattson. And while I can't speak about racist microaggressions in the group as a white person, I do get the vibe from some people that they might have a few harmful comments about my pronouns if I were to share them. People act like California is all liberals and allies, but you can probably talk to any older white woman in Burbank or practically anyone in Orange County and realize that's not true.

"Okay, you're definitely buying me ice cream," Anderson says, but he shuts off the car.

"Deal."

With everything that's going on, I don't think there's been a single day not worthy of Ben & Jerry's, if such a thing could exist.

We're a bit early, but a good amount of the group is gathered. Immediately as Anderson and I walk up, Terrance and Margaret wave me over. They look as cute as ever in matching lavender shirts with a little heron embroidered on the shoulder.

"Bianca, hello!" Terrance says when we approach. "And who is your friend?"

"Anderson Coleman, nice to meet you, sir." Anderson holds out his hand.

"Terrance." He shakes it before gesturing to Margaret. "And this beautiful young woman is my wife, Margaret."

She smiles at Terrance before also shaking Anderson's hand. "Nice to meet you."

"Are you also a birder?" Terrance asks.

"No, just here with Bianca," Anderson says.

"Welcome nonetheless." Terrance looks a little disappointed but regains his smile when he catches my gaze. "Oh, but Bianca. Let me show you this barn owl photo we captured. He's a beauty."

Margaret starts some small talk with Anderson as Terrance pulls out his camera to show me the collection of photos. I don't get to see owls much, so the close-up angle is even cooler. Terrance has a real eye for photography.

"You should submit your photos somewhere." I don't know

anything about photography, but Terrance's work looks top tier to me. "These are really good."

He almost looks a little embarrassed.

"That's what I say," Margaret adds, overhearing.

"Well, maybe." He closes out of his photos.

Jillian steps in front of the group. She's tall, so I can see her despite the cluster of birders standing around. "Hello, everyone," she says. "Glad you could all make it to the weekly hike. I know we've heard the spiel before, but let me take a moment to go over our general rules . . ."

Right as she starts, Elaine Yee jogs up to the group, hair in a high ponytail that reveals a new undercut.

I slide my hand over the underside of my ponytail. Would I look that cool with some of my head shaved?

She meets my eyes, and though my first instinct is to look away, I manage to give a small wave.

She smiles and waves back.

And it's like my chest fills with bubbles. I immediately turn toward Jillian to hide my blush and ridiculously big smile.

Anderson seems to study me, but I keep facing forward. He definitely saw that small interaction and, based on my embarrassment, knows everything. He's too good at reading me. I stay focused on Jillian until she gets the hike started and we move out as a group.

Once we're on the trail and there's some distance between everyone, Anderson leans toward me and keeps his voice low. "Do you like her?"

I shove my hat down and will my face to cool. "Shut up."

"Why?" Anderson sneaks another look. "It's a good fit. You both are weirdly into birds . . ."

"Sure," I say. "But I don't know if she's . . . if she'd be into me."

While I like it, I know not everyone is comfortable with the word *queer*, and I don't know if Elaine is any part of the LGBTQIAP+ community. As much as I may read into comments, it's a lot more likely that she's straight.

"It'd be cute." He thinks for a minute. "She's not part of the weird bird stuff, right? She seems artsy and cool, like the poem-writing type." He lifts his eyebrows like a warning.

"No way." I brush the thought immediately aside. "And even if she was, that's fine."

Anderson makes a face. "What do you mean, 'that's fine'?"

"Like, that's fine. She can ruin my whole entire life any day." I can't help but sneak glances at her. The way she lights up when she makes a find has me swooning on the regular.

Yeah, if anyone has to kill me . . .

"I really worry about you, Bianca." He steps to the side. "I'll do recon."

My chest seizes. "No, no, Anderson, do not . . ."

He's already walking toward her, and I'm not about to yell at him and get the attention of everyone. I guess I'll wander off into the mountains and live off the land and hope that no one ever finds me again ever.

Now they're talking.

I'm going to cry. What is he saying? We've never really talked about crushes outside of the realm of fictional characters—or anything relating to our love lives, even if mine is nonexistent. It's kind of nice we're at this point, or it would be, if I wasn't so embarrassed.

Dammit.

I look off in the other direction, using my binoculars to hide my eyes. This is horrible. This is the absolute worst. I take back everything I said about him being my platonic soul mate.

I want to turn back. This is seriously the worst. This is . . . I spot a California towhee. It hops along a branch before taking off.

Anyway. This is the worst and also how dare he.

If I so much as catch one murmur of my name, I'll have to flee the state and open up a stray cat sanctuary in Colorado.

"You see that towhee?" Jillian asks from near me.

She's a godsend. At least I don't have to suffer through this alone.

"Yeah," I say. "Beautiful."

"Sure is." She looks off a little wistfully before returning to me. "I'm glad you brought a friend. Or is he . . ."

"A friend, yeah," I interrupt.

She smiles. "Well, I'm glad. It's great to share your passions with friends. It took me forever before I was able to get my partner to look at a bird."

"It is nice." I need to get my mind off Elaine and Anderson. "I have my essay mostly done for the application. Should be ready soon."

She clasps her hands together. "Perfect, I'm so excited for you!"

"Thank you," I say. "For everything. I really look forward to coming every week. It means a lot to me."

I swear, her eyes look glassy. Everything about Jillian is so sincere.

"Of course," she says. "You don't know how much I appreciate you, Bianca. I'm always gushing about you at work, which is why you'd be perfect for the internship."

"Thank you."

"Don't mention it." Jillian gives my shoulder a squeeze. "Now, I'll let you get back to your birding."

She moves on, past where Anderson and Elaine are walking. My joy from the conversation with Jillian evaporates as nerves swing back to the forefront.

I pretend to look at a bird through my binoculars as I slow my breathing.

After another minute, Anderson taps my shoulder. "You good?"

I glare at him. "Not cool."

"What? We had some small talk. A quick introduction. A few comments about having brothers. I explained we're friends and I made you drag me along, and she happened to mention the time she tried to get an ex-girlfriend into birding . . ." He gives me a pointed look.

I can't remember how annoyed I was. It's like I forgot everything about everything except for this.

"Ex-girlfriend?" I repeat. "She said that?"

He nods. "And I got confirmation."

"Really?" Do I dare to hope?

"She flat out said she's pansexual." He says this like he's giving me the secret to happiness, and honestly, this kind of feels like that.

Because, sure, Elaine Yee might not like me, but at least the reason she won't like me isn't my gender. If anything, it'll probably be the fact that I spy on people or the fact that I have an ever-growing list of everything I'm afraid of and she's basically half of it. But there's still a *chance*.

"Is it wrong that I'm excited?" I ask.

"It would be weird if you weren't," Anderson says. "You got a shot, my friend."

He practically squeals along with me. It's silly, but I don't even care.

"Wait . . . weren't you supposed to be figuring out if she was possibly involved?"

Anderson frowns. "Right . . . well, priorities. She seems uninvolved enough, and you should talk to her."

I bite my lip. It's like for a moment I forgot you have to talk to people in order to get them to like you. It really puts a damper on things.

"I should . . ." I start.

"But?"

"I don't initiate conversation really," I say.

Anderson crosses his arms. "And how do you expect to meet anyone new?"

"Like their tweets and pray to Sappho?"

He shakes his head. "How's that worked for you?"

Well, I didn't expect to be attacked like this in my own home.

It'd be better to completely change the subject. Anderson doesn't care about looking at birds, even if he might pretend for my sake, so I take out the *Rules of Flight* book. It currently sports a book slipcover with small Pusheen illustrations—no one should be able to tell what it is.

I hold up the book to Anderson.

"Maybe we should take another look at this?" I ask. "We might be inspired by the whole birding thing."

He doesn't seem sold on us getting inspiration, but he nods. "Can't hurt."

Anderson takes the book and flips through the pages. While there is a good amount of space between everyone, we keep our voices low.

He opens to a random page and starts skimming the poem. He whispers the last two lines aloud. "'To stop the time on your life's ticking clock / Reset your mind and simply join the Flock' . . ." He looks at me. "I don't know what this means, but this is some weird-ass, creepy-ass, freaky-ass shit."

"I didn't think birding was that bad."

Both of us turn to Elaine Yee, standing right there, a smirk on her face that makes my heart race.

"It's this book we were assigned for English class," Anderson says. "The poems are kind of unsettling."

That's a good way of putting it.

"Really?" Elaine asks. "Like horror?"

Anderson looks at me. "Something like that."

"You can look if you want," I say.

I don't think Elaine is involved with the Flock. And double agent or not, she's still talking to me. That's a win.

"Sure," Elaine says. She takes the book and meets my eyes. "I love Pusheen."

"Ha, yeah," I say.

Ugh.

Elaine scans through the poem Anderson had it open to. "Definitely a little weird." She flips through some more. "Interesting that they are Shakespearean sonnets in style."

"They're what now?" I ask.

"Sonnets," Elaine repeats. She stands closer to show us the text. I focus my eyes on the book and not on how I can literally feel her next to me, which makes my palms sweat from more than the sun overhead. "It has three stanzas in the right rhyming format, followed by a couplet at the end. And it uses iambic pentameter—the ten-syllable lines mirror a heartbeat in rhythm. Which works a lot for romance and passion." She makes a face. "Not sure any of that is included here, but hey."

"Could there be some kind of code that has to do with it?" Anderson asks.

He seems a little excited at the prospect.

Elaine tilts her head to the side. "A code? Isn't it for English?"

Anderson and I share a look. I had basically already forgotten our excuse. "Our teacher is really into mysteries," I say. "She creates these extra credit assignments where you have to solve a puzzle based on poems and then do a presentation on the meaning."

I hope she doesn't notice my pained expression, or she figures it has to do with the assignment being too hard.

We don't go to the same school, so it's not like she'll look into it.

"Oh, that's really cool," Elaine says. "But if this is a puzzle-solving thing, I'd be down to help. I've got nothing going on today, if you're working on it later."

"We'd love some help," Anderson agrees before I have the chance to think about backing out.

Which I definitely would have done.

"Although I don't know much about Shakespearean sonnets," Elaine admits. "At least, no more than the basics."

It's not like Anderson and I do either. He's smart, but it's not like we spend that much time on Shakespeare in school. And if he did have a secret fascination, I think he would have brought it up by now, or found a Shakespeare Funko Pop! to add to his collection. An additional mind would be helpful, even if it isn't the safest to tell others what we have on VQ and the Flock. Maybe we don't have to tell her too much.

I can't pass up a chance to spend time with Elaine Yee, and Anderson would never forgive me if I did.

There's one clear option of where to go for help.

"The thing is . . ." I start. "I know someone who does."

TWENTY

THEREFORE I LIE WITH HER

There are currently sixty-one items on my ever-growing list of fears, and yet it's hard to imagine a nightmare worse than Elaine Yee sitting at our kitchen table with my mother hovering as I convince her to help us with a weird murder book.

Which might have something to do with the people who want me dead.

Fantastic.

"Anyone want a snack?" Mom asks, already putting together a plate of cheese and fruits. She sets it on the table between Elaine and Anderson. "Oh, let me grab some cookies."

If she learned anything from her mother-in-law, it's that you must have cookies on hand for when people come over. Dad may be the better cook, but Mom isn't a bad baker. Nonna said she's basically Italian after she taught Mom to make pizzelles.

Since then, one Sunday a month, she'll go ham on the pizzelle iron and make like a hundred or so to keep in storage. Always vanilla, never anise.

She makes a plate, adding some chocolate chip biscotti.

"Mom, you don't have to be so extra," I say, trying to keep my voice low so Anderson and Elaine don't hear over at the table.

She gives me a look. "You never have friends over besides Anderson, and he's basically family. You're giving me this."

It's the kind of look she has when she pulls out my middle name. Or worse, the confirmation name I had to get as a sham to keep the grandparents happy, despite Dad and me both being atheists and Mom mostly claiming she's "spiritual."

The whole confirmation *do you believe in God still check yes or no* thing was kind of weird, but looking at saints was cool. When I picked a name, I went with Saint Francis of Assisi because I read online that he was gay.

I shut up and let my mom fill the table with snacks.

"So," Mom says finally once she gets everyone to eat something. "You're all studying Shakespeare?"

"Well—" Elaine starts.

"Yes," Anderson interrupts. "Yes, we are. And we love him. The control of language, the deep emotions . . ." He looks at me for help.

"The dick jokes," I add. Helpfully.

Mom rolls her eyes but smiles. "There are plenty, that's true."

I look at Elaine, hoping she can gather from my expression that we will explain more later. Anderson must have the same thought as me, which is that my mom will be less than thrilled to know we're still investigating the murder that caused a threat to be left on my doorstep.

Our parents didn't exactly say to stop trying to investigate the murder, but I think they assumed that was implied.

Their mistake.

Looking into Elaine's brown eyes makes my heart practically flutter, but she gives a small shrug, and I guess she's going to go along with it.

And Elaine Yee is in my house. This might be a dream.

She looks so good.

I quickly snatch a pizzelle and try to hide my shame.

"Basically, we want to know about sonnets," Anderson says. "Bianca thought, since you're a theater professor, you could probably help."

"Oh, we can absolutely talk about sonnets," Mom says. "Let me get some paper."

Not only does she get printer paper, but she also returns with a book of Shakespeare's complete works.

"I don't know if we need the book," I start.

"Oh, there's an app you can use too," Mom says. "It has every Shakespearean play and sonnet for free."

Elaine and Anderson pull out their phones and start looking, like we're actually taking a course on Shakespeare and need to follow along.

"Now," Mom says, "you probably know the basic format of the sonnet." She opens the book to a random sonnet, which ends up being 138. "Three stanzas that follow the rhyme scheme of *abab*, *cdcd*, *efef*, and a couplet that rhymes, *gg*. The same letters indicate endings that rhyme." She writes the small letters next to the lines in pencil, directly in the book. "Each line is written in iambic pentameter, which you can break down in those awful English class readings like . . ." She takes the first line from the book. "'When *my* love *swears* that *she* is *made* of *truth*' . . . That kind of trash."

I would make a comment about her language, but she's just getting started. My mom gets a little too into this stuff. If I interrupt her, she might kill me before anyone involved in Feathergate even gets the chance.

"But that's not how you read Shakespeare," Mom continues. "Yes, when performing, you'd use your diaphragm and vocal techniques, but it can sound conversational. It has universal themes, and when done right, you'd be surprised by how much you actually understand. So, say we want to break this down like an actor, not an English teacher."

She grabs one of the printer pages and I take a second cookie.

"You can take the words that aren't like *the*, *a*, *is*, and *of*, and search the dictionary meaning, the denotation, and then write out your own meaning, the connotation. In class, I'd have students go deep into a stream of consciousness, really pull from their experiences and themselves, and I welcome you three to sit in on a class . . ." I give Mom a look, and after a sheepish smile, she continues. "But, anyway, for the sake of it now, let's take the couplet at the end of this sonnet."

She writes the two lines in big text.

"Side note," she adds. "Try to work with the first folio version if you can. His punctuation was intentional, unlike the punctuation and removed capitalization editors later changed and fucked up."

She has it out for people in the English field, I guess.

I eye the paper.

THEREFORE I LIE WITH HER, AND SHE WITH ME,
AND IN OUR FAULTS BY LIES WE FLATTERED BE.

Immediately, my face blushes at the *lie with her* part because Shakespeare is like inherently sexual. And now I'm thinking about sleeping with girls while Elaine Yee sits like a foot away from me and this is so much.

"The words I'd use here are *therefore, lie, her, she, me, faults, lies, flattered, be.*" Mom circles them. "These are where you can draw your connections. Pronouns and proper nouns can often have a lot of meaning. I'd also pay close attention to the last word in each line. Those hold a lot of importance."

My mind sort of focuses on the pronouns. Now that I'm thinking about pronouns for myself and the ones that represent me, it's all too easy to see that reflected in this poem.

"And our personal relationship with the text helps us understand it, even if we each have different connections."

She continues on with an example using one of the words, but my eyes keep going back to that *therefore I lie with her.*

That doesn't have to be a specific person to me.

It can be the pronoun that I no longer have an attachment

to. This different me that I allow as a shield because I'm afraid of letting the world see who I really am. I'm afraid of what will happen to that person.

I lie with *her* because I am a *they*, and because I want to make it easier for people. I suppress and ignore myself around others because I'm afraid of how everyone will react.

I look over the sonnet—it's like *she* is this female lie I've been spinning. I know she's not me and *she* knows it too, but we hold on to each other because it feels like it's safer.

No matter how much it actually hurts.

And, suddenly, this poet guy who has been dead for forever seems to have a solid grasp and understanding of my relationship to my gender and why I need to clutch on to this fake female identity I'm not comfortable with.

"Bianca, you okay?" Anderson asks.

Without meaning to, I started tearing up to a noticeable degree.

No better way to look cool in front of your crush than to cry the first time they see you outside your club.

"I'm fine," I start. "I just . . ."

I can't exactly explain everything *now*.

Mom reaches out and puts her hand over mine. "We get a lot of tears in acting class. You'd be surprised by the emotional release Shakespeare can offer. I usually have tissues on hand or have someone grab toilet paper from the restroom."

FEAR #43: ACTING CLASSES

"I'm good," I say. "Really."

I can't bring myself to look at Elaine, because no matter what her reaction is, I'm better off not knowing. I hear her voice, though.

"The last words have importance?" she asks my mom.

I can't be sure if she intended to do it, but that subject change is basically a godsend. Mom completely shifts her attention from me as I wipe my eyes with the sleeve of my shirt.

"Definitely," Mom says. "I do another exercise off the last words of each line. And another one with the couplets. Sonnets have power."

"I believe it," Elaine says.

I really hope that's not in reference to me.

An alarm goes off on Mom's phone. She eyes it. "Oh. I have to send out a quick schedule change for our rehearsal. But any questions, and you know where to find me."

"Thanks, Mom," I say.

She gives a wave to Anderson and Elaine as they thank her, and then goes off to her computer in the other room.

"I have an idea," Elaine says. "For the weird sonnet book."

"Let me get it," I say quickly. I want the excuse to flee for a moment so I can pull myself together.

I tossed my bag on my bed before asking Mom for help, so I rush over to it. The telescope is the first thing I see, still pointed out the large window. There is no way I can let Elaine Yee take one single look inside my room.

Puck stretches on my bed, opening her mouth wide in a yawn as her back arches. I scratch her on the butt before she settles back into the sheets. I give myself a quick glance in the mirror. My eyes aren't too red, although they are a little glassy. I wipe at them again.

I don't need to focus on how the rest of me looks right now.

Instead, I snatch up the book, pulling off the Pusheen cover because it isn't really needed now, and head back into the kitchen, where Anderson and Elaine talk over snacks.

"Got it," I say. For some reason I feel the need to announce myself even though the book is obviously in my hand.

"Did we try looking at the last words of the sonnets?" Elaine asks. "You were looking for some kind of hidden message, right? That could be a start."

We can use any kind of start. I sit back down at the table and open the book to the first sonnet, keeping it flat so that Anderson and Elaine can see.

I grab the paper and write out the last words.

Told
Heard
Old
Bird
Grace
Soar
Chase
More
Flight
Earth
Might

Curse

Never

Sever

I stare at the page of words for a while, but I don't really see anything in them. The first letters of the words don't spell out anything, and I'm not sure reordering them would make a difference.

"Well," Elaine says, looking as puzzled as I feel. "It might help if I know some context."

It's quite the story, and I don't really know where to begin.

"Bianca saw a guy get murdered and we think it's because he had information on this weird group called Valley Quail, which might be related to this book, and they also threatened Bianca a few times." Anderson practically counts off points on his fingers before deciding he's satisfied with his abridged version of events.

Elaine looks between the two of us. "What."

She doesn't even say it like a question.

"I did witness a murder," I admit. My skin is itchy. She probably won't believe me. Do I have to show her my room? I feel light-headed. "And, um, people are threatening me for looking into it. So we want to solve it before they try to kill us, too."

Anderson gives a sheepish and guilty smile. I don't know what else to say, so I keep looking back down at the list of words.

The minute that passes feels like an hour under high sun.

"Oh, and our high school is somehow involved," I add. "So, it's not actually an extra credit project. I just found this book in a teacher's office, and we think it's connected to the case."

"Huh," Elaine says finally. "What if we focused on the couplets?"

Both Anderson and I look at her like she suddenly sprouted a pair of wings.

"You're cool with this?" Anderson asks.

"You think I have something better to do than solve a murder and uncover a conspiracy?" Elaine asks. "Because I don't, and I know I'll be great at it. This is what all those episodes of Buzz-Feed Unsolved prepared me for."

She's so cool. I can only stare in awe for a moment.

"The couplets?" she repeats.

"Yeah, let's try it," I say. "The final two lines of each couplet?"

"Maybe just the last words," Anderson says. "I feel like the message won't be that long."

I start going through the book and writing out the final words from each couplet, until we have a complete list on one of the leftover sheets of computer paper.

Never/Sever
Balk/Talk
Outside/Abide
Fleetings/Meetings
Only/Lonely
Muse/Use
Code/Bode
Shames/Names
For/More
A/The

Flock/Clock
Rot/Not
The/Huh
Done/One
This/Bliss
Knife/Life
To/Knew
Choose/Lose
Next/Text
Strife/Life
To/Who
Rain/Gain
Early/Surly
Word/Bird
Gets/Lets
A/The
Worm/Firm
Lever/Clever
Birds/Herds
Met/Get
The/A
Lest/Best
Follow/Hollow
Preach/Each
Holy/Lowly
Squirm/Term
And/Sand

From/Come
Home/Roam
Flew/To
Your/Tour
Together/Forever
Nest/Best
Health/Commonwealth
North/Forth
Could/Oakwood
West/Test

Writing these words out over and over is going to have me thinking in rhymes pretty soon. But it definitely feels like we're getting somewhere. This has to be an excuse to hide a message, because a lot of these lines seem forced. Who ends sentences with *the*, *a*, or *to*? If Ms. Richards caught wind of this, she'd have a field day with her red pen tearing it apart. The poetic skills of the writer are really bad—I can't imagine someone publishing this for the enjoyment of reading it.

"Wait . . ." Elaine says.

She stands to look over my shoulder at the paper, hair falling so close, it could practically brush against my skin. I freeze up. If we touch even the smallest amount, my heart will go off the deep end.

I really hope I smell amazing.

Or, more realistically, decent.

"What if we only use one of the words from each couplet?" She takes the pen from the table, and after analyzing the words for a moment, starts crossing out half of them—one of each pair in alternating order.

What we're left with is actually cohesive. I read it out loud, to see how it sounds.

"Never talk outside meetings, only use code names, for the flock not the one, this life to lose, next life to gain, early bird gets the worm, clever birds get the best, follow each holy term and come home to your forever nest, commonwealth north oakwood west." I pause after I finish the end of the list. "Well, that definitely sounds creepy."

Anderson and Elaine nod in agreement.

"It's like rules for a cult or something," Anderson says. "Whatever this flock is . . . which might also be Valley Quail?"

My stomach drops. Hopefully I'll be able to keep down those cookies.

"What I'm interested in is the last part," Elaine says. "It seems like a location. Maybe that's where they go to meet?"

Commonwealth North, Oakwood West.

She's right. Those could be street names. I open up my maps app, setting my phone down so Anderson and Elaine can see, and look for the intersection. And Commonwealth does intersect with Oakwood. At the northwest corner, there looks to be an office building, or one of those shopping centers, as it has a Jamba Juice and a taqueria displayed.

Something tells me they aren't meeting over smoothies or al pastor.

That's when my phone buzzes loud against the table. A call

from an unknown number. It's definitely not Mom, since she's home, so that means . . .

"I think the killer is calling again." I put my phone down on the table like not touching it will help. "Do I answer?"

"Put it on speaker," Anderson says. "I'll record with my phone."

He gets his voice recorder app open and I answer the call.

"*Hello?*" Someone on the line says. "*Who's there?*"

It sounds grainy, like we're listening to a recording instead of someone speaking in real time. I don't think it's the killer on the line, as the man's voice is filled with fear.

"*Nate,*" a deeper voice says. "*It's been a while.*"

My heart pounds in my chest. Is Nate alive? Have they been keeping him captive this entire time?

"Who's Nate?" Elaine whispers.

"Our dead neighbor's missing nephew, shhh." Anderson's attention, like mine, is locked on the phone.

"*Stop . . .*" Nate says from the line. "*You don't have to do this, I won't say anything . . .*"

His words mumble into pleas, and then a scream pours through the speakers.

The call ends.

No. He couldn't have . . . they wouldn't . . . Tears prick my eyes as the hairs on my arms rise. They killed him. Just like they killed Mr. Conspiracy. And no one cared, no one was able to do anything about it.

Why would they share that?

"Shit," I say. "That was Nate. He's dead, too. Oh my God." I rub my eyes, but I'm shaking. Those were his last moments. This isn't right. "That had to be from a while ago, right? They couldn't have kept him alive all this time just to kill him now?"

I need validation that there wasn't anything we could have done.

"It was probably from January." Anderson swallows. "Or February. When he first went missing."

Elaine is completely still. She doesn't seem to know how to respond, and I can't blame her. It's not even my first interaction with a murder, and I'm certainly not taking it well.

I try to breathe, but the air comes out in quick gasps. "Shit," I manage to say again.

Anderson steadies me. "Hey, it's okay."

"No one was there for him," I say. "They killed *two* people, Anderson."

"I mean, you're here for him now," Elaine says. "We all are. That has to count for something."

I bite my lip. It's hard not to believe it when she says it. Maybe we can make a difference. Even if it's too late for Mr. Conspiracy and Nate, this Flock might have future victims we still can save.

"Exactly." Anderson points at his phone. "We have evidence now. We just have to prove who's involved. And we might be able to do that by checking out this location."

"Should we go?" I ask. My heart pounds in my throat.

I pull back up the location on my maps app. After that call, it's hard not to feel terrified, though a shopping center with a taco joint and smoothie shop hardly feels like it'd be connected to actual murderers.

"We should definitely go," Elaine says. "We just have to be safe about it."

Anderson nods. "Let's go Monday. We can meet up after school, and if we notice anyone or anything suspicious, it will seem like we're just getting food."

I'm glad he didn't suggest trying our luck tomorrow—I have enough to stress about with the support group. I don't need potential run-ins with murderers on top of that.

Still, this feels like a bad idea. Whoever VQ is, they didn't hesitate to kill people. I got their message loud and clear. I might be next.

I blink, feeling the leftover tears between my eyelashes. It would be so easy to say no, to stop here.

But Nate offered to stay silent, and that didn't change anything.

We have to solve this. We might not have any other choice.

"Okay." I take a deep breath to steady my nerves. "We'll go then."

Anderson nods and Elaine smiles right at me.

"It's a date," she says.

And, despite literally everything, the horrified patter of my heart lightens to an excited flutter.

TWENTY-ONE

A FAMILY NEXT DOOR

As if I wasn't nervous enough for our Monday plans of meeting up with Elaine to investigate a possible murder hangout, I have the nonbinary and trans support group to go to. Ronan offered to come, but he has a D&D campaign with friends, and I wouldn't want to take him away from that. Since Anderson is coming already, I'll be okay.

The chalky taste of Tums on my tongue, I knock on his door.

Mrs. Coleman opens it and immediately pulls me in for a hug. "Bianca, how are you?"

"I'm good, Mrs. Coleman, you?"

"Doing fine," she says, ushering me inside. "Anderson said he was going to give you a ride somewhere. He broke his wrist training last night, so I can drop the two of you off."

Anderson broke his wrist? He should've texted me. But it's

kind of nice he didn't accidentally out me by giving details.

"Is he okay to go?" I ask.

"I'm fine, don't worry, it's my left hand," his voice says. I jump and turn to the hallway, where he walks in with a cast around his wrist. "Although now I'm out of training for two months. Maybe I can do some one-handed Jiu-Jitsu . . ."

His mom gives him a light slap on his good arm. "You'll be out longer if you mess it up more."

He rolls his eyes and lets out a long sigh. "Well, I can help you train, Bianca. And, like . . ." He looks toward his mom for permission. "Watch the others, I guess?"

"As long as you don't make that injury worse, sure," Mrs. Coleman says.

"Why didn't you message me?" I ask. "We don't have to go."

"ER was wild. But we're good, promise," he says. Something about his smile makes me instantly believe him. Anderson looks at me. "You ready?"

I shrug. "I'm never ready, but I end up having to do stuff anyway."

Mrs. Coleman laughs, and I kind of feel guilty keeping the support group from her. I mean, if she didn't mind Ronan's gender, I feel like she'd have to understand where I'm coming from.

"It's a nonbinary support group," I say. "That we're going to." I pause and swallow before awkwardly adding, "Because I'm nonbinary."

"Oh." Mrs. Coleman pauses for a moment before pulling me into another hug. "Thank you for telling me. Let me know if you need anything, I went to some groups for trans families before." She smiles and looks at me. "And correct me if I misgender you."

I kind of feel bad with how well everyone is taking this. Almost like a terrible reaction is overdue or something. I swallow. Hopefully that won't come from my parents.

"Thanks," I say. "Really." My heart is still rapidly beating from the thought of telling Mom and Dad. "You can come in and stay for the meeting," I say. "If you want."

Which is how I end up bringing along two people who aren't my blood family to the group. To be fair, not being alone does make me feel a lot better—although I end up walking in by myself. I really have to pee, so Mrs. Coleman and Anderson drop me off at the door to look for parking.

I should've planned for parking issues: I live in Los Angeles. I should have used the bathroom before we left.

I rush inside the center and manage to find the bathrooms without talking to anyone. They are gender neutral, too, which is another win, although when I walk back into the lobby, Mrs. Coleman and Anderson still aren't here. A big part of me wants to wait for them before entering the room with the group name on a sheet taped to the door, but I feel like they'll be way prouder of me if I at least find us seats. I glance through the little window, keeping back slightly so I won't be seen.

It's a nice room. Kind of looks like a small space at a hotel where they do conferences and stuff. A bunch of chairs are set up in a semicircle, and three people are sitting.

Looking at each other.

Oh hell no, I can't do this.

I retreat back into the lobby.

"You here for the trans and nonbinary group?" a voice asks.

I turn around to a person about my age. They're Black, darker than Anderson and Mrs. Coleman, and their hair is in braids. They have a really cute floral romper on, jean jacket tied around the waist. They are so gorgeous I have to amend Fear #13 to

FEAR #13: BEAUTIFUL PEOPLE

I don't want to assume their gender because even though they present traditionally feminine, that doesn't define their identity or pronouns. I also feel like scurrying back to the bathroom. Some people are too attractive to talk to, and they can't all be secret geeks like Anderson.

"Yes," I manage to say.

"Great to meet you!" They hold out a hand. Their nails are painted in the bisexual flag colors, and the middle two fingers are kept short. "I'm Layla, she/they. Either set of pronouns is fine to use."

I shake their hand. While I can use *she*, I might as well get used to using they. I don't want to be one of those people who only uses the pronoun that's easier.

"Bianca. They/them," I respond.

"Is this your first time?"

"Yeah," I admit. "I have some people coming . . . I'm kind of bad at this stuff."

"No worries," they say. "You already did the hardest part by showing up."

That's reassuring, but I'm not totally convinced that's accurate.

I'm pretty sure the whole point of these groups is to share things about yourself and personal experiences.

"You don't have to talk if you don't want to," Layla adds, like that's a common fear. "It's also nice to be around other people like us."

Like us. I've never really been included in anything besides GLAOE, and it's not like this. Getting into birding was something I chose, and I'm happy to know other people with the same interest, but this feels different. It's a new kind of community that understands my identity. It's not about how much I know, it's a place where I can focus on getting to know myself.

"Cool," I say, after what was definitely too long of a pause.

I really wish I was better at talking to people. I get ready for Layla to walk in the room and leave my awkward ass out here until Anderson inevitably drags me in.

"You have an Instagram?" Layla asks. "You can reach out to me there if typing is easier."

They're so cool and friendly, and typing *is* way easier. Despite my Instagram being a glorified stalker account with maybe one photo of me among many shots of birds and Puck, I nod.

"Yeah, that'd be cool."

They pull out their phone and open the app so I can search for myself. I find my account and hand it back.

"Followed," Layla says. "Message me anytime."

I smile. "Cool, thanks."

Dammit, it's like my vocabulary is reduced to one word every time I have a social interaction. But with the way they're holding their phone, I can make out the case.

"Is that Luna?" I ask, even though it obviously is.

How many good-looking people are actually anime fans?

Layla lights up though. "Yeah! You watch *Sailor Moon*?"

I nod. "I watch a lot of anime."

"I'm a huge fan. I do a lot of cosplay too. Who's your favorite guardian?"

"Sailor Uranus," I say. "Race car drivers are hot. Lesbian icon. Screw the English dub."

"Hell yes," Layla says. "Bianca, we are definitely going to be friends."

The door opens and Anderson and Mrs. Coleman walk in. Anderson practically double-takes when he sees Layla.

"This is my support group support group," I say as they approach.

"That's so awesome you came for Bianca," Layla tells them, "I'm Layla, she/they."

"Anderson, he/him."

Sometimes I forget how cool Anderson is normally because he mostly acts like a dork around me. But, I'll give it to him. He's got a killer smile.

"Alicia," Mrs. Coleman says. "She/her, I'm Anderson's mom."

"Nice to meet you both," Layla says with a smile. Their eyes land on Anderson's arm. "What happened?"

"I train Jiu-Jitsu," Anderson says. He tosses them a smile. "You should see the other guy."

"You mean the guy who rolled over your wrist accidentally?" Mrs. Coleman asks.

The look Anderson gives her is priceless.

"Layla and I were talking about *Sailor Moon*," I say, making a note to look at Anderson. "She's a big anime fan too."

Both Mrs. Coleman and Anderson look like Christmas came early.

"Too?" Layla asks.

"*One Piece* is literally how Bianca and I became friends," Anderson says.

"Oh, so you're only into Shonen stuff," Layla says.

"Tell that to the masterpieces that are *Fruits Basket* and *Ouran High School Host Club*," Anderson counters.

"Damn, all right." Layla actually does look impressed. She turns to us. "I wish I could talk more, but I should finish setting up."

"I can help," Anderson says. There's that smile again. "I've still got one free hand."

He's too overpowered. He took his flirting to fifth gear. I'm so jealous. I'm an awkward mess if Elaine is even in the general vicinity.

"Thank you," Layla says, and the two of them walk off.

Mrs. Coleman and I stand in the lobby for a second, because we both know better than to immediately follow after.

"He needs to teach me his ways," I say.

"Oh, he gets his charm from me," Mrs. Coleman says after a laugh. "That gorgeous person won't run away at the sight of his room? I hope he marries her."

Honestly, same.

After enough of a moment has passed, we walk inside and write our names and pronouns on name tags before taking seats in the middle of the room. Mrs. Coleman casually looks over to Anderson and Layla, grabbing chairs from across the room to fill out the other half of the circle, before looking back at me.

"I feel like there should be snacks, I'll bring something next time."

I can't argue against food, and it also is immediately reassuring that she's open to a next time.

"We can have my dad help make them, he always wants to cook and bake." I swallow. "If I tell him it's like . . . anime club."

Mrs. Coleman laughs. "I'm surprised you two didn't start one of those already."

I look at her. "Thanks for coming with me."

Mrs. Coleman sets her purse on her lap and reaches out to lightly touch my shoulder. "Of course." She pauses, almost weighing her next words. "So your parents don't know?"

I shake my head.

"Do you not want to tell them?"

"I don't know," I say. "I just don't know if they'd accept me. I guess it can be different when it's your kid."

"But because you're their kid, that might not matter," she says. "I can't promise it, and it might not be easy. When I first found out Ronan is a boy, I was definitely confused, and I didn't always do everything right. It can take time. The important thing is that Ronan's my son, and I love him no matter what. His gender, what he needs to do to match his outside to his inside . . . that falls into the 'no matter what.' And any person who doesn't support their child in living their life as their true selves has no right being a parent." She meets my eyes. "And if your parents don't realize that, fuck them. You got a family next door."

I can't say how much this means to me. Even if Anderson and I have been friends for a while, it's different to hear it like that directly, especially when I need it most.

My eyes are watering, so I pull Mrs. Coleman into a hug to try to keep people from seeing.

They definitely notice, but no one says anything, and I feel like they might be used to it. I'm not sure how to feel about that, so I don't really think about it.

I move back into my seat to brush at some tears. "I think my dad will be okay with it, but my mom's a different story. She's done a lot for me, so I don't want to complain, but she's kind of like the stereotypical white feminist." Mrs. Coleman makes a knowing face at that and I continue. "Like, I don't think she'd disown me or anything, but she won't get it. She'd only ever see me as her daughter. I'm realizing that's never what I was or who I am."

Mrs. Coleman nods. "It's been almost two years since Ronan first came out, and it still feels new to me. You don't stop loving someone just because you can't understand them." She holds up one finger. "That doesn't mean you have to tell her if you don't want to."

"Seriously, thank you." I don't know how to convey what I'm feeling. It's not my strongest trait to begin with, and I'm normally not this emotional in front of people I don't know well.

"I guarantee our Thanksgiving has better food anyway," Mrs. Coleman says. "Consider yourself invited."

I forgot that's coming up. The invitation is nice, and dinner with the Colemans sounds like heaven compared to the usual Torre Thanksgiving: pizza delivery, since Dad always works and Mom would burn water if she tried hard enough. I love my mom and my sister, but I'd need like ten espresso shots to keep up with their energy.

Anderson joins us after a bit.

"I'm in love with them," Anderson says once he sits down.

"Did you get their number?" I ask.

He grins, causing Mrs. Coleman and me to both freak out a little as the meeting gets under way.

"She does *cosplay*, Bianca," Anderson says quickly.

"I know."

At least now I'm able to focus on how happy I am for Anderson and dry some of my tears. He doesn't ask about them.

"Let's start with some introductions," a person across the circle says. They have a buzz cut and killer eye shadow. "Name, pronouns if you'd like to share them, and something good about this week. I'm Lex, they/them, and I got a new bed for my cat and he actually uses it."

I'm glad that we don't all respond *Hi, Lex* like at AA meetings in movies.

My one solace is that the introductions go around the circle, so I can anticipate my embarrassment bubbling up. I keep rubbing my damp palms on my pants. What happened this week? I found out a teacher in my school may be involved in a poetic murder cult? I got threatened with a bloody cat toy and followed home? I'm going to investigate the creepy lair of said cult that killed at least two people?

Everyone's staring at me. Because it is my turn.

"I'm Bianca," I say. "They, uh, them . . ." Oh no, that sounded like my Italian uncle saying my pronouns. Abort intro. But people are still watching me, because I didn't complete the instructions. "I . . . um . . . well, I, uh, actually came out this week."

To like four people and kind of a fighting gym, but hey.

The announcement gets me gentle applause and congratulations and my face heats up so much.

FEAR #17: BEING THE CENTER OF ATTENTION IN ANY CIRCUMSTANCE

I could give another huge hug to Mrs. Coleman when she puts me out of my misery to start her introduction.

The rest of the meeting isn't that bad. It's an open discussion, the weekly topic being how our gender identity affects our relationships, and while my mind is constantly going, I don't say anything.

FEAR #37: OPENING UP TO STRANGERS

And this is a big enough group that I'm getting some anxiety from

FEAR #1: PUBLIC SPEAKING/HUMILIATION

So I stay quiet. But Layla was right. No one pressures me to speak, and it is nice to listen and be around other people who have similar experiences, even if I'm only getting started on my own journey with gender.

It seems like no time has passed when everyone begins packing up their stuff.

"Well, I'm super down to come next week," Anderson says, stealing a glance at Layla.

"Me too," Mrs. Coleman adds.

"I'd like that," I say.

It's not like I'll be any more open to sharing next week, but it will be nice to have them here.

My phone buzzes. It's a text from Elaine, which sets off a quick flutter in my heart.

Elaine: We still on for tomorrow?

I type in a quick

yeah

Coming back here next week with Mrs. Coleman and Anderson will be great.

If I'm not killed at the cult hideout, that is.

TWENTY-TWO

BIANCA TORRE LAUGHS IN THE FACE OF DANGER

Since Elaine couldn't meet until five and I'm a big ball of nerves given the nature of what we're doing and who we're doing it with, Anderson takes me back to the MMA gym to help me train. I officially joined, and while the membership is kind of expensive, my dad was into the idea of me learning some self-defense.

School went by without any issue. And even though *The Rules of Flight* burned a hole in my backpack, I didn't notice any teachers giving me death glares or strange looks like they knew I took it.

I close my eyes and release a breath. My glove makes contact with the bag.

Anderson coaches me by calling out combinations and occasionally making anime references for motivation.

I fix my stance and uppercut the bag, alternating between my left and right hand as sweat drips down my face.

"They're looking great," Rafael's voice says. I turn my head slightly to see Rafael watching us as he walks by. He catches my gaze. "When are you going to train with me, Bianca? What's this guy have that I don't?" He smacks Anderson's good shoulder.

"Charm," Anderson responds. "Beauty. A fantastic sense of humor. Raf, what do you have that I don't?"

"A black belt," Rafael says.

Anderson looks back at me. "Well, he's got me there."

"I'm not sure Jiu-Jitsu is for me. Maybe a striking class . . ." I say. "I have the app now, so I can check the schedule."

I'm mostly appeasing him. He has been great about my pronouns and super welcoming, though. Maybe I could try one class and stand way in the back. If Anderson goes with me.

"Okay, but if you ever want to grapple, we can find a time to train with you and Mr. Charm and Beauty over here." He shakes his head but keeps on a smile. "Let me know."

The issue with using training as a distraction is that it works a little too well, and before I know it, I'm rushing home to take a quick shower so I'm not disgusting when Elaine arrives.

My hair's wet as I walk outside to wait with Anderson, so I throw it into a small bun. Maybe I should cut it short. It might help a little with not presenting so female, which would be great—although certain androgynous styles make me look like a thirteen-year-old boy, which is not how I want cute girls like Elaine to see me. But there might be some smaller adjustments I can make to inspire some euphoria.

Even if I'm perceived a certain way, I kind of wish I wasn't perceived at all.

Can I label my gender as, like, awkward void cryptid?

Or I'll just buy a flannel from the men's section and wear a baseball cap, I don't know.

Maybe I can ask Layla for some help. Sure, their gender expression seems to stay traditionally feminine, but they might have an idea of what would work for me. I followed them back on Instagram, and while reaching out by DM is another thing entirely, it's a nice thought.

"You ready?" Anderson asks once he jogs over from his apartment building.

I probably should've taken the time to look a little nicer instead of wearing a sports bra, baggy shorts, and a loose T-shirt that has a few crows on it and says *murder*. It's kind of on brand for the moment though.

"You know the answer to that," I mutter.

"No, you're not, but you're here, and that's what counts," he says. "I'm making some small talk so I don't freak out, because I've been texting Layla and she's amazing."

His voice is a little higher than normal and he's practically showing dimples. It's so cute to see him like this. Our anime crushes don't exactly inspire the same behavior.

"Did you see the Boa Hancock cosplay she posted?" I ask.

"Yes, and I can honestly die happy after it." He holds a hand up to his head. "Bianca. I'm falling hard. We were up until three last night talking."

My eyebrows raise. That's exciting for him *and* impressive. "Did you ask her out?"

I'm not really sure how that works given my lack of experience, but maybe I can learn something for the future. If I could be one-eighth as smooth as Anderson, that'd be a dream.

"Not yet, you can't rush these things." Anderson rubs his eye, almost like he's hiding his expression. "And I already like her too much for it only being twenty-four hours since we met. I can't seem, like, too clingy."

"Wouldn't seeming like you're really interested be a good thing?" I ask.

"Bianca, you sweet, sweet cinnamon roll," Anderson says. He puts a hand on my shoulder and looks directly into my eyes. "No."

His phone lights up. "See? That's her. And I'm so excited I might tear up a little, but I'll give it a few minutes. Keep it chill."

"Oh."

Who knew there were so many rules to this? There's no way I'm ever going to be good at flirting.

"Is there a specific amount of time you have to wait?" I ask. "And that doesn't apply to full conversations, like late-night stuff, right?"

Before Anderson has a chance to answer, Elaine pulls up and parks at the curb. She waves. I start to walk toward the back seat of her car, but Anderson beats me to it. He grins.

My heart beats a little faster. I dry my palms on my ass,

regretting not wearing longer shorts, and open the door to the passenger side.

Elaine wears an open flannel with high-waisted shorts and a crop top underneath. She looks so cute and put together and I want to run away.

"I love that shirt," she says.

"Thanks," I mumble, focusing on not fleeing and instead getting into the car and strapping in.

I'm so close to her. Jesus.

"Sorry I'm late, I had college counseling after school."

"Must be nice." Anderson sprawls out in the back. "Us public school kids basically just get a thumbs-up from the guidance counselor and a link to the Common App."

Elaine puts the intersection into her GPS and then starts driving. My muscles are so stiff, and my hands are folded over my lap like I'm in Catholic school church.

"We actually don't live that far from each other," Elaine says, sending me a glance.

I'm not really sure how to respond to that. I should probably say something like *oh really? We could do some evening birding hikes, or you could come over to Discovery Channel and chill.*

"Oh," I say in a high-pitched voice. "Nice."

You can take a person out of their comfort zone, but you can't take the lesbian sheep out of the person, I guess.

"Also, I shared the address with my brother in case things go south," Elaine says. "If he doesn't get a check-in text from me every half hour, he's bringing backup."

"Smart thinking." Anderson leans forward between us. "How far are we from the cult hideout?"

Elaine glances at her phone, secured on the dash. "It's like ten minutes away."

"Great." He falls back against the seat. "Right around the corner."

"I mean, the cult book was found at our school," I say. "Who would want to go far for their cult meetings? In Los Angeles traffic?"

At least they can laugh at that.

"How'd you know the book was related?" Elaine asks. "When you saw it?"

"It had the same symbol as something Mr. Conspiracy uncovered," I reply. I can't remember if we clarified the nickname or not, so I add, "The guy who was murdered."

"And we think it has to do with some money laundering company called Valley Quail," Anderson says from the back seat. "Which we've also been referring to as Feathergate. Or the whole thing as Feathergate? Either way. Our school has been allocating funds there saying they are an educational supply company, but we can't find anything on them. It must be a cover."

Elaine takes this in as she drives.

"Okay," she finally says. She cracks a little smile. "Guess I missed a lot, huh?"

"You really should've joined the investigation earlier," I say. "I mean, you weren't here for the first few threats on my life and everything."

I hope she gets my sense of humor and doesn't think I'm actually into death threats.

"I always miss the good stuff." Elaine laughs. "But the fan favorites are usually introduced later in the story."

I'm not sure what to say so I smile a little. Does it look forced? That little exchange of conversation was probably a step in the right direction. Totally natural. I can do this.

"It's okay," I add after a moment. "It seems like we're getting into the exciting part, so maybe you have perfect timing."

"All those years of practicing piano with a metronome finally paid off."

She plays piano? That's cool, although not really an in for a conversation since I don't do anything remotely musical—aside from being forced to learn the words to the show tunes that Kate belts in the shower or rehearses for her performances.

The car falls into silence, and for some reason, that makes me more uncomfortable. I'm fine being alone, but when I'm with other people, the whole awkward-pause thing isn't my favorite. Especially because I'm with Anderson, and I can be myself around him.

"Thanks for helping us out," I say to Elaine. "It might be dangerous."

"No problem," she says. "I need to do something besides read books and watch birds." Her eyes sneak in my direction for a moment. "And Anderson told me you have a mean left hook, so I'll have you to protect me."

Anderson may have exaggerated and needs to stop telling

people about my training progress, but the way she says that makes me want to buy him dinner for doing it.

The idea of me protecting anyone from anything is laughable, though. I'm literally the poster child for the flight response. But I feel like that's not something to say on a first date.

Not that this is a date. It's totally not. Anderson is here, for one, and Elaine doesn't like me like that.

I'm getting too into my head again.

"Uh, yeah, of course," I say. "I laugh in the face of danger."

FEAR #26: DANGEROUS SITUATIONS IN GENERAL

"Very badass," Elaine says.

Anderson at least has the decency to not call me out and, with her response, sneaks a thumbs-up to me.

Elaine pulls into the shopping center that matches the location from the book and parks in one of the empty spots. There is the Jamba Juice, the taqueria, and a liquor store that is currently chained up.

"Are we sure it's here?" Anderson asks. "Something tells me the murder cult is not going to be meeting at Jamba."

I scan the storefronts. There has to be something weird about this place.

We walk back and forth a few times around the shopping center, but there's literally nothing out of the ordinary.

"Maybe this is a setup?" Elaine asks.

Anderson takes out his phone. "I'm sharing my location with Ronan. Just in case we're jumped."

Perhaps this wasn't our best idea.

"Is it possible they just meet over tacos?" I ask.

"We need a new game plan." Elaine tosses her hands up. "This is a bust. We might as well get smoothies and figure something else out." She looks around. "Plus, it is a lot less suspicious if we talk inside."

Anderson and I both shrug. Smoothies sound like a better idea than standing around outside a potentially dangerous area.

We head into the Jamba Juice. It doesn't take long to get our orders, and we sit around the table.

"What do you know about this Feathergate company itself?" Elaine asks.

Anderson looks at me, but I don't have much to offer. "Not a lot."

Elaine frowns. "Do they have a website or something?"

"We couldn't find one." Not that Ronan and I looked all that deeply into it, but the name seems too specific not to yield any search results.

"What about VQ?" Anderson drops his voice to mouth the abbreviation. "That's what Mr. Conspiracy called it."

Elaine types into her phone and scrolls a bit. Her eyes lift to meet mine. "Is this the weird bird symbol you were talking about?"

The web page she shows us features the exact symbol from the book, with *VQ INC.* lettered in a bright text on top of it. Underneath, it says *Established 2018*.

We *really* didn't look that hard, I guess.

"This has been going on for a while then. Is there anything

else?" To see the screen, I have to lean in closer to her. My palms sweat and my heart skips.

"No, there's some vague mission statement, but I doubt it would help."

Without warning, her face turns to mine, and we're only like two inches apart. My eyes have no choice but to drop to her lips, which seem really soft and probably taste like her smoothie.

"I'm going to the bathroom," I quickly announce, and turn my head before either of them can see my blush.

Real smooth, Bianca.

If I'm lucky, the bathroom will have a window big enough for me to crawl out of so that I never have to face Elaine again. Thankfully, there's no one using the restroom, so I can go right in and lock the door.

I didn't actually have to pee, but since I'm in here, I go for it anyway.

It's a nice bathroom. Clean, well-stocked. It's a little weird that there's a storage closet on the inside. I don't normally see those in public bathrooms. The closet door is riddled with doodles. After flushing and washing my hands, I walk up to it.

Reading what people have to say is a lot easier than hearing it. It's almost like a different form of watching them—a small window into the lives of strangers.

And it gives me an excuse to recover before going back out to Elaine.

The writing on the door is mostly just initials, swear words, a few penis doodles, and the drawing of the Valley Quail symbol.

What the hell?

The door has a keypad to get in. Is it possible that *this* is what the book was referring to?

It seems to require a four-digit passcode. I try 1234, but that doesn't work. I shouldn't be doing this. I don't know what's on the other side, and just because the symbol is on the door doesn't mean this closet has anything in it. Maybe someone involved in Feathergate had to poop and decided to kill time by making a carving.

I think back to the website. A lot of people use certain years for PINs.

I type in the digits 2018.

The keypad flashes green and unlocks. My heart pounds wildly. I slowly open the closet door. Except it isn't a storage closet.

It's a stairwell.

And while I can't make out what's at the bottom, I can see what hangs from the wall leading down.

Three plague doctor masks.

I try to give a little laugh but end up feeling some acid in my throat.

Shit.

TWENTY-THREE

NOT A PEEP

I take a few quick pictures of the doorway and the stairwell leading down with my flash off, then quietly make sure the door is firmly shut and locked before rushing out of the bathroom.

My mind is a mess of *what is happening oh my God oh my God*, but I try to keep my cool until I make it back to the table.

"I found it." I keep my voice low, but it definitely is more of a whisper-yell. "The evil lair is here in the bowels of the Jamba."

Anderson blinks, looking up at me. "What the hell are you talking about?"

My experience spills out of me, a rush of words trampling over each other. I take out my phone and show them the pictures. Anderson nearly spits his whey protein shake in my face.

"They have a secret entryway in the bathroom?"

I nod.

"I'm a little confused," Elaine says between sips of her own smoothie. "What do plague doctor masks have to do with anything?"

"The killer had one on." I rub my hands on my knees.

"We should go down there then," Elaine says.

"No, we shouldn't!" I blurted that too quickly. I don't want to seem scared in front of her, so I add a quick, "It's evening. Any of them could be there. And what if they have weapons?"

"Fair points."

"Yeah, I'm not really in the mood to take on a weird cult today," Anderson says. "I didn't even finish my drink."

It's hard to hide my relief. "Maybe we should head back to the car? Someone involved could be anywhere, and I'd rather watch the entrance through locked doors."

Anderson and Elaine nod, and we grab our smoothies and exit. I try not to walk too suspiciously fast as we get to the car, but I still try to open the handle before Elaine can unlock it. Finally, we get in, the entrance of the store still in view.

"Okay," Elaine says. "Basically, this confirms that the book and symbol are definitely connected to the person who murdered Mr. Conspiracy." Excitement lines her voice. She ties her hair back into a loose ponytail. "We can assume the person you saw, the person who killed him, was part of the Flock."

"The Flock?" I ask.

"It's what they call themselves in the poetic cult handbook, might as well use it."

"You pick up on murder investigation stuff very quickly," I say, trying to keep my voice light.

She gives me a grin. "What can I say? I'm a fast learner."

It's not like she said anything suggestive, but the way she's looking toward me makes my lungs feel like they're filled with helium. I want to float and flee at the same time. She still doesn't break my gaze. I cross my legs, heart rate quickening.

"That means someone at our school might be the killer," Anderson says with a mouthful of acai. "I bet it's Coach Roberts. Complete dick."

My face starts heating because for a moment I completely forgot Anderson was in the car with us. To be fair, he finally responded to Layla's text and was keeping to himself, but it had a lot more to do with Elaine being next to me.

She's helping out, it's not like she's interested in me. I have to remove the word *date* from my vocabulary until this is done, she gets bored of me, and we go back to occasionally saying a few words to each other on birding hikes. Otherwise, I'm going to get my own hopes up for no reason, only to be really disappointed in the end.

"I doubt it's Coach Roberts," I say. "It was in the office with the English and history department, so it has to be one of them, right?"

"That's true . . ." He bites his straw as he thinks. "It's probably not Ms. Richards or Mrs. Garcia. They don't seem the type."

He's not wrong. And with the way Ms. Richards critiques my

writing, I don't think she'd let a book of mediocre poetry slide.

"Ms. Schmidt, the Euro teacher? Now, I could see her killing someone," Anderson continues.

"I mean, someone doesn't have to be an obvious murderer." Elaine tucks loose strands of hair behind her ear. "They are involved in this Flock, which implies multiple people, and doesn't mean they were the one to kill the guy. They could've let it happen without doing the dirty work."

"True." Anderson looks off like he's trying to go through all the teachers in the English and history departments to figure out who could be the most murderer adjacent.

"But why would they leave the book out?" I ask. "Like, it was way obviously in the open."

"Maybe they were trying to test you." Elaine sips her smoothie before returning it to the cup holder. "To see if you're actually still investigating the murder. They might not know how much you know, but if you took the book, it definitely seems like you're looking into them."

Great. This makes me feel great.

"Awesome," I say.

"And with the bird references?" Elaine asks. "It seems like someone is targeting you directly."

Another nice thought.

"I mean, Mr. Conspiracy used bird references before I got involved," I say.

Anderson leans forward. "It is a possibility that a birding group is involved."

Yeah, that probably is important to mention. Elaine's eyebrows raise.

"It can't be ours. But if it is, I bet it's Mr. Wattson," she says.

"Who's randomly judging murderers now?" Anderson teases.

A bit of color rises in Elaine's cheeks. "Well, we can't rule out the possibility. If anyone was laundering from our group . . . But is there any evidence that points to GLAOE specifically?"

I shake my head. "I can't imagine there being tons of bird clubs in the area, but no." I sigh. "And we don't know if that's a real connection. All this started with Nate, who was an avid birdwatcher. It could be because of him?"

Anderson blinks like he never even considered that. I can't blame him for focusing on the birding group possibility either. "I don't know," he says. "*Maybe.*"

"We should look into it either way," Elaine says. "But our group isn't meeting again until the weekend. So, what's the plan now?"

"I think we're looking at this from the wrong angle," I say. "This location is a great start, but there could be something else we're missing with Feathergate."

"You do have to catch me up a bit more on that," she says.

"I'll send you pictures of the school's budget documents. We can also look more into the sonnet book." I brought it with me, concealed by the Pusheen cover, so I hand it to her. "We can try to figure out what they're planning, apparently there's something going down on the eighteenth."

Elaine leans the book on the steering wheel and begins

flipping through the various sonnets.

"Yeah, that doesn't give us much time. It's possible there's more hidden in here, but this also could be one of a few things the cult members are given. That would be smarter than putting it all in one place. You know, in case someone happens to steal it."

She looks directly at me and I feel my cheeks heating. I take a long sip of my smoothie, willing the cool drink to prevent the spreading blush from being that bad.

"What they didn't prepare for is a Shakespeare-obsessed mom," I say. "If the next book is based on Stanislavski or Meisner acting techniques, they better watch out."

"No idea what that means," Anderson says.

I'm not sure if Elaine does either, but it gets her to smile, and that's honestly enough for me.

"Other than the address, I'm not sure what to get from this . . ." She looks at me, then twists to Anderson in the back seat. "Any ideas?"

I completely forgot the entire message, so I have to read over it a few times. It doesn't seem to give any clearer information. Not that poetry has ever been a strong suit for me. I think I maybe tried to write a haiku for an assignment in class once and got a C on it. That's about the extent of my knowledge.

"The 'this life, next life' thing is kind of unsettling," I say. "Do you think that has something to do with killing Mr. Conspiracy? Or Nate? To, like, rebirth them or something?"

"No, they definitely killed them to silence them," Anderson

says, leaning forward to see the paper. "This makes it seem like only the cult people are reborn. Which, along with the money they're stealing, is probably what gets people to join."

"Great to know what we're dealing with," Elaine says.

Despite the sarcasm in her words, her eyes are wide and shining. I feel like she really did watch a lot of true crime or something, because this seems to be right up her alley.

I'd be happy to follow her every idea to see her face illuminate like that.

"Wait, we should show you Mr. Conspiracy's diary," Anderson says. "It's mostly . . . pretty out there . . . but if there was a code in the cult book, maybe he left some kind of code for us too."

"Did you know him?" Elaine asks.

Anderson and I share a look. "Kind of," I say finally. "We both had connections to him, even if we weren't super close."

"Well, I'll still try to help. Fresh eyes and all." It's like she's trying not to sound eager. It's not exactly working, but the excitement is a little contagious.

"We took pictures of the pages. I can share the folder with you." I open it up on my phone and hand it over to Elaine to type in her email. "Are you sure you want to do this though? Like, they have been threatening me."

Maybe I am being a little paranoid. But the concern seems valid enough to add

FEAR #62: CULT MEMBERS MURDERING THE GIRL I LIKE

"Fortunately, the threats have been limited to Bianca,"

Anderson says. "It makes helping out a lot easier."

I'm glad that's the case, even if he is teasing and I'd much rather there be no threats at all.

"They probably won't even know I'm involved, it's fine." She winks at me. "If they kill you first, then I'll get worried."

"Great," I say. "Thanks."

Elaine hands me back the poetry book. "I'll take you two home before I get into it. I'll text you if I can find anything, but we can also meet up soon."

I can't argue with that. Even if it doesn't lead to any more information on the Flock, it's an excuse to hang out with Elaine again.

"Sounds good."

The drive home goes by faster, and I'm not sure if that's because it doesn't feel quite as awkward. Elaine parks in front of my house.

"Thanks for trusting me with this," she says as I open the door.

I tuck a loose strand of hair behind my ear. "Thanks for helping."

She gives a thumbs-up, and I exit the car along with Anderson.

"See you soon." He waves.

"For sure."

Once we're both on the sidewalk, she waves back and drives off. My heart races long after her car disappears around the corner.

"You're getting better," Anderson says. "There is hope for you yet."

I look over. "That's actually reassuring."

"Speaking of potential crushes, I'm gonna FaceTime Layla."

"Because you're playing it cool, right?"

"Ice cold." He grins.

"See you."

He pulls me in for a one-armed hug. "Text Elaine."

I hug him back before gently shoving him away. "That's a bad goodbye."

Anderson laughs it off and already starts pulling up Layla's contact info as he jogs back to his apartment. I pull out my keys and unlock the front door before stepping inside. Dad should be at work. Mom has class, and it's tech week for Kate, so she likely won't be home before ten a single night this week.

I send a text to our family group chat to let them know I'm home. Mom immediately likes it, but doesn't respond otherwise. It's part of our post-threats arrangement, along with keeping my location visible.

"Hello?" I call to the empty house.

Nobody answers, but I suppose nobody breaking in would.

I shut the door behind me quickly and lock it. I'd dead bolt it too if Mom wasn't due to come home soon. I can't explain this bad feeling that nestles in my chest, being home alone. My first thought is to ask Anderson if I can go over his place, or if he would want to come over and watch *Your Name* or *Spirited Away* for the twentieth time. I don't want to interrupt his call with

Layla, though, because I do like them both.

It's probably leftover paranoia from the previous threats.

My bedroom door is slightly open, but as I approach, I hear Puck doing a weird mix of her bird chirp and a growl.

Is there a bird outside the window?

A little excitement rises in me. I could actually use some quiet birdwatching to get my mind off everything. Maybe a little people-watching too. If I can handle it. It has been a while, and it might be too much after the whole mask discovery today.

I walk inside, and instead of my telescope grabbing my attention, it's the words on the outside of my window, written in blood.

My heart stops. My breathing comes too quickly, and my vision blurs.

Against better judgment, I walk closer.

Next to the blood, there's a small bird hanging from a string. I recognize the little gray-vest plumage of an olive-sided fly-catcher, though it's hard to be sure with the blood staining the feathers. There's a hole on the outside of its belly that has some of the inside peeking through. Its neck is bent at an unnatural angle, body too stiff and still.

Tears start burning my eyes.

FEAR #10: BLOOD

FEAR #56: ANIMAL CARCASSES

My heartbeat is too fast. I'm light-headed. I'm breathing way too quickly. I need to slow my breaths. Measure them.

It doesn't work. It's like my body is shutting down. I'm dizzy.

I glance back at the lettering next to the hanging bird. This time I know the blood isn't fake.

I briefly register the words before my vision goes white.

NOT A PEEP.

TWENTY-FOUR

ANDERSON COLEMAN IS AFRAID OF SOME THINGS

I can't stay here. I manage to scoop up Puck and make it out of my bedroom, shutting the door behind us. I stumble down the stairs, Puck squirming out of my arms, but not going far. I barely make it to the couch before falling over. I only feel a slight reprieve as my face presses into the cushion. I'm not sure if I narrowly avoid passing out or if I do pass out a little as I lie on the couch with my eyes squeezed shut.

Puck sits down next to me and starts to lick the hair of my forearm. I let her. If anything, the scratchy tongue is kind of soothing.

When I regain a small sense of equilibrium, I reach for my phone in my pocket. I can't stay in the house. I'm not sure Mom or Dad have access to their phones, and I know Kate doesn't.

I want to call Anderson. I shouldn't be alone. I would hate to interrupt his call with Layla. Still . . .

What if the person who did this is still nearby? I at least have to make sure the Colemans are aware in case someone tries to target Anderson too.

I call Ronan.

He picks up on the second ring.

"Is everything okay?" he asks.

He must know that I'm not the type of person to call unless it was some kind of an emergency. Normally, the very idea of having to talk on the phone fills me with dread.

FEAR #20: PHONE CALLS

But hearing a familiar voice right now is reassuring.

"Can you come get me?" I ask. It's probably not the best way to start, but I don't know how else to say it. "Not alone, though! Or maybe I can come over, if that's okay? I . . . I was threatened again, and it's a little worse this time."

While I think murdering a bird and using its blood to write a creepy message on the second floor is a bit more than *a little worse*, I don't really want to go into the details right now.

"We'll be right over," Ronan says.

"Okay," I say. "Thanks."

Ronan hangs up. I hate how scared and small my voice sounds, but I'm not necessarily out of danger yet. Ronan must run over, hopefully with Mr. Coleman, because barely a few minutes pass before there's a knock on the door.

I stand up slowly but don't answer it immediately.

"Bianca?" Ronan's voice calls. "We're here."

I unlock the door and open it up to Ronan and Anderson.

"I didn't mean to interrupt your call," I say.

"Shut up." Anderson puts his good arm around me and pulls me in. I'm not one for contact, but this is welcome. I can barely stand up on my own without shaking. "Where is the threat?"

"My room," I say. "The window."

Ronan checks his phone. "Mom is reaching out to your parents. You're going to stay with us, so we'll need to grab your things. Are you good to go in the room again or should Anderson and I go for you?"

As much as I don't really want to be greeted by the sight of the bird in there, I'm not sure I could handle the embarrassment of my two male friends picking out my underwear. "I can go." I shift on my feet. "I shouldn't leave Puck though."

Like she wants to make sure of it, Puck starts circling around our legs and brushing her side against them. Either way, if someone is willing to mangle a bird, I'm not sure how far they'd have to stretch to move on to pets.

"Mom loves Puck, so it shouldn't be an issue. I'll ask her." Ronan already starts typing out a message. "Anderson, you can help Bianca."

Anderson leads me to my room and walks in first. I try to look anywhere but the window. Of course, it's the first thing he sees.

"That's a real bird?"

I nod.

"Okay." He rubs his forehead for a second. "Get whatever you need, I can help carry it."

"Am I spending the night?"

"They know where your bedroom is, I think so."

"Is that okay?"

He waves away the concern. "I think this is a special case and it's probably better you aren't at home, especially not by yourself."

He's right. I have to remind myself how easily they can get to me.

I blink back tears as I grab the one large duffel bag I have and start tossing in random articles of clothes, deodorant, and whatever other essential items I'll need for the night. I make a note to grab my toothbrush from the shared bathroom. I try to keep it to what I actually do need, and not anything extra. Anderson doesn't really know how to help, so he stands in the way of the window, partially to block my view and partially to take a bunch of pictures of what the Flock did.

I can't stop my hands from shaking, and tears keep falling.

"Bianca . . ." Anderson starts, and there must be something in the way he says it.

I break. The tears flood and I collapse, burying my face into the mattress.

"Hey." He steps over and sits on the bed next to me, reaching down to put a hand on my upper back. He moves his fingers up and down, scratching the fabric. It does feel kind of nice. I don't lift my head, but I don't tell him to stop either. "You know," he says. "It's okay to cry in this situation."

I twist my head to the side facing him without moving the

rest of me. "That's good, because it's happening."

I let the tears fall into the comforter, not bothering to hide my sniffles as Anderson rubs between my shoulder blades. I'm not sure how much time passes with Ronan and Puck waiting downstairs, but Anderson doesn't say anything.

"Was I wrong?" I ask. "To get us involved in this?"

"Maybe," Anderson says, "but I also think it's the right thing to do."

My tears blur my vision, so I don't really have to face him, even if I keep my head turned in that direction. "I'm scared," I say.

"That's okay—"

"No, you don't get it. I'm not scared just because I was threatened. I'm scared of all of this. I'm scared of everything." My voice tinges with more and more emotion as I keep talking. I try to lower it. "A person with a list of fears longer than the Dressrosa arc of *One Piece* is not cut out for this kind of thing. What the hell was I thinking?"

"You weren't thinking," Anderson says, stifling a small laugh. "You were following your gut, because you're compassionate and brave."

It's impressive that he gets a laugh out of me in this state. "Really? Me, brave?"

He flicks my back. "Yeah. You're like the bravest person I know, because despite your list of fears, despite the fact that so many things make you uncomfortable and scared, you never give up. You push through."

I blink away my tears and rise up on my elbows so I can see him. "That's not . . ."

"Would you say I'm brave?" he asks.

"I mean, yeah," I start. "You're cautious, because you're smart, but you're brave."

"Fear number one," he says. "Death. Fear number two: never amounting to anything. Fear number three: dying and not even getting to say goodbye to my family." His voice is quiet as he lifts a finger for each new thing. "Fear number four: not being able to protect my little brother. Fear number five: never actually finding anyone to love me. Fear number six . . ." He twitches a finger. "Crocodiles. Fear number seven, and this is a new one: weirdo bird cults. Fear number eight: hospitals. Fear number nine: ventriloquist dummies. Fear number ten: anything happening to you." He holds my gaze. "And that's the start of my list. Nobody is fearless, Bianca. Nobody. What matters is that despite your list, despite how long it is and how scared you are, you don't give up."

Now the tears aren't falling because of the dead bird hanging outside my window, but because that was maybe the sweetest thing anyone has ever said to me, and it means a lot. I was wrong for putting distance between us by labeling him as just an anime friend when he's been so much more than that for a long time.

He's been here for me through everything, and I need to make sure that I'm always there for him too. So when he is afraid, when he breaks down and cries, he also sees the strength in that.

His eyes water a little and I pull him into another hug. "Thank you, Anderson, for everything."

"Hey, I chose to get involved in this. I owe it to Mr. Conspiracy too."

"Doesn't matter, I just want you to know how much I appreciate you."

I can't see his smile, but I can picture it based on the sound of his voice. "Enough for all four days of Anime Expo?"

I snort through my tears. "Hell, I'll even cosplay if you ask me to."

He swallows. "That might just be fear eleven for me."

We both laugh, so I pull away.

"Crocodiles, huh?" I ask. "I didn't know that one."

Anderson's expression shifts back to neutral. "I mean, yeah."

"We live in Los Angeles."

"I've seen videos. They are scary. Being eaten alive *and* drowned? No, thank you." He gives my shoulder a shove. "And what the hell? That stands out to you, but ventriloquists don't?"

"No, those are terrifying. You know they're on my list too."

FEAR #34: VENTRILOQUISTS AND ESPECIALLY THEIR DUMMIES

He shakes his head but keeps the smile. "Fair."

"Seriously," I say. "Thank you for sharing that. I needed this."

Anderson shrugs. "Me too, honestly. I'm scared," he says. "Really. But I don't think we should stop, and I don't want to. Mr. Conspiracy lost his life over this, Nate probably did too, and we're maybe the only people he has to care about figuring out why. We shouldn't give up."

"Okay," I say.

It would be so easy though. To shove the investigation behind us and pretend nothing ever happened. For me to drop the diary and the poetry book off at the police station, where it will probably collect dust because the killer covered their tracks by leaving a forged suicide note, and neither Anderson nor me would have to think of it again.

But whatever this Flock is, if they were willing to hurt someone once, they'll definitely do it again. Not to mention, just because they're threatening me to stop doesn't mean *they'll* stop threatening me even if I do. I'm already a liability.

Anderson's right. We can't give up. No matter how scared we are.

"Okay," I say again, like I needed the reassurance.

Anderson zips up my bag and tosses it around his shoulder. "All right, let's go home."

TWENTY-FIVE

RETURN OF THE JAMBA

While Puck and I settled into the Colemans' apartment, my mom got in contact with the police. She brought me to the station to give them a copy of the recording of Nate, but based on their tone while questioning me, I'm not sure anything will come of it. It kind of felt like they assumed kids were bullying me for being weird. I wasn't feeling all that hopeful as we got back to the Colemans' apartment.

Mom and Dad decided to stay at a hotel and Kate is staying with Yoneta, since it would be easier for their pre-preview rehearsal schedule. I would rather actually get murdered than stay with my parents alone in one room, so I was all kinds of relieved when they agreed to let me stay at the Colemans' apartment—although I'm half convinced Mrs. Coleman wants me around just so she can keep playing with Puck. They seriously love each other.

With everything going on and it taking so long to actually get to sleep, Anderson, Ronan, and I ended up missing all our alarms and we arrive to school late, just in time for the end of third-period English with Ms. Richards.

"This is ridiculous," I say. "Class is basically over."

We delayed going to English while getting our things from our lockers, but the secretary wrote the time on our passes, so we can't take that long. It's unfortunate. Especially because I've barely done homework since Mr. Conspiracy's death.

Anderson studies my face and seems to catch on. "If she doesn't ask for our homework, I won't mention it."

"I appreciate that."

I open the door and step inside. Ms. Richards doesn't react much to Anderson and me walking in so late—just gives a little nod to acknowledge us. She's in the middle of explaining something about the new book we're starting, I guess. Anderson and I put the passes on her desk and head to our seats.

I can't focus on the words Ms. Richards is saying. She places a copy of the book in front of Anderson, not stopping her lecture, and then puts another on top of my unopened notebook.

I don't look up at her, but I mutter a thank-you.

As she initiates a discussion or something that involves student responses, I hope she doesn't call on me for any reason. My heart is in my throat, and all I can think of is *The Rules of Flight*, still in my backpack under the Pusheen cover.

FEAR #51: GETTING CALLED ON IN CLASS WHEN I'M NOT PREPARED

I can't help it though. It's like my mind refuses to register any words around me, only a little ringing that may or may not be in my mind.

I focus on the book now placed on my desk. I can barely take it in. I'm too on edge.

Someone at the school is involved. A real person who knows where to find me and can at any moment of the day. For all I know, they could be waiting outside the class right now. They already targeted my bedroom—it wouldn't be much of a stretch to leave another threat for me at school. Or worse. It can't be that hard for a teacher to get me alone.

I grip both sides of the new book. Its cover is worn, and I flip through the yellowed edges. It makes a strange noise, so I don't do it again, and instead run my pencil back and forth on the folder sitting on top of my books, coloring it darker until I leave an indent on the inside.

The bell rings and I brace myself for the open hallway.

"Bianca, can you stay a minute?" Ms. Richards asks.

My hands shake when I think about the threat. I'm really not in the mood to talk about my falling grades or the fact that I had no time to open the book on gender.

I gather my things and approach her desk as the rest of the class files out.

Ms. Richards smiles. "I have your essay corrections and wanted to give them back. It's really well done, though."

She hands over the page. For something that's really well done, there are a lot of red marks, but I'll deal with that later.

"Thank you," I say. I step back. "I'll see you tomorrow?"

I start to turn on my heel when she asks, "Bianca, are you sure you're okay?"

I stiffen. Am I really being that obvious? The acting skills weren't passed down to me like they were to Kate, I guess.

"I'm fine."

"Your mom called again. From what I understand, you were late because there was some incident last night?" She shifts in her chair, head tilted to the side.

Jesus. It feels like my mom talks to the administration here more than she talks to me.

"Yeah, it was a small thing, but I'm good." I smile as best as I can. "I'm great. She's probably just stressed about Kate's show. The preview is coming up, you know."

"I'll be there, I volunteered to help sell tickets."

"That's nice of you."

She waves it off. "I volunteer for everything around here. Especially when it comes to the arts."

Normally I would want to talk more, but I'm not really feeling it today. "Is that all?"

Ms. Richards stands from her desk. "I'm glad to hear you're okay." She takes a step toward me. "I just want to make sure. You seem to be rather . . . preoccupied."

I shake my head. "No thoughts here." She's being a little strange, maybe it would help to lighten the mood. "I'm sure you could tell based on my last assignment."

Apparently, I'm not as funny as I think I am sometimes, because her lips remain in a straight line. She steps closer, practically towering over me in her heels.

"I'm only trying to help." Now her smile returns full force. "It's what I'm here for."

My phone buzzes in my pocket. I'm not sure if Ms. Richards can hear it, but that's a good cue to leave. What if something happened to Mom, Dad, or one of the Colemans?

"Appreciate it, really. Thanks again for the edits!" I rush out of the room before she can stop me. Once I'm in the hallway, I check my phone.

My heart stops.

It's a text message from the unknown number. There's no words, only a photo.

Of Elaine Yee in the Jamba Juice parking lot. It's a tight shot, but I can recognize the bright sign advertising a smoothie behind her.

Soon enough, a message follows:

Tell anyone, and she's dead.

They have Elaine. I send her a flurry of messages, and call twice, but there's no reply and it goes straight to voice mail. I want to throw up.

Instead of going to chemistry, I look for Anderson. It's his free period, and my best bet is to check outside.

Sure enough, as I head out to the courtyard, he's smiling at his phone. My guess is that he's talking to Layla, which is really sweet and would make me so happy if not for the fact that my own crush is likely in imminent danger.

Fuck.

"Anderson, get up, we're leaving," I say. "Tell Layla it's an emergency and I'm sorry."

He looks at me, and while he's probably used to seeing me cry, his eyes still widen at the sight of my face. "What happened? And where are we going? The cafeteria?"

"No," I say. I show him the text. "We're on a rescue mission."

"They got Elaine? Okay, we just have to get to the Jamba basement, but I can't drive . . ." He looks back at his phone to go through options. "I'll message Ryan. He'll take us."

"Will he have his phone on?"

Anderson gives a quick laugh and calls Ryan. My parents are both working, and I know Anderson's parents work day shifts as well, so I don't think we have many other options anyway.

Anderson starts walking back into the building so we can grab our stuff and meet Ryan. While the main office would probably notice us leaving, there's a door in the science wing of the building that's never attended, especially now that class has already started. It's almost too easy to slip out, but I think the whole focus is to keep the side doors locked so that no one can get in. I don't think they care as much about people leaving.

We start walking off campus toward the sidewalk. Apparently, Anderson told Ryan to drive out of the parking lot, take a right, and look for us. My heart is in my throat. What if we don't get there in time?

I keep checking my phone in case Elaine responds.

"Do you think she went there by herself? Why? Or did they kidnap her? How did they know? Oh my God. They must have stalked us on the bird hike. What if they have eyes everywhere?"

"You're spiraling, take a deep breath. We'll handle it," Anderson says. "Are you okay?"

"I've been better. Are you okay?"

"All things considered," he says. "Sure."

"Do you think they are going to kill her? I mean, they can't just kill teenagers, right? Like she actually has a family and friends and it would be all over the news . . ." I take a breath. "Okay. I am spiraling."

"Understandable." He frowns. "What do we do?"

"We can't call the cops. If they hear sirens, they might actually kill her regardless. Or take her somewhere else."

Before Anderson can respond, a car pulls up next to us on the curb, lightly tapping the horn. We both look over to where Ryan Pérez waves from the driver's seat. I climb into the back before Anderson can pull that move of his again, forcing him to take shotgun.

"Thanks for getting us," I say. "It means a lot."

"No problem, my friend. Anderson says it is an emergency. Where to?"

Anderson has the location saved in his phone, so he navigates. The traffic isn't terrible, although the trip feels much longer than it actually is. Ryan is extremely easygoing and doesn't question anything, not even when we arrive in the lot.

I don't see Elaine's Subaru anywhere, or any sign of her at all. Did they straight-up abduct her?

"Do you think they brought her inside?" Anderson asks.

We both race out of the car as Ryan goes to park. Anderson and I enter the Jamba Juice and make a beeline for the bathroom. Ryan manages to squeeze in with us at the last second and I lock the bathroom door.

"You two are certainly interesting," he says.

Anderson approaches the keypad on the storage closet as my phone buzzes. I look down. It's a call from Elaine. I pick up.

"We're here, are you okay?"

"Here? Like at my school?" She doesn't sound like someone who is in danger, only someone who is extremely confused.

I'm relieved, but also not feeling great about our situation, whatever it is.

"I got a text from the murderers. It was a picture of you in the Jamba Juice lot. It seemed like a threat, so Anderson and I rushed over?" I don't know why it's hard to say. It feels kind of strange since Elaine seems to be completely clueless about her own kidnapping.

"I was in AP Bio. I had my phone on silent. I'm so sorry." She really does sound shocked. "In the picture, what color shirt was I wearing?"

"Plaid." Immediately as I say it, it hits me. "That was from yesterday."

"Yeah. I'm really sorry, Bianca."

"No, it's not your fault. I'm just glad you're safe." I sigh into the phone.

A small moment passes before Elaine speaks again. "So . . . you were going to rush over and save me, huh? That's pretty romantic, actually."

My face heats. "Ha ha, yeah, talk later. Bye."

I quickly hang up the phone.

"Oh no, Bianca." Anderson winces. "That goodbye was so awkward."

I ignore him. "Elaine's fine. She's at school."

"That's good," Anderson says. "But I don't get what they were trying to accomplish here then."

I glance back at the closet door. They took a gamble in baiting me with the sonnet book because they wouldn't know whether or not we cracked the code.

Unless they saw us making a beeline for the bathroom.

My skin tingles as my stomach drops. "We need to get out of here."

Anderson practically shoves Ryan out the bathroom door, and together, we run back into the parking lot. Ryan is either the most adaptable person ever or used to quick getaways, because we hop in the car and he floors it.

"I have no idea what's going on," he says as we put distance between us and Jamba. "But I think I'm into it."

Anderson laughs from the back seat. "Can you take us back to my apartment?"

"Of course." Ryan looks between us. "And I've got something that will help." He points behind him with his thumb.

I glance over to a box on the seat. Anderson opens it to reveal a small bag filled with marijuana flowers. He nods in appreciation. "Nice."

"I'm reading a nice calming indica for you two." Ryan grins, shooting me a quick look. "Bianca, you in?"

Normally, it would be an immediate no. It should be an immediate no. I mean,

FEAR #15: LOSS OF CONTROL

And getting high or drunk can lead to that.

But after the week I've been having? And the fact that it's only Tuesday?

Maybe being too in control all the time isn't the best. Yeah, I'm driving the bus, but with my anxiety and decision-making skills, it's like driving a bus that's on fire.

I take a deep breath and smile.

"Sure, Ryan. I'm in."

TWENTY-SIX

A FIELD GUIDE TO NORTH AMERICAN BIRDS AND MURDERS

Anderson, Ronan, and I are getting ready for school when my dad drops by the Colemans' apartment. Mrs. Coleman opens the door and he's carrying about four massive aluminum trays of food. He's not exactly a tall man, so I can barely see him over the tower.

"I wanted to bring dinner," Dad says to Mrs. Coleman. "We really appreciate you letting Bianca stay here."

Mrs. Coleman helps him navigate to the counter to put the trays down. She sneaks one of the corners open to take a peek. "Actually, it was a ploy to have your cooking again, so mission accomplished."

"Aren't you staying at a hotel?" I ask.

Dad scratches the back of his head. "Well, I popped back home. Just the kitchen. I don't know how long we'll be away and I couldn't let the food we had go to waste."

Based on the catering he's trying to pass off as a dinner for five, I don't really believe this was made just from what was lying around in the fridge. But it was nice of him, and pasta is literally my dad's love language.

Ronan joins Mrs. Coleman in peeking at the food. "Is that lasagna? Mr. Torre, you are a hero."

Dad waves off the comment. "No worries at all. There's not enough lasagna in the world to repay you for this."

"I don't know about that."

"Can I get you some coffee?" Mrs. Coleman asks.

Dad shakes his head. "I have to sleep before my next shift. Thank you, though."

Mrs. Coleman takes a seat in front of her coffee, and Puck immediately jumps onto her lap. I swear, I'll have to bring her over for playdates when this is over. "Of course."

Dad glances between Anderson, Ronan, and me. "You three need a ride to school?"

Since he's already leaving, it would be a lot easier than having Mrs. Coleman drive us before work. "Sure, thanks, Dad."

Ronan grabs a Pop-Tart and gathers his things. Anderson and I are ready too. As much as I really don't feel like going to school, everyone agreed that I'd be safer around people. It'll be a lot harder to kidnap or kill me from class, presumably.

Sure, it would've been nice if I actually did my homework, but it's been a rough few days.

After we say our goodbyes to Mrs. Coleman, the four of us head to my dad's car. We're early enough that the traffic isn't too bad.

"There haven't been any more threats, have there?" Dad asks.

I glance over to Anderson and Ronan in the back seat. I'm not sure if yesterday really counts as a threat. I mean, technically they threatened Elaine, but they didn't actually endanger her. It was probably just a test.

And I completely failed.

"Not yet," I say.

Dad rolls his eyes at the "yet" part. "That's the spirit." He gives a little smile. "I'm sure the police will figure out who is doing this in no time. Just stay together and be observant."

"Yep."

"And when in doubt, go for a double leg, Bianca," Anderson adds.

Dad laughs.

As much as I like the bit of training I've done with Anderson, I really doubt I'd be able to fight anyone. It's not the nature of a lesbian sheep.

Dad pulls in front of the school. Ronan and Anderson get out of the car first. I look back toward my dad.

"Love you." It seems like a good enough time to say it.

His eyes are bright. "Love you too, kid. Be safe."

I nod, though I'm not really sure I can promise that.

Anderson and I have different homerooms, and Ronan's is practically across the building, so we have to split up. I'm not exactly alone in the crowded hallways. I check my phone to seem less obviously by myself, and half expect another threat. Instead, I have a new Instagram notification, which is almost harder to believe. I open the message.

Layla: it was great meeting you on Sunday! Hope you can come again this weekend!

My heart's a little full at that. Assuming I don't get brutally murdered before then, maybe I can go back.

I'll definitely try, thanks:)

Layla: We should grab coffee sometime either way! Anderson talks so much about you, I feel like we're basically friends already

I smile. He really does seem to like her. It can't hurt to both tease and help him a little. Especially with how he's acted around Elaine.

For sure! And trust me, it's not nearly as much as he talks about you

Layla: Maybe Sunday after group?

Layla: And only good things, I hope

Only the best

Sounds good, let's plan on it!

It's actually exciting to consider the prospect of getting closer to Layla. I barely recognize myself, making new friends.

Okay, maybe it is a little soon to consider her a friend, but she said it first.

I'm smiling despite myself.

Until I catch sight of the *Little Shop of Horrors* posters begging people to go to the preview on Saturday, November 18.

The same day we're supposed to meet with Mr. Conspiracy's connection, and the same date written on the Post-it note stuck in *The Rules of Flight*.

I squeeze the strap of my backpack. Since it's Wednesday,

that's only three days to figure out what those events are about, or if they're related, and we don't have much evidence. We barely know anything about the Flock, it feels like.

Not compared to what they know about us.

But until I can figure out what Mr. Conspiracy had on them, there's not a whole lot to go off. I stop.

Mr. Conspiracy left his book for me, which means there might be something in there that only I would get. That other people might have missed.

With a different Pusheen cover disguising the diary, I flip through the pages instead of paying attention in first period. If he did leave clues for me specifically, he knows that I like birds. And stalking people, sure, but I don't know if there could be a clue left based on that one.

Wait, I remember seeing a random list of birds when we first looked through it. Anderson and I figured it was just research ideas of what he could draw for me next. I skim the pages until I land on it. There's a little note Mr. Conspiracy left at the top.

I was going through the second edition of my Peterson Field Guide to Birds of North America, and these birds stood out to me. Especially the last two, which make a great combination.

    pink-footed goose
    common merganser
    great blue heron
    golden-winged warbler

I blink. What does he mean about a great blue heron and a golden-winged warbler making a great combination? They aren't similar at all.

Unless this is code for some kind of combination or password? Maybe the birds correspond to numbers? I reread the page. Why would he specifically mention which field guide he was using if it were only meant for himself?

Thankfully, we're able to use personal laptops to take notes in this class, so I go through my ebook library until I find the right Peterson guide. If this diary was left for me to decode, it was a bit of a gamble on Mr. Conspiracy's part, but I have nearly every ornithology field guide in recent history. Plus, I could have just bought the guide if I didn't have it already.

Using the table of contents to get in the right group, I open to the first bird. The pink-footed goose is on page 100.

If it is some kind of combination, page numbers based on the table of contents are probably the only way to keep it consistent. To be safe, I zoom out so I have the pages set to what should match the printed copy. I can always confirm it once I get home.

I go through the book until I find the numbers for all four birds and jot them next to the names.

pink-footed goose 100
common merganser 84
great blue heron 342
golden-winged warbler 717

If just the last two are supposed to make a combination, that would be 342–717. Or, if it's like my locker combination lock, maybe 34–27–17.

But what are the 100 and 84 for?

I lean my head against my desk. I was so excited about potentially figuring something out, I didn't think about where I'd go with it.

"Miss Torre?" my teacher snaps from the front of the room. "Care to join us?"

I glance up, and my stomach twists. The *Miss* is bad enough. The sound of it hisses against my ears and sinks into the pit of my stomach. But the eyes turning in my direction are worse.

FEAR #17: BEING THE CENTER OF ATTENTION IN ANY CIRCUMSTANCE

I should just apologize quietly and pretend to pay attention. That's exactly what I would have done two weeks ago.

Of course, the Bianca of Before wouldn't have broken into an apartment with Anderson Coleman, or smoked weed with Ryan Pérez, or planned a coffee meeting with another nonbinary person and hopeful friend.

The Bianca of Before definitely wouldn't have Elaine Yee's number in their phone and plans to text her immediately with this diary update.

So instead of apologizing, I close my laptop and gather my things.

"Sorry," I say. "I'm feeling sick."

Before I can be offered a pass to the nurse or asked any further questions, I'm out of the classroom and into the hallway. I have to find a place where I can text Anderson and Elaine about my latest breakthrough.

Once I turn the corner, my breathing comes in and out too quickly, and I nearly start hyperventilating.

Did I really just walk out of class? Am I seriously skipping right now?

I might throw up. *Holy shit.*

I run down the nearest stairwell and sit in the corner, knees bent and head in my arms, until I calm down. Then I take pictures and send them to Anderson and Elaine.

Anderson: whoa, I can't believe it

Anderson: Is Bianca Torre actually ditching??

Anderson: WITHOUT ME?!

I laugh to myself. He really does have a way of making me feel better, even if I know for a fact he isn't the type to ditch class either. The one time we went to see *Kiki's Delivery Service* in theaters as part of an event during the school day, we had our moms call us out.

My phone buzzes again. I try to think of a funny comeback to send to Anderson when I unlock my screen, but the message isn't from him.

Instead, it's a picture of Ryan, Anderson, and me walking toward the Jamba Juice door, clearly coming from the direction of the bathroom. Another message comes in below it.

Gotcha.

TWENTY-SEVEN

KATE TORRE MAKES A COMEBACK

Despite the creepy message yesterday, there was no movement from the killer during school on Thursday. I've spent most of the time since then trying to figure out what the code could mean, but I'm stuck. It's like I'm missing something, and the bird connection alone isn't enough.

Even Anderson and Elaine haven't been able to crack it yet, and it's hard to not want to move on to something else with Saturday approaching. After so many dead ends and near panic attacks, I almost want it to just be the eighteenth already, so we can get this all over with.

It's evening when I get a text from Elaine Yee.

Elaine: Are you free tomorrow?

I have to reread it five times, and I still can't believe it's actually there on my screen. I glance at Anderson, lying on his bed and working on a sketch. I spring up from the sleeping mat rolled out on his bedroom floor and practically shove my phone in his face.

"How do I respond?" I ask.

He looks a little annoyed, until his eyes focus on the phone and he makes out the message. "You say you're free."

"Is this . . . asking me out?" It seems like a bad question, but I can't hide the hope that's in my voice.

"I think so," Anderson says. "It has to be, right?"

Yeah

I text back quickly.

I don't just have butterflies in my stomach. I have hummingbirds. Hummingbirds on crack. At a rave.

"I may throw up," I say. "Hold my phone, I can't look."

I toss it to Anderson, who manages to catch it, and wait for Elaine's response.

I mean, if she's the one asking, I don't really have to worry about getting rejected. It has to have a good outcome, right? But if we do go out, what am I supposed to wear?

"Oh," Anderson says.

"Oh? What does that mean?"

He holds out my phone and I quickly scan the new messages.

Elaine: Great, I think I found something in the diary. Not obviously related to your code . . . but maybe? I'd love to go over it with you and Anderson!

My stomach sinks and my face heats. I can't look at Anderson, so instead, I return to the sleeping bag and lie flat on my stomach, hands at my sides and face buried into the pillow.

Of *course* she wasn't asking me out. I'm so silly and ridiculous.

"Bianca?" Anderson asks cautiously. "You good?"

"I'm never leaving this room," I say, voice muffled by the pillow.

I'm not sure I can add **ASSUMING IT'S A DATE WHEN IT ISN'T** as its own entry to my list of fears, but I'm on the fence about it.

Maybe it can be 13.5, right under **BEAUTIFUL PEOPLE**.

FEAR #13.5: ASSUMING IT'S A DATE WHEN IT ISN'T

Then my phone starts vibrating, enough that I can hear it from my state of self-despair, which means it's a call. I reach my hands out and pull myself up.

"Anderson, if that's her, don't answer. I can't face her. I don't think I can handle staying in the state. Now is the time to finally move to Colorado and start my stray cat sanctuary."

"I'll join you," Anderson says. "Make a mountain art retreat or something." He turns my phone toward me. "It's Kate, though."

I reluctantly stand to grab the phone back from Anderson. While I'm tempted to ignore the video call, I haven't talked to Kate in what feels like forever, and it's kind of my fault that she's not able to come home.

Or entirely my fault, but whatever.

I accept the call. Kate has her stage makeup on, since they likely just got out of the dress rehearsal. They only have one rehearsal left for the preview that will make or break the show. On one hand, I really want it to go well. On the other, Mom will make me see it again in December for the actual two-week run if it succeeds, I'm sure.

"How's it going?" Kate asks. "I've barely seen you. Can't

believe they had to threaten your life during tech week."

At least the first part of that seemed to have some genuine concern. "Yeah, next time I'll tell them to be more considerate so they can murder me on your schedule."

"It's basic human decency," she says. "But really."

"I'm good," I say. "Chilling with Anderson. Alive, so, that's a plus."

I turn my phone toward Anderson so he can say hello.

"Hey, Anderson, my sister treating you well?" I hear her ask.

Sister. It's like the word is a slap.

I haven't told her yet, so it's not like she could have known, but I've hardly had the time with everything going on.

"We're doing great," he says. "Solving murders, drawing bad comics. The usual."

"Hey, yours are getting pretty good!" I twist the phone back to me. "He's right about mine though. They're awful."

"Well, you're good at identifying birds at least?"

I'm not upset about being bad at drawing—it's more Anderson's thing that I'm happy to enjoy with him—but that comment makes me feel worse. Like that's really all I'm good at.

"Thanks," I say. I think she's still staying with Yoneta. She looks to be in a living room or something.

I should tell her about my gender.

"Hey, Kate," I say.

"Yeah?" Her voice is a little confused and cautious. Probably because it was weird to try to get her attention when we're already FaceTiming and she's looking right at me.

"Um . . ." I glance over at Anderson like he could help, but I'm pretty sure he's confused too. "Well . . . maybe don't call me your sister."

Kate lifts a contoured eyebrow. "Because . . . ?"

"Because I'm not," I say. "I'm nonbinary."

I'm not sure that's the best way to come out. Maybe I should have led into it a little bit more. What if she thinks I'm accusing her of something, or somehow mad about it? It's a lot to take in, and I probably should've thought about that more.

At the same time, maybe I don't have to keep thinking of other people's comfort before my own identity.

"Oh," Kate says. "Cool, that's great." I know she wants to be supportive, but she also doesn't know quite what to say. "So, I call you my geek sibling?"

"Yeah," I say. "Geek sibling, or Bianca. Either one."

She cracks a smile at that. "And your pronouns?"

"They/them," I say. "I don't necessarily like she/her, but I can live with it because I'm not out to everyone . . . but stuff like woman, girl, sister . . . those kinds of words really bother me."

"Okay," Kate says. "Okay. I'll try to avoid that, slap me in the face if I mess up."

I don't know why she and Anderson have to be so violent with their suggestions.

"I can point it out, and you can learn from there," I say. "Don't make it a big deal, you can correct yourself and move on."

"Whatever you need." Kate adjusts the phone and the way she sits. "Are you going to tell Mom and Dad? About anything?"

Right, because it's not only my gender, it's also my sexuality. Hell, you can add the fact that I'm investigating a murder against their wishes. Either way, it's ridiculous that books and movies seem to separate a queer person's life into pre–coming out and post–coming out, like it is one big event.

Every day has to be a coming out. To every new person I meet. Unless I can walk around with a shirt that says Anxious Nonbinary Lesbian, I'll never be off the hook for coming out.

And it's tiring.

"No," I say. "Not anytime soon."

Although I do kind of want that shirt.

I almost expect her to argue. To assure me that Mom and Dad will be super accepting, so why couldn't I tell them? When there are so many people who have to come out to parents that are so much worse than mine? That I'm selfish. A coward.

But she doesn't.

"Okay," she says again. "I'm really glad you decided to let me in." She actually tears up a little bit, although that might be stress about the show opening soon. "I'm sorry," she says, wiping the corner of her eye. "I . . . I'm so happy I get to know the real you, and I'm sorry for everything I did before to prevent that or make it hard."

Toward the end of the sentence, her voice breaks a little.

"You're so dramatic," I say, though now I'm tearing up and I sound just as bad.

I'm not taking back

FEAR #40: PEOPLE MAKING A BIG DEAL OUT OF THINGS

But it isn't so bad when it's only the two of us.

Well, and Anderson, who is kind of awkwardly sitting and smiling across the bedroom. He doesn't seem nearly as uncomfortable as I would be if the situation was reversed, so maybe I'm finding it awkward for him.

"I'm an actor," she says. "You know this."

I look up at Anderson, wiping my eyes. "Never date an actor," I say.

"They're right," Kate adds from my phone, voice a bit pinched.

It's such a relief too. Maybe I don't need everyone to know, not anytime soon, but it's nice to have my sister on my side.

"I mean, Layla's a cosplayer, but that's different," Anderson says.

"I wouldn't know," Kate says. "But wait, who's Layla and why didn't I get all the details?"

"Why would you?" She's so nosy. This is why I limit talking about Elaine. A little smile creeps up on my lips though. "They're adorable," I add, which gets Anderson to retreat back to his bed.

Although it reminds me of my own embarrassing assumption from earlier about Elaine asking me out. Of course it was about the investigation. I should probably give up on social interactions and go back to the telescope now. Anderson and Layla can visit me on occasion for anime watch parties and tell me tales of the outside. I'll get another cat for company like Queen Elizabeth and I'll undoubtably have to give it another ridiculous Shakespeare name like Malvolio—Meowvolio—but it's fine. It'll be fine.

"What are you thinking about?" Kate asks.

She always calls me out on getting lost in my thoughts.

"Nothing," I say.

"Okay . . ." Kate's face lights up. "Oh! I almost forgot. The weird company y'all are investigating—their name is Valley Quail, right?"

"Yeah," I say. "Why?"

This gets Anderson to scramble back to the end of his bed to watch Kate from over my shoulder. "Did you hear something about them?" he asks.

"Yeah, get this." Kate leans in close to the camera like she's telling a secret, even though nobody else is around. At least, as far as I can tell. "I spilled some of the info about the budget to my sophomore mentee—obviously not saying anything about the murders and stuff—and guess what? She found documents with that exact name at her family's bakery. She specifically remembered it because they were listed as an egg supplier, and they don't use eggs, it's a vegan bakery." She pauses for dramatic effect. You'd think this was her college audition monologue based on how into it she is. "So suspicious, right?"

"Yeah, the company is fake," Anderson says. "It's a front."

"Exactly," Kate says, looking very proud of herself.

"Who was the sophomore?" I ask. "Does she know anything else about the company?"

"Joanna Mayfield, I don't think you know her," Kate says. "And no, I did not endanger the life of my theater mentee. Joanna's clueless." She gives me a look. "Just so we're clear, I know nothing and I'm not involved. I can't die. There aren't any understudies."

"Right, that's why you can't die." I roll my eyes.

Joanna Mayfield. The name does sound familiar, but I can't place it. Maybe she's one of the theater kids that randomly follow me on Instagram.

Regardless, that doesn't seem as important.

Anderson and I look at each other and I almost see a glint of fear in his expression. This might be way bigger than we imagined.

Kate practically speaks my exact thought aloud.

Her voice cuts through my speaker. "What the hell have you two gotten yourselves into?"

TWENTY-EIGHT

A MESSAGE FROM MR. CONSPIRACY

It's hard for me to pay attention in any of my classes, but at least that seems to be the case for everyone right now. Not only is it a Friday, but next week we only have two days of school before Thanksgiving break. Every class feels like twice the amount of time it should be, but we finally make it to the end of the day.

I try to grab my things from my locker as fast as I can. I have to meet with Anderson so Elaine can pick us up. I know school is a relatively safe space, but I still want to get out of here as fast as possible.

Valley Quail might be planning something tomorrow. We don't have any more time to waste.

"Bianca?"

I twist around to face Ms. Richards. "I wanted to check in— did you hear about that internship yet?"

It's really sweet of her to follow up on that, but does she have to do it *now*?

"Oh, I just submitted the application." It isn't a lie. I literally did just submit it earlier. "I probably won't hear back until next month at least."

"Got it," she says. "Just make sure to keep me updated."

I close my locker, but she doesn't step out of the way.

"I'll see you at the show tomorrow, right?" Ms. Richards asks.

I nod. "Not like I can miss it when my sister's a lead."

Ms. Richards gives a little laugh. "Of course not. I'm excited for it, seems like there will be a big crowd, and they'll pull in some money. I just hope nothing goes wrong."

I frown. I don't really know what would go wrong. Did the PTA do something to sabotage the puppet again?

"Yeah . . ." I shift the weight of my backpack on my shoulders. "Well. I'll see you then."

Ms. Richards steps out of the way, giving me a little wave goodbye, and I rush over to Anderson's locker. He zips up his bag as I approach.

"Hey," I quickly greet. "Ready?"

He grabs his things. "I'm ready."

Despite the last bell having rung a few minutes ago, the intercom dings again with an announcement.

"Bianca Torre, please report to the office," the voice says. "Bianca Torre, report to the main office."

Anderson looks at me. "Should you go?"

I wince. It's probably about missing class. I really don't want to deal with that now. I'll have more time on Monday.

If I'm around on Monday, that is.

"I'd rather not."

"Let's go out the science door."

He's right. If we try to slip out the front door, they'll see me from the main office. Anderson shuts his locker and starts heading in the direction of the science wing. I pop his lock closed before following.

I squeeze my eyes shut for a moment, staying close to Anderson. I'm going to get in so much trouble for this. I'm not sure what they do to students who blatantly ignore the rules and office sentencings. Can I maybe pull off the excuse that I was already outside the building? Or listening to music and didn't hear it?

Anderson and I manage to make it to the science door, where Ryan Pérez sees us as he's walking out.

"Oh, Bianca," he says, voice loud, "they want you in the office."

Other people around us, including a science teacher, turn to look.

Anderson grabs Ryan with his good hand and shoves him all the way out of the door. I try to be quick without arousing even more suspicion.

Anderson keeps pulling Ryan in the direction of the football field, until the senior parking lot separates us from the door. He stops behind someone's Ford Raptor.

"What the hell, man?" Ryan asks.

"We have other priorities," Anderson says quickly. "We can't go to the office, Bianca's dealing with a lot right now."

"Dude, I feel." Ryan looks at me. "They schedule detentions at the most inconvenient times. Like, my whole life isn't school, you know?"

"Yeah," I agree. "Exactly."

Especially not when my other current priority involves murderers threatening my life.

"You seem stressed," Ryan says. "I've got an indica strain that has high CBD if you want. Help you relax a bit."

"Next time, Ryan. Promise."

"I will look forward to it, Bianca Badass. I'll go to the office and cause a distraction. I actually already have detention for like ever. My pipe fell out of my pocket in Mr. Meyer's class."

"You'd do that?" I ask.

It's only a matter of time before they realize I'm not coming and that science teacher mentions they saw me leave through the side exit. And we have to wait for Elaine to get here.

"Of course. You're my bro now," he says, like that's a joke but also kind of serious. Ryan pats my head. "Don't get too stressed, friend. I care about you."

I almost tear up a little at that.

"I'll try my best."

He nods and gives a quick fist bump to Anderson before turning toward the school. He takes a deep breath, looks back to give me a wink, and then drops in a freaking sprint toward the main entrance.

"What's he going to do?" I ask Anderson.

"Who knows?" He shrugs. "Either way, Ryan Pérez is a god-damned hero."

I pull out my phone. "I'll see how close Elaine is. Maybe we can meet her on a side street, like where Ryan picked us up last time."

He really *is* a hero.

Anderson bites his lip. "I'm not going with you two."

I turn to him before I can finish typing the text to Elaine. "What? Why not?"

"I think you and Elaine should have some time alone."

I open and close my mouth a few times. "That is pure silliness," I finally say. "It's not a date. We both know that now."

I hate how much I'm blushing at the reminder.

"Probably because I'm always tagging along," Anderson says. "She hasn't had the chance to think of it as one . . . but if it's just the two of you . . ."

My stomach tightens.

"I don't know . . . I'm probably not ready for just the two of us."

"You'll be fine." He gives a signature Anderson Coleman smile. "Promise."

"What are you going to do?" I ask.

He shrugs. "I'll chill at home. Catch up on some homework. Work on my drawings. Talk to Layla. Don't worry about me."

I don't get the opportunity to protest because Elaine's car pulls in, and she has a clear view of us, so she turns in our direction.

Oh God.

Anderson puts his hand on my shoulder. "Good luck."

Then he's walking away. I can't go after him and leave Elaine hanging. I try to calm my breathing and not pee my pants as I wait with eyes a little too wide for Elaine to stop in front of me.

I hear the door unlock and I pull it open.

"Anderson's not coming?" she asks.

That's not disappointment in her voice, right?

"No," I say. "Something came up."

If she is feeling anything negative about that, she doesn't show it. Instead, she gives me a wide smile.

"He's missing out," she says casually. "Because what I uncovered is so good, you'll die."

Yeah, if the masked murderer doesn't get to me first.

"Can't wait," I say, crawling into the passenger seat.

For someone who really shot down the idea of this being a date, even without specifically intending to, Elaine is kind of giving me mixed messages—especially when she pulls the car over on a fairly secluded street, which feels like something you'd do to hook up with or physically harm someone.

And at this point, not sure I'd really argue with either option.

"Is everything okay?" Elaine asks. "You seemed pretty freaked when I picked you up."

"I'm always freaked out. And I think I've gotten like four or five threats at this point so it might just be residual freak-out."

"I'm so sorry."

"It's okay," I say. "I mean, I'm not dead yet."

"I'm really glad for that." She smiles. "We have so much stuff to do together."

I glance over at her. What does she mean by that?

A bit of pink stains Elaine's nose and cheeks. "Like, there are so many good bird hikes in the area."

My heart flutters. If she's a little embarrassed, did that mean she had something else in mind?

I can't think straight. I don't want to assume again and be disappointed, but at the same time, it's hard to shake that little bit of hope and suppress the oncoming smile.

"I'll have to live then," I say quietly, "for the bird hikes."

She is really close. Can you overheat from proximity to another person?

"I'm holding you to that," Elaine says.

She can hold me to, or against, anything.

Dear God, now *I'm* blushing.

"But, um, yeah. Off topic, but I do use *they*, you know, for pronouns."

My voice is so awkward. I thought I would be more used to saying it by now, since I did have to separately tell, like, four people. But it's different when it's someone I've had a hopeless crush on for months.

With the way she's watching me, despite the better judgment of my head, my heart keeps thinking that maybe this doesn't have to be so hopeless.

"Are you out to a lot of people? If you don't mind me asking?"

Elaine quickly tacks on the second question.

I shake my head no.

"Thanks for trusting me," Elaine says. "It's weird. Basically everyone at school knows I'm pansexual. I mean, I had a girlfriend last year for a bit . . ." She tilts her head back to the headrest. "But my family has no idea. I don't really know how they'll take it. Some part of me feels like I'll wait until my wedding day to tell them." Without turning her head, her eyes dart to me. "Other times I feel like I should graduate, move far away from here, and never tell them at all. Like maybe as long as I know who I am, it isn't as important for everyone else to . . . I don't know." She gives a little laugh. "I think I'm scared."

I have to tuck my hands under my thighs to keep them from shaking, but I'm hanging on to every word. In a lot of ways, I relate. I don't know why I'm struggling so much with the idea of telling my parents. I think I've accepted the fact that my very Catholic nonna in Italy isn't ever going to really know me. I'm not sure if that hurts me or if I've become numb to it.

Is it self-preservation, or fear?

"I'm probably not going to tell my parents either," I say. "Not everything."

"I feel like in all the movies and books, coming out is like the goal, right? Like you aren't true to yourself if you don't come out to everyone. But doesn't it matter that I know? That I'm okay with myself?" Elaine scratches her arm. "I feel like the goal shouldn't be to need everyone to know. It should be to find people you can really let in."

She looks directly at me with that line, and my heart beats in my throat.

"Our happy coming-out story doesn't have to be to everyone. I don't think life is actually like that." I shrug. "I think I'm always going to be misgendered because I don't look how people expect nonbinary to look. The people who matter know, and I know. Maybe that's enough."

"I feel you." Elaine sighs. "I still wish I wasn't so afraid sometimes."

If there is anything I can relate to, it's that feeling. Her eyes look a little glassy, and I kind of want to reach out to her, but I'm not sure how she'd feel about that. Instead, I keep my voice as soft and steady as I can.

"You know," I say. "I have a list of everything I'm really afraid of. It's constantly growing and shifting. Coming out to my parents? That's currently number eleven."

I could probably add another in this moment.

FEAR #65: TELLING PEOPLE ABOUT THIS LIST

My heart is beating heavy in my chest, and I keep squeezing my hands together under me.

"I never listed it out," Elaine says. "But I feel like that would be top ten for me."

I smile. "Fair."

"It's hard to believe you have a whole list of fears given what you've dealt with recently." Elaine shakes her head. "You're pretty brave."

"Well, brave or not, I'm still afraid of everything."

She gives a little smile that makes my head spin. "Even me?"

Especially you.

"Should I be?" I ask.

Elaine laughs, but her face looks nearly as red as mine.

"I don't want to make you scared," she says. Her voice is quieter than before. "Maybe a little nervous."

For me, that would be an understatement. I have a whole mix of emotions right now and despite the nerves tingling through me, I'm practically giddy.

"I think I've made that obvious," I say without meeting her eyes. I look down at my legs. "But I have to figure out this whole cult thing."

"And make it out alive," Elaine teases. "For our first solo bird hike."

"Of course."

"In case it isn't already implied," Elaine says, "I'd like it if Anderson was busy for that one, too."

My chest is going to burst. I don't know if it's a heart attack or an alien spawn, but I seriously can't handle this. I'm smiling and my face is completely hot. I hope I'm not imagining this right now.

Elaine looks as embarrassed as I do, like she didn't quite expect herself to actually say that.

"Speaking of figuring out the cult thing," Elaine starts. "I found something."

"Really?" I ask.

"Along with the code he left for you. There's an address." She takes a breath. "It took me a while, but I think I got it."

That does help break the tension in the car a little bit. Although looking at her makes my blush threaten to start up again. I try to rein my mind in and focus.

"Great," I say. "What was it?"

Elaine pulls out her phone and opens the notes app. "Okay, so I saw that Mr. Conspiracy would occasionally mention going to Chandler's. Which seems weird, because that's not his nephew, and according to you and Anderson, he didn't really get out much."

I nod. I must have skimmed over that part, or assumed it fell under the "off-topic rambling" sections I thought he included in case the book fell into the wrong hands.

"But it got me thinking, what if Chandler isn't a person. What if it's the street?"

"What's on Chandler?"

"Look." Elaine pulls up a picture of a page from Mr. Conspiracy's diary on her phone. I read from her screen and really try not to notice how close we are.

Another trip to Chandler's. 11:30, 4th time this week.

"Did he really go four times in a week? That seems excessive. Or did he write those numbers to mean something else?"

"I thought that too." Elaine's eyes sparkle as she looks over to me. "So I looked up 11304 Chandler Boulevard, and guess what's there?"

My heart skips. "What?"

"The post office." Elaine drops her phone onto her lap. "Maybe

Mr. Conspiracy left something there for you."

Excitement builds in me. This might be a leap, but it makes sense. And at the moment, it's the biggest lead we have.

"Well, there's only one way to find out," I say.

TWENTY-NINE

THE FLOCK FOLLOWS THROUGH

Elaine and I try to act as inconspicuous as possible at the post office. Nerves make my skin crawl, but we pretend like we know exactly what we're doing as we walk inside.

We're about to get in line when I freeze. "Wait. How could he have left something for me if he didn't know my name?"

I don't think I can walk up to the worker and see if someone left a package for Stalker Birdwatching Teen.

Elaine bites her lip, looking around the office.

"What if he had a post office box?"

I spin to view the wall of boxes and step closer—all of them have five numbers on them, most starting with a one.

"The code I found . . . it could be to get in the box." I find the pictures I took. "He said the last six digits were a combination, so maybe the first few are the box number. Is there a 10084?"

Elaine scans the labels a lot faster than I do and finally stops on one. "Here."

It's closed with a combination lock. My palms sweat and my heart pounds in my chest. This might actually be it.

"Okay," I say. "Let's see if this works."

I bite my bottom lip. If there's one thing I can do, it's a combination lock. Elaine shows me the code. I spin the dial three times before circling to the right numbers. I hold my breath as it stops on the seventeen.

And I pull.

The lock pops open.

Elaine and I look at each other, both barely able to contain ourselves, until we realize there are other people around us, and they're certainly not as thrilled about getting a lock right.

"I can't believe that worked," I whisper.

"Neither can I," Elaine admits. "We make a good pair."

My face heats. "No, yeah, um, for sure."

I cringe at myself and pull on the metal door, and there's not much inside. Just a flash drive, sitting right in the middle of the box.

I pick it up and close the door, locking it shut. The flash drive has *256 GB* printed on the side, and that seems like a decent amount of space. We don't really use them much in school, but my dad has a few where he saves photos.

"What do you think is on it?" Elaine asks.

I meet her eyes. "What he has on Feathergate. It has to be."

Elaine nods, her eyes wide.

"I'm staying at Anderson's house. I can ask if it's okay for us both to go back and check it out," I say. "I really don't think he'll mind. He'll want to see it too."

Elaine checks her phone quickly, and her expression falls. "I have to get ready for my shift tonight."

I blink. I didn't know Elaine had a part-time job. How does she have so much time for everything? I feel like I have basically no hobbies other than birding and I somehow end up kind of busy.

"Where do you work?" I ask.

"An escape room. Might be why I'm so good at puzzles." She smiles. "You should definitely come do one of the rooms sometime."

FEAR #54: ESCAPE ROOMS

"Yeah," I say, my voice a little too high.

Even if they can't *actually* lock you in, I don't like the idea of it. I'm not exactly the best under pressure, or with puzzles, and literally the whole point of escape rooms is that you need multiple friends to do them with.

Not for me.

"Come on, I'll take you home," Elaine says.

I keep the flash drive tucked in my hand. It's too important to accidentally drop on the floor, and I don't know if someone from the Flock might be watching or following me.

"Thanks," I say, still with my hand closed into a fist around the small piece of plastic.

We walk back to her car and get inside. Luckily, the post office isn't far from home. It makes sense that Mr. Conspiracy used the closest one. Placing the flash drive in the lockbox was probably the only time he actually left the apartment.

I can almost imagine it, but it's hard to think about him. I've only seen the man on two occasions: when he was terrified or dead. It's not exactly like I have good memories.

My stomach grumbles, so I clench my jaw.

If I throw up in Elaine's car, I will literally drop everything and flee the country. I can dry fish in Sweden or whatever I would need to do to never be found again by anyone.

"We'll talk tomorrow about what's on there, okay?" Elaine says. "Speaking of . . . are you going on the hike?"

I forgot to mention the meeting with Mr. Conspiracy's informant. If Anderson and I do show up, it will conflict with the GLAOE meeting time.

"Um . . . maybe," I start.

"Do you need a ride?" she asks. "I can pick you up in the morning."

"I might be late," I admit. "Anderson and I have a potential lead."

"No worries. Just let me know." Elaine's smile is big. "I'm really glad you got me involved in this. I've been wanting to talk to you for a while now."

I shouldn't take that in any special way besides friendly.

"Yeah, we are the only high schoolers in the birding group," I tease.

"I mean, I only joined because of you," Elaine says.

It's like the words slip out, because her body stiffens immediately after saying that. And my mind just about goes blank. It's silent, aside from the quick beating of my heart.

"I just . . ." Elaine's nose reddens as she darts her eyes between me and the road. "I was on a hike by myself when I saw GLAOE, and you, on one of the hikes. And I just . . . you seemed to feel the same way about birds as I do, so I wanted to talk to you. I was too nervous, but I gathered up enough courage to ask Jillian about the group and join. Clearly, I haven't been great about approaching you. It's been . . . what? Three months now?"

I don't know how to speak. Is Elaine Yee basically admitting that she was intimidated by me? That it wasn't just me? And if that's the case, does that mean her feelings are similar to mine?

I'm about to get a nosebleed.

"Better late than never," I manage to say.

"Yeah," she says, but she's not really looking at me. "Hopefully I'll see you tomorrow."

It's only then that I realize the car is stopped and we are in front of Anderson's apartment. This is probably the worst timing, and while I want the conversation to continue, I'm definitely not brave enough to get it back on track.

Could she have meant . . . ?

I can't stop smiling. I look away to try to hide it.

"Okay, have fun at work," I say as I get out of the car.

When she drives off, I walk into the building. I'm a little lighter on my feet than normal. The flash drive is tight in my hand as I make it up to the Colemans' apartment. I open the door, ready to immediately share the news with Anderson. But his shower is running, so I have a few minutes to kill before he's out.

I open my phone and see six missed calls from my mom.

FEAR #42: PISSING OFF MY MOM

I press the phone icon on her name. Squeezing my eyes shut, like that will help at all, I listen to the rings and prepare myself.

"Where the hell have you been?" Mom immediately asks as soon as she picks up. She doesn't give me time to answer. "I got a call from school that you've skipped a bunch of classes this week. You're supposed to be texting me."

This is bad. I should have known they would call my parents. To be fair, she should have been checking my location. But that's probably not the best thing to bring up.

"I . . ."

Mom doesn't let me continue. "And when they ask you to come to the office, you ignore them?"

Dammit. Between trying to crack the code and finally getting the flash drive, I completely forgot about that.

It's like Mom doesn't want to give me a chance to explain myself, because she sighs into the phone.

"I know things have been hard, and there's a lot going on right now, but you can't keep missing classes, okay? A day, sure. Not multiple classes so you're nearly failing!"

"Okay," I say. "Sorry."

There's so much more I should say if only I could get the words out.

"Promise me you'll go to every class starting Monday, and really focus on homework?" Her voice tells me I don't have much of an option.

"Promise," I say.

"Good." She sounds a bit calmer and more controlled now, almost a little apologetic, as she adds, "You know you can tell me stuff, right?"

Ha.

"It might help if you actually talked to me instead of just calling the school when something happens to me."

I don't know why I say that. I could've just kept silent to appease her.

"What are you talking about?" Mom asks. "I haven't . . . shit. I have to start my evening class. We can talk about this later, okay? I love you."

I sigh.

"Love you too," I say. "Bye."

Distracted by the call, I didn't notice the shower turn off. Thankfully, Anderson is clothed when he enters his bedroom.

"Hey," he says. "How did it go?"

"It went well," I say. "Look what we found."

I hold up the flash drive. Anderson sits on his bed and reaches over to grab it.

"This is Mr. Conspiracy's?"

"Yeah, he left another hidden message in his journal that led us to a PO box where it was stored."

Anderson whistles. "What's on it?"

"Not sure yet, Elaine had to work and I just got back. Plus, you'd be mad if I looked without you."

"You're right about that." He stretches his arm over his head. "Is Elaine coming with us tomorrow?"

"No, she's going on the hike."

Anderson takes a deep breath. "Speaking of . . . do you think it's a good idea for us to go to the meeting? The Flock could be behind it."

"They killed Mr. Conspiracy, so why would they still show up? They don't know that he left us the info."

Anderson wipes a few water drops off his forehead and adjusts his glasses. "If it's not the Flock, there's still no guarantee that this informant guy will show up—maybe he could've seen that Steven died?"

"*If* this ex-member knew his real identity, which is a big *if* knowing Mr. Conspiracy."

"All right, so in the event that this meeting is separate from whatever the Flock has scheduled *and* the ex-member is planning on showing up, these Feathergate people are stalking you. What if they follow us to the meeting location and compromise it?" He scratches the top of his head. "I'm just saying, maybe it isn't the best idea?"

He has a point. Their focus has been on me the entire time. If the Flock follows me, I'd lead them right to Mr. Conspiracy's contact.

Unless they followed me somewhere else, and I give Anderson the opportunity to talk to the informant without worrying about the murderers.

"You're right. They're after me." I look up at Anderson. "So what if I don't go? I'll do the bird hike with Elaine. If we're followed by the killers, at least we won't be alone. I'll share my location and everything. Maybe you can take Ryan with you to the meeting for backup. You don't even have to talk with them. If it looks dangerous, just leave."

"Basically, you would be the diversion."

I nod. It could work.

Anderson smirks at me. "Or is this you just wanting to spend more time with Elaine?"

"Two birds." I press my hands to my face to cool it down.

"That makes sense though. We can both share our locations with Ronan and our parents, in case they follow either of us."

"Yeah, but since we'll be going around the same time, I'm sure they'll follow me. You're not the one who has been getting threats."

"And I'm happy about that. Can Elaine drive you tomorrow?"

"Yeah, she already offered. Kate has to be at school all day getting ready for the performance. My mom will be there too."

Mom may not be one of the ridiculous PTA parents, but she's definitely a stage mom. Which I feel is kind of worse.

I text Elaine about the change of plans, and that I actually will be going on the hike tomorrow. She immediately agrees to drive me.

"Okay, stop smiling into your phone, I want to know what Mr. Conspiracy dug up," Anderson says.

I stick my tongue out at him but get moving. I take my laptop and place it on his bed, still kneeling on the floor. Anderson plugs the USB into the port, and I open the drive.

Luckily, we don't have to do any hacking or code cracking. The flash drive has one folder, labeled VQ.

"Whoa," Anderson says. "This must be where Mr. Conspiracy backed up his info on them."

"Doesn't that mean the police would have this info too?"

Anderson shrugs. "I doubt they looked through his entire computer, it's a closed case."

I open the file. There are a number of documents containing budgets from the high school, bakeries, law offices, laundromats, and even pet shops. Plus a map of what seems to be the secret lair under Jamba Juice. There's a range of businesses funneling money to Valley Quail, Inc.

"This is wild," I say. "They really are everywhere."

Mr. Conspiracy has some Valley Quail, Inc., bank statements too. I widen my eyes at the amount.

"That's a lot of zeros."

"Jesus," Anderson says. "And look at those transfers . . . the same amount of money is going into personal bank accounts every month." He points to the paper that shows all the transactions. There are twenty separate accounts that receive the transfers on the first of each month. "So, everyone involved is stealing money from their jobs, putting it into this corporation, and then sending it off to their personal accounts." He whistles. "This is big. They killed Mr. Conspiracy so they can keep this covered up."

Mr. Conspiracy clearly put a lot of work into getting these files together, and it should definitely be enough to incriminate the group.

"Wouldn't he have gone to the police with this already?" I ask.

Anderson shrugs. "Maybe he went at some point, and they didn't believe him? Maybe he was planning something bigger, to really nail them? He had the ex-member meeting scheduled. I don't think he considered dying first."

It still would be really bad if the cult finds out we have these files now.

"What's that?" Anderson asks.

He's pointing to a file labeled *The Flock*.

I click on the file. It's a Word document of Mr. Conspiracy's notes. It's a list of birds, connected to the individual businesses.

"What does that mean?" Anderson asks.

"I think these are the members," I say. "Remember in that message from the sonnet book? It says they use code names. These must be the code names."

I start reading the list.

ACORN WOODPECKER—K & M Associates

NORTHERN CARDINAL—Mayfield Vegan Treats

GREEN HERON—Marco's Pet Supplier

I keep scanning the list for our high school. The em dash to the left of it connects to RED-WINGED BLACKBIRD.

"We don't know who these people are," Anderson says.

"No, but we know where to find them."

I close out of the document. I don't want to keep looking at the code names.

I continue scrolling through the rest of the files and come across another Word doc, this one titled *TO THE GIRL WITH THE TELESCOPE.*

It's not like I can be mad at a dead man for misgendering me under the circumstances, and there's no way that's intended for anyone but me, so I hover the mouse over the document.

Anderson reads the title, eyes widening. "Oh, wow," he says.

I'm about to click it when glass shattering echoes from outside. Anderson and I look at each other and move toward the window. It's kind of strange to view it from this other direction. To see my house, my own bedroom window.

My own bedroom window, which was broken into.

By a person in loose black clothing and a plague doctor mask. They are straddling the sill, ducking through the shards of glass, the blade in their hand glinting in the light from the streetlamp.

Anderson's eyes are wide. "That's the . . ."

I don't hear the rest of the sentence. It's like I'm taken back to the night I saw Mr. Conspiracy. The blood. The way his rigid body paled.

Only this time, they came for me.

If I was at home, I would be a body on the floor, like Mr. Conspiracy.

Panic strikes through me. Puck is here. Kate is at the final dress rehearsal. Mom and Dad are at work or the hotel. They're safe.

I call 911 as the person disappears into my room.

My breathing starts coming quickly, my vision growing splotchy.

Oh no.

I reach out and grab Anderson's good arm. He steadies me.

Puck meows as if she can tell something is going on.

I can't breathe, and the minutes feel like hours as Anderson sends off quick texts to his family.

The sirens blare in the distance, getting closer.

The person in the mask appears back in the frame of my bedroom window, starting to climb over.

Anderson and I both watch as the figure in the mask kicks one leg through the jagged opening and angles it toward the raised, empty flower bed at the side of the house. That's probably how they climbed up, and it makes a nice enough crash pad. The figure doesn't immediately jump. Instead, they look over.

Directly at the two of us.

A moment passes with them staring through the creepy holes of the mask, no way to tell where their eyes are. But we're practically across from them, in plain sight.

I push Anderson out of the way so neither of us are visible.

Anderson finds his voice first. "Do you think they recognized us?"

I can barely hear him. Between the sirens growing in volume

and the pounding of my own heart, the world around me and within me is nearly deafening.

I cautiously move back toward the window, trying to not be so obvious about showing myself while looking to see if the person is there.

But they're already gone.

THIRTY

A COMPLETELY UNEVENTFUL BIRDING HIKE

The night was filled once more with talking to cops about the break-in, being unable to give much of a description, and Mrs. and Mr. Coleman speaking with my parents. I didn't want to mention anything about Feathergate to the police yet. I'm not sure they'll believe me. Someone broke in, but that doesn't mean it was a murderous money-laundering cult. Even the cops said it was probably someone from school messing with me.

I need to figure out who is behind all this first. For Mr. Conspiracy.

And maybe it's wild to admit, but for myself, too. We've gotten so deep into this, can I really just step aside when I don't know if they'll actually see the investigation through?

Anderson, Ronan, and I stayed up late. Our parents decided that I would still stay at the Colemans', along with Puck, while Kate remains at Yoneta's and my parents go back to the hotel.

The Colemans reported the incident to apartment security, and the other people in the building were told to not let anyone in. Not that it would stop someone from breaking in, but at least they were made aware of the potential danger.

Ronan and Anderson are deep asleep when my phone vibrates at six thirty in the morning to wake me up. Anderson sleeps on top of his comforter, with Ronan curled up with Puck at the end of Anderson's bed.

Trying to not make so much noise that I wake up Ronan, I tiptoe over to Anderson and nudge his shoulder.

"Hey," I whisper. "Wake up."

He slowly opens his eyes halfway. "No."

"I have to leave soon to go to my birding group even though someone tried to kill me last night. And you should get going too."

Keeping his eyes mostly closed, he holds out his good arm like he's going for a hug. I pat him on the head instead.

"I'll be ready in, like, five minutes."

"Text me if anything bad happens," I say. "And drive away if it seems unsafe. You're sharing your location?"

"I've been sharing my location."

"Sounds good. We'll keep each other updated?"

"You got it," he says. "Don't die."

"Not before I find out what the One Piece is," I assure him.

As if he doesn't have to get up soon, Anderson closes his eyes again with a little smile. I'll text him to make sure he gets there on time.

My phone lights up. Elaine's on her way. I probably should

have set the alarm for a little earlier. I have on clean clothes, but the lack of sleep is definitely visible on my face.

I walk into the kitchen, where Mr. and Mrs. Coleman are already awake, sipping coffee. It's like they never sleep in.

"Morning, Bianca," Mr. Coleman says. "Want a cup?"

"Yes, thank you," I say. I'm on a few hours of sleep at best, but I can chug it down.

He starts pouring me some, and it's nice to have regular coffee instead of my dad pushing the Italian espresso that Nonna ships him. Although that wouldn't necessarily be unwelcome, considering how strong he makes it.

It sort of makes me miss it. Just waking up and smelling the espresso, seeing Mom and Dad in the morning. Not having murderers after me.

A lot changed in just a few weeks.

"You're up early," Mrs. Coleman says. "It's been a night."

"I have my birding hike," I say. Mr. Coleman hands me the warm mug. "Thank you." I look between them, both having done so much for me, and my eyes prick. "I'm so sorry," I say. "I didn't stay out of it and now you're all involved. If anything happens to any of you . . ."

"Hey." Mrs. Coleman pulls me into a hug. "It'll be okay. We're going to take precautions, and make sure that no one is alone at home until it's figured out."

"No weirdo is going to kill you or my sons," Mr. Coleman adds. "Not while I'm alive."

Mrs. Coleman pulls away enough to make eye contact. "Do

you need a ride to the hike today? If that'll make you feel better, I think it should be okay to go. We can go with you, if you'd like."

"One of my friends is going to pick me up."

"Okay," Mrs. Coleman says. "But text me the exact location right now, in case anything happens. You call immediately."

"Got it, thank you. I'm sharing my location with Anderson and Ronan too." I copy the name of the trail and address from the invite and text it to Mrs. Coleman. "I really can't thank you both enough."

Mr. Coleman waves it off. "If you make it big as some fancy ornithologist, make sure to take care of us." He gives a smile. "I wouldn't mind a beachfront property."

I really doubt I'll get the big bucks from studying birds, but if I ever win the lottery, the Coleman family would be the first people I'd spoil. Then again, after seeing Jillian's mansion, maybe there could be something to it.

"All right," I say, smiling. "If anything, I'll split the cost with Anderson and Ronan to get you both a house in Malibu."

"That's all I ask," Mr. Coleman says with a wink.

After I down the coffee and put the mug in the dishwasher, Mrs. Coleman walks me outside to wait for Elaine. I'm not sure the cult will try anything when the sun's up, but it's nice to not have to be on my own and out in the open.

"So," Mrs. Coleman says. "Who's this friend?"

I can already tell by her tone of voice what she's asking.

My face heats up. "It's not like . . ." My hope from yesterday keeps creeping back up. "I mean, maybe it's a *little* like that."

Mrs. Coleman nearly does a little dance in excitement. "Aw, you and Anderson can double-date."

I'm bright red now, I know it. "Well, it's not anything yet, like . . . I definitely like her."

"Well, she has no reason not to like you," Mrs. Coleman says. "Unless she's trash."

While I'm hopelessly embarrassed, it's also really nice to talk about this with her. It's not like I can go to my mom and mention my crush on a girl. Even if I don't like making a big deal of things, that's probably not the best way to come out.

Elaine's car pulls up, and Mrs. Coleman pinches my arm when she sees her. "Oh, she's *cute.*"

And I'm a literal shaking tomato.

Elaine parks at the curb, and upon seeing Mrs. Coleman, gets out of the car for a moment. She walks up to her and holds a hand out. "Hi, I'm Elaine Yee, Anderson's friend and Bianca's, uh, friend. Also."

Mrs. Coleman gives me a pointed look before smiling at Elaine and shaking her hand. "I'm Alicia. Anderson's mom because I birthed him, and Bianca's second mom because I like them."

That gets me right in the feels. I would kill a man for this woman.

Which is good, because with a murderous cult at my heels, I might have to.

I swallow the rising bile and put on a grin. "Hi, thanks for the ride."

"No problem," Elaine says.

She smiles back at me and it lights up her whole face. Her brown eyes practically sparkle gold in the rising sunlight, and I keep looking between them and her lips, painted a rose color that I'd really like to taste.

I turn away.

"I have the address, call if anything happens, or if you have the slightest bad feeling at all," Mrs. Coleman says. She looks at Elaine. "You take care of each other."

"We will," Elaine says. "Promise."

"Holding you to that," Mrs. Coleman says. She lets the two of us get into the car and waves us off. "You kids have fun."

We wait for Mrs. Coleman to walk back into the apartment building, and then head toward the meeting location for the hike. Just to be safe, I double-check that my location is shared with Anderson and Ronan.

Anderson has already sent a quick *One Piece* meme. At least I know he's awake now.

"What was on the flash drive?" Elaine asks.

"Everything he had on Valley Quail and Feathergate was backed up on it. It connects everything to the Flock. We know that there are twenty members." I almost mention that Mr. Conspiracy also left a document for me, but I was too nervous to read it. I'd rather wait until this is all over, whatever *this* ends up being, so I don't feel like I failed him. Looking at his words now would be too hard. Besides, it would be hard to explain that document without also explaining my casual stalker tendencies, and that's not exactly the best topic of conversation for someone I'm really into romantically.

"They are stealing money, then." Elaine tightens her grip on the wheel.

"Yeah, from at least twenty different businesses," I say. "I mean, there could be more. This is just what Mr. Conspiracy uncovered."

"Maybe I can come over after the hike to look at it?" Elaine asks. "If Anderson wouldn't mind."

"I doubt he'd mind," I say. "We were kind of interrupted last night."

Concern washes over Elaine's features. Her eyes dart to me for a second before returning to the road ahead. "What happened?"

"One of them broke into my bedroom," I say. "At my actual house—I'm staying with Anderson." I lean back into the chair. I try not to think too hard about it, to say the words like they aren't connected to me. "They had the same mask and large knife as the night Mr. Conspiracy was murdered, so . . . I think they wanted to do the same to me."

Elaine pales, and her mouth opens for a few seconds before she speaks. "Are you all right?"

It seems like that's what everyone has been asking me lately, and I'm starting to feel like I never was. Before seeing Mr. Conspiracy bloodied and lifeless, I was stuck in my bedroom with a whole list of fears I never faced and limited interactions outside my family that didn't take place silently through multiple layers of glass.

That wasn't exactly all right either.

"I'm good," I say, "really."

Because that's the kind of thing you say, even if you're not.

Elaine gives a small smile. "You ready to potentially put yourself into more danger?"

I glance toward her, leaning back in my seat.

"No," I say. "But I seem to be really great at it anyway."

The birding hike is very calm and uneventful, unless I count the vermilion flycatcher Terrance snapped a picture of toward the start of the trail, which is an extremely rare find this time of year in Los Angeles. Everyone politely and quietly clapped. It's almost like everything is completely normal.

One key difference on this hike is that Elaine and I walk together. We don't talk a lot. Mostly we pay attention to the surroundings, point out any possible sightings, and trade our note-covered field guides back and forth.

Occasionally, as we walk along the trail, our arms brush. Tingles shoot through my skin at the mere touch, but I don't pull away.

And neither does she.

"Bianca, Elaine, did you see the flycatcher before it flew off?"

We turn toward Jillian, smiling brightly in her matching shorts and T-shirt, both somehow the exact same shade of lavender. Even the frames of her glasses have a purple accent.

"I did," I say the same time Elaine says, "I didn't."

"I saw the picture though," Elaine adds.

"Wish I didn't miss it." Jillian turns toward me. "I'm glad you caught it, Bianca. You're such a natural observer."

"Thanks, Jillian." I'm not really sure what to say to that, but her tone definitely made it seem like a good thing, and it would make sense for her compliments to be a bit more on the quirkier side.

"I'm so glad you made it today," Jillian says. "We are all so proud of our two youngest birders."

Now I'm a little embarrassed.

"I'm glad you welcomed me into the flock—I mean, fold!" I try to hide my wince with a smile.

"I'm happy to help," Jillian says. "Because I know that you'd help me in return. Right?"

It's a bit odd for her to say it like that, but I can't really speak to anyone saying things that sound more awkward than intended. It's practically my special talent.

"Of course."

Jillian is all smiles. "Oh, by the way, are you two free tonight? I was thinking of doing a little get-together dinner party at my house."

"I have my sister's musical performance tonight."

"Oh, it wouldn't be until later, so you can come after! Let me know!" She clasps her hands together. "Well, I won't bother the two of you any longer. Don't fall too far behind the rest of the group." She winks at the two of us.

Elaine blushes nearly as much as I do.

What is Jillian suggesting?

She keeps up her pleasant attitude, turning on her heel to greet Mr. Hawthorne, an older white man who I believe is a lawyer or something. He definitely has that look to him.

"That was strange," Elaine says. "But sweet."

"Jillian has mastered the fine line between them," I say. "I didn't know there was something planned for tonight."

"Maybe she just decided on the spot." Elaine shrugs. Then, she immediately twists her head to the right. "Wait, what's that?" She points to a bird rustling in one of the trees to our left, but I can't quite make out the features.

We stop, and I lift my binoculars to get a better view.

Before I can focus on the bird, I'm yanked back. My heart stops.

FEAR #3: MURDER

I turn around to see Anderson.

"What the hell?" I ask, trying to keep my voice low. "Weren't you meeting with that guy?"

"I was, and I have urgent news. Ryan's waiting for us in the parking lot." He looks more serious than I've ever seen him. "We have to go. Now." He starts to pull me with his good arm, but can't grab onto Elaine. "You too, Elaine, let's go."

"What did he say?" My eyes widen. "You know who it is?"

"Yes, and that's why we need to get out of here. *Now.* It's this group. They're the Flock."

My stomach churns and my hands start shaking. I wasn't prepared for this. Even Elaine looks like she saw a ghost. "Everyone?" I ask.

"Everyone who joined before you did, at least." Anderson looks to Elaine. "Unless you have something to share?"

Elaine frowns. "No, but you can't be serious."

She's right. How could it be nearly everyone in the group? Some of them seem the type, maybe, but not . . .

"Jillian too?" my weak voice presses.

The get-together she was mentioning . . . is that what the sticky note was about?

No, that's . . .

Anderson nods. "Jillian is practically the helm of it. The contact Mr. Conspiracy found used to be part of the group but got out of it and changed his name. And it gets worse. Look at what he had."

He holds out his phone to show us a photo. It was clearly taken at a wedding, featuring Jillian in a straight white dress, holding a bouquet of flowers and kissing the cheek of a smiling . . .

"What the fuck?" I blurt.

But it's unmistakable.

Ms. Richards and Jillian are married.

While I must admit my next thought is *so cute*, that's immediately followed by an *oh no*.

Not only is Ms. Richards the person at our school who is involved, but Jillian is too?

Guess that internship is no longer on the table.

I don't know if I'll make it to spring.

Tears spring to my eyes. I can't believe I've been with this group for a year . . . I trusted most of them. I definitely trusted Jillian. She's part of it.

They're all part of it.

And Ms. Richards on top of it?

I'm such a failure.

We have to get out of here.

The edge drops from Anderson's voice. "Can we leave now?" he asks, softly but with urgency.

"Yeah," I say. "Please."

There's a metallic click from behind us.

I turn to see Jillian, holding a handgun aimed directly at my face.

My breath catches, heart pounding in my throat.

I don't know if I want to completely alter the numbering on my list, but at the moment, there might be a tie for first.

FEAR #1.5: GUNS

"Unfortunately, none of you will be leaving," Jillian says as she takes a step closer, not moving the barrel from my face. She talks directly to me now. "To think I chewed Jeffrey out for trying to kill you. I said you'd understand, that you'd stay quiet if I could talk to you first. That's what this day was supposed to be about. You finally accepting us." She sighs. "Made a real clown out of me, Bianca."

I don't know what to say to that, other than "Jeffrey tried to kill me?"

"I like how you focus on that, and not the fact that I wanted to save you." Jillian rolls her eyes. "Where the hell is my credit?"

Anderson starts to make a move, and she points the gun at him. "You better not try anything. I was a state-ranked shooter and I'll kill the three of you right now."

I have to do something to get Anderson and Elaine out of this. Or at least buy us some time to run away.

"Wait," I say. I hold my hands up and take one step toward Jillian. Two. "I'll stop all of this, and none of us will say anything. No one else knows." I take a deep breath. "It's like you said. I need to understand. You can't doubt me if you never tried to explain."

Now I'm barely a foot from Jillian and the gun. It's not like I can reach out and punch her. She'll definitely shoot me first, and then Anderson and Elaine.

My breath catches. "Don't hurt them. I'll hear you out. I promise."

Jillian thinks for a long moment. She doesn't lower the gun.

"Okay," she says finally. "Party will start early."

I'm about to let out a breath in relief, when Jillian brings the handle of the gun down on my head and everything snaps to black.

THIRTY-ONE

ENTER THE FLOCK

I hear voices before I see anything, but I can't make out what they're saying. Death is likely somewhere on my list of fears, but my head is pounding too much to actually think of the numbers. As my vision starts to return, I first notice candlelight.

There are a lot of candles. Like a there-was-a-holiday-sale-at-Bath-and-Body-Works number of candles.

Or like . . . a sacrifice-a-nonbinary-teen-birder-who-pissed-you-off number of candles.

Tears prick my eyes.

"Bianca?"

At least I think someone says my name. I'm groggy and the world is unclear, like I'm suspended under water.

I blink a few times, the top of my head in searing pain as my senses slowly return to me.

I'm not sure I can trust them though, because the sight in front of me is incredibly strange. I'm in a large room, with lanterns spaced out on the wall, revealing strange bird paintings on every surface.

In the center of the room, there's a stone statue that has the same bird-and-sword design from Mr. Conspiracy's journal and the sonnet book, except the swords look real.

Surrounding the statue are a bunch of people wearing crimson robes and matching masquerade masks with feathers and long beaks. Despite their disguises, I can recognize them as members of the GLAOE.

Jillian, masked and robed, stands at the opposite side of the room, on top of a podium, so that she is above everyone else.

They remain motionless.

I try to wiggle free, but my arms and legs are both tied to the chair I'm sitting on. I have some blood and spit dried on my shirt.

FEAR #46: SWEAT AND OTHER BODILY FLUIDS

FEAR #10: BLOOD

And I can't even wipe the blood or spit that's on me. My skin crawls.

They didn't take me alone. They couldn't have.

I turn to the right, where Anderson and Elaine are in the same predicament as me. Elaine is awake, her own eyes filled with fear. Anderson groans, just starting to wake up.

"Are you both all right?" I ask.

"We're alive," Elaine says. "I think they drugged us. I'm not sure how long we've been out."

"I have to pee so bad," Anderson says. "I'm gonna get a UTI."

Guess the gun to the head wasn't enough. I feel terrible. I glance back to the cloaked people I've spent my Saturdays with for the past year. Still no movement from them.

My eyes catch some motion to the left of me, and I twist to see Terrance and Margaret, also tied up. They don't have any blood on them, so they might not have had a gun to the face, at least.

"You're not part of this?" I whisper.

"We had no idea this was a cult cover," Margaret says, voice low. She seems really drowsy too.

"Looking back, the website was a little outdated and weird . . ." Terrance shakes his head. "But we just really like birds."

They both try to shrug, but can't really do it with the ropes on. They are surprisingly calm given the situation. I'm on the brink of a panic attack.

I can't believe I've dragged more people into this.

"I'm so sorry," I say. "I didn't know they'd bring you here too."

"It's not your fault," Margaret starts. "We—"

Whatever the end of that statement is, it's entirely lost by the sound of an extremely loud cuckoo clock going off at the other side of the room. While it's hard to see in the dim lighting, it looks like it's already five. We've been gone all day?

Except Ronan should have our location. He would have shared it when we didn't come home. They have to be looking for us, don't they? Did Ryan see something when they left with us?

"Ca-CAW!" Jillian yells once the clock stops.

"Ca-CAW!" the rest of the group responds.

"Oh, hell no," Anderson says. "This is some real white-people shit."

"Mm-hmm," Terrance and Margaret agree.

He's not wrong. Terrance, Margaret, and Elaine are the only nonwhite members of the group, and the people standing in the circle with their ridiculous costumes on are extremely pale.

Jillian chooses to ignore us in the back, if she can hear us. Instead, she raises both her hands into the sky, red sleeves drooping.

"The Flock before the One," Jillian says, voice booming.

Mom would really appreciate her projection techniques. That's definitely from the diaphragm.

"The Flock before the One," the rest of the group repeats.

"The Flock before the rest," Jillian says. The group follows with the same line.

The next part they say in unison.

"And once this shallow life is done, we return to our true nest."

They do one more ca-caw call-and-response, and I'm starting to think that whatever I may have been drugged with was a hallucinogenic, because there is no way this can be real.

"Now," Jillian says to the crowd. "Today we are gathered to determine the fate of our fellow birder Bianca Torre for continuing to investigate our operation despite multiple warnings—a complete betrayal of the Flock."

"The Flock before the One," the group chants, facing me.

"In addition," Jillian continues, "we have on trial fellow birder Elaine Yee, for conspiring with Bianca. And fellow birders Terrance and Margaret Bryant for . . ." Her voice loses the theatrics as she looks back at the couple. "Honestly, a wrong place, wrong time thing, I'm sorry about that."

"The Flock before the rest," the group says in response.

"Lastly, on trial is Bianca's friend . . ." She trails off, looking toward Anderson.

"Anderson Coleman," he says. "Nice to meet you all."

Now is probably not the time to be polite.

"Weird circumstances, but you as well," Jillian says. Then she switches back to the cult-leader voice. "Anderson Coleman, for also conspiring against the Flock."

"The Flock before the One!"

My skin pricks, and the ropes around my wrists feel incredibly tight. This is too weird. I can't even feel my full range of emotions from the betrayal because my mind is too busy trying to process what the hell is happening in front of me.

"You might want to let us go." I'm almost surprised I have my voice. "Our phones were sharing our location."

Jillian glances at me. "We stopped the location share after texting your parents that you're fine and not to worry. Try again."

I don't really have anything else up my sleeve. I was kind of banking on that.

"Any other warnings? Interjections? No?" Jillian's voice returns to her booming, cult-leader tone. "Now . . ."

"I'll have you know I'm trained in Jiu-Jitsu," Anderson says. "I just got my blue belt, which basically means I'm dangerous to an untrained person."

Jillian blinks. "Okay. Go ahead."

Anderson frowns. "Well, once untied, I'm an extremely dangerous person."

None of the cloaked members seem scared. Jillian raises her voice again. "*Now*, we shall start the ceremony."

It goes quiet for a moment. I try to pull at the ropes, but they are too snug.

"Can I interrupt with a question?" Anderson asks.

The rest of us turn to look at him. Excluding the Flock members. They're really into the whole creepily-staring-straight-ahead deal.

"Oh. My God." Jillian throws off her mask. "Make it quick."

Anderson tries to lift his shoulders in a shrug, but being tied up with his wrist already broken has to seriously hurt. I wish I could seem as calm as him.

"If you are all part of this cul—this lovely group. Why let other people into GLAOE?"

It's a valid question. I certainly didn't think it was a cover-up for a money-laundering scheme when I reached out through the website. They could've said they weren't accepting new members.

Jillian blushes. "Well, Bianca reached out and seemed really passionate and so knowledgeable about birds! I couldn't just ignore someone like that. I thought it'd be a good opportunity to actually start the birding hikes. When Elaine reached out, and then Terrance and Margaret . . . I mean, we already had the hikes at that point, so it seemed easier to go along with it."

It would almost be sweet that she did this for me . . . and if I wasn't hearing about it while tied up and if they weren't threatening my life, I might be a little moved.

"I guess it is a good cover," Anderson says. "Okay, proceed."

I glare at him, and he bites his lip a little. I guess there's not much we can do at this point. Distracting Jillian isn't the worst idea. Maybe she'll remember how much she likes me and decide not to kill us.

Unlikely, but worth a shot.

"Thank you." Jillian spins to address the rest of the still-masked members. "Now, Northern Cardinal and Red-Winged Blackbird are otherwise occupied, so they will agree with the overall decision of the Flock."

I don't know who they are based on bird names alone, but I don't see Jeffrey present. Or Ms. Richards.

If they aren't here, what are they doing?

"As Belted Kingfisher, I have made the decision to give Bianca Torre the opportunity to repent her crime by joining the Flock."

"Return to our true nest!" the group says in response.

I'm really starting to get freaked out by the whole chanting thing. I might have to tack that on to the bottom of the list.

FEAR #66: CULTLIKE CHANTS

Jillian steps off the podium and walks across the room toward me. The rest of the members turn their bodies without actually moving from the spaces they stand in.

"I'm serious, Bianca. Tonight we planned to initiate you. Of course, it wasn't supposed to go exactly like this . . . we didn't expect that you knew Steven or would bring friends . . ." She gives an exaggerated sigh before smiling. "Oh well, sometimes you have to improv."

The rest of the group encourages her with another loud CA-CAW.

"The Flock is more than a collection of like-minded people; we are a family," Jillian confides. "We share common beliefs, values. We share a similar love that will carry us on from this life to the next one."

No one else who's tied up dares say anything. She's so close now, and she has the gun at her side. The last thing we need is to set her off by interrupting her passionate speech.

"We are trapped in this life," Jillian continues, "tethered to the dirt with our clunky bodies, our greed and desire for material goods. People are the scum of the earth. So much of humanity is garbage, Bianca. Humans are filled with hatred. And the worst of them, the most vile and disgusting beings, are the ones in power. It is beyond redemption, beyond saving." Jillian holds up her gun as she speaks, like she's admitting that she is part of the problem.

"People suck," Anderson agrees.

Dammit, Anderson. For a moment, I'm terrified Jillian will point the gun at him. Instead, she nods, glad he, too, is following her diatribe. "Exactly," she says with glassy eyes. "People *suck*. The only thing to do now is to rise above it."

Jillian turns to me. "What animal is there that is freer than a bird?" She gets a faraway look before gesturing to the statue behind her. "They are able to soar above the garbage riddling the earth, as they are kings of the sky. They rule a different realm, closer to the heavens. They are the perfect beings." Her face is alight, eyes sparkling like a kid's as she looks right at me. "Haven't you ever wondered what it's like to taste flight?"

She doesn't continue, but actually seems to be awaiting a response.

"Well, yeah," I say, because maybe Anderson is right and it's a smart idea to agree with the woman carrying a loaded weapon. "Of course."

"That's what this is about," Jillian says. "We have simple rules, group prayers, ways to strengthen our bonds—methods of purifying our human vessels to be reborn as birds in the next life."

I'm silent for a moment. She sounds so sincere.

"Oh," I say. A moment passes. "But what does that have to do with the money?"

Jillian actually blushes again. "Well, that was more of Kaitlin's idea," she says in a low voice. "But it's a great point. We have to partake in these disgusting human urges like material greed so we can be completely cleansed for the next life."

"Kaitlin . . ." I say. "Red-Winged Blackbird?"

"Oh dear. I slip up sometimes." Jillian gets redder. "When you love someone . . . Plus, once you get used to a certain lifestyle, you have to maintain it, right?"

Ms. Richards is behind the money laundering? Does that mean Jillian was telling the truth when she said she really didn't want me dead? Not that it matters in this situation, but it might be good to play that card.

And while she may not be a good sapphic role model, at least Jillian wasn't actively trying to kill me.

Just . . . trying to convert me to . . . a bird . . .

Could be worse.

"You too can rid yourself of humanity and the filth that comes along with being human," Jillian says, and she's really selling it. "This life doesn't have to be the end. In the next life, you can soar."

"Really?" I ask. "I can?"

"Of course," she says. "If you join the Flock."

"The Flock before the One," I say.

"The Flock before the One," the group repeats.

Jillian smiles brightly. "I knew you would understand."

Anderson gives me a look, trying to speak out of the corner of his mouth. "Bianca, do you really believe—"

"Of course I do," I interrupt. "People do suck. And I've gone through so much hardship in my life. And I'll only be going through more now. For being nonbinary, for being awkward, for being a lesbian. There really is no fixing it. But I can fix my next life . . ." I meet Jillian's eyes. "Return to my true nest."

"Yes," she says. "Yes, exactly."

I hope Anderson and Elaine realize I'm bluffing and don't give me away.

"I'm so glad you told me," I say. "I needed this opportunity, this family."

Jillian takes the mask with the beak and places it on my face.

"Ca-caw!" I call.

"Ca-caw!" the crowd yells back.

And then a phone starts ringing, sounding a lot like my ringtone.

Jillian steps away to where the phones are, and my chest seizes. Who is that?

FEAR #47: BEING CAUGHT IN A LIE

Jillian picks up my phone, and she can clearly see something in my notifications that makes her entire expression fall.

Oh no.

She walks back over to me, still silent. But something is definitely different. She holds up the phone to my face, where the notifications are visible. I see past the absurd number of missed calls to look at the new text messages.

> **Kate:** Are you going to be able to stop investigating that weird-ass murder cult so you can come to the preview? Mom said you're out?
>
> **Kate:** Come celebrate Valley Quail not killing Audrey II
>
> **Kate:** can't wait for you to see the puppet looks so good

Oh no no no no.

"Well, that was before I knew the reasoning," I say weakly, but she doesn't seem to buy it.

"You lied," Jillian says slowly. "How many people know about Valley Quail?"

"Just us," I say. "Mostly me. And, well, Kate."

And Ronan. And Kate's sophomore mentee? Maybe that's a stretch.

Can she tell that I'm literally thinking about how I'm lying now?

"I see," Jillian says. She turns to the rest of the Flock. "It looks like we go through with attending the musical tonight. Red-Winged Blackbird is in charge of ticket sales, so we can use that petty cash to hem the new robes."

"Jillian, I was wrong before," I say. "I didn't know, but now . . ."

She gives me a glare. "Too late for that." Her expression is hard as she looks back at the rest of the cloaked group. "I hear the show is great," Jillian says. "It's a shame that the leading lady dies at the end."

She tightens the grip on her gun. I know the plot of *Little Shop of Horrors* enough now to know that the character of Audrey does actually die, but that's definitely not what Jillian seems to be implying. My stomach clenches.

No. They're going to go after Kate.

"She wants to be a good actress, right?" Jillian teases. "I'll make her death scene a little more method."

Kate revealed what she knew, and now they want to silence her too? Would they actually kill her when her character is supposed to die in the show?

"No," I say. "No, please . . ."

Jillian ignores me. "We'll return for judgment after the play.

Meeting adjourned," she says. "Ca-caw!"

"Ca-caw!" the Flock responds, before they slowly exit the room and head up a staircase, until only Jillian remains.

"I never wanted it to come to this . . ." she says. "I don't like violence, you know. But I had to be born a human."

"You don't like violence, but you killed two people. Maybe more." I shake my head. "Nate was one of you."

"Nate *betrayed* us!" Jillian snaps. "If he actually cared, he wouldn't have tried to turn us in and ruin everything we built. Besides, he's free now, Bianca. Can't you see that?" Her eyes shine with tears as she puts on a smile. "Just like you'll be."

She steps toward me and uses the barrel of the gun to tilt my chin up to her face. The metal is cold against my skin. My heart beats wildly in my chest. Elaine and Anderson say something, voices pleading, but I can't make out the words.

It's just me and Jillian, and the gun between us.

"Guess I'm not getting that internship, huh?"

She narrows her red-rimmed eyes. "Those are terrible last words."

I can't move. I don't know what to do. Is this really the end?

"What would be better?" I ask, voice low. "I'm sorry? I've always looked up to you, and it really sucks that you want me dead?"

She doesn't move the gun, but uses her other hand to wipe her eyes.

"Of course I don't want you dead, but what am I supposed to do?" Her voice echoes around the room as she takes a deep

325

breath. "I have to kill you. Just like Nate. Just like Steven. No loose ends."

My mind flies in circles, trying to think of any way to save myself, but I'm out of options. The only thing I can do is try to convince Jillian.

"Belted kingfishers spend most of their time alone," I say. "I was a lot like that, and maybe you were too. Maybe that's why we got along so well." My voice trembles a little. "You don't have to be alone, Jillian."

"I'm not," she says, moving her finger to the trigger. "I have the Flock."

My eyes squeeze shut. I can't help it.

"No," I hear her say. "I can't."

I open my eyes to see the tears streaking her pale face. The hand holding the gun drops to her side.

"I can't . . ." she repeats, shoulders shaking. She tries to compose herself. "Someone else will have to do it later. It's not like you five are going anywhere."

I can't argue that. I'm glad for the extra time, and for my brain matter to not be splattered against the wall.

"Please don't hurt my sister," I say weakly, as if I can ask for more.

She looks down to me. "I really liked you, Bianca. And it would have been so good." She wipes at her face. "I'll pray that you'll join us in the next life." A fresh tear spills down her cheek as she gives a sad smile. "I wish things could have been different in this one."

With that, Jillian leaves, heading up the stairs. The five of us are alone and tied up.

My own eyes fill and my heart nearly pounds out of my chest.

I thought I was afraid before, but I had no idea what fear was.

What was I thinking getting into this?

I'm nothing more than a lesbian sheep, who keeps finding new things to be afraid of.

FEAR #67: NOT BEING ABLE TO SAVE MY SISTER

THIRTY-TWO

REAL-LIFE ESCAPE ROOM

Jillian took my phone, and the rest of the cult members grabbed everyone else's, so it's not like we can contact anyone. Plus, our parents seem to think we're just fine.

The cuckoo clock goes off again, the little bird shooting out of the wooden clock as the noise plays.

"It can't be six," Anderson groans. "I'm dying."

Six. Kate's show starts in a half hour. I don't even have the full length of a musical before my sister gets a hit taken out on her.

"What did they give us?" Elaine asks. "That we've been out for so long?"

"They have vets and doctors in this group," Terrance says. "Who knows?"

"They're after my sister," I say. "We need to get out . . . we need . . ." My eyes start burning. I don't know what we can do. I feel more trapped than I've ever been.

"We have to think of a creative way to get out of here," Elaine says. "Like an escape room."

FEAR #54: ESCAPE ROOMS

Which seems a lot more valid now, though I'm assuming this is much worse.

Anderson looks at Elaine. "Something tells me the cult didn't leave riddles and puzzles to guide us to the exit."

"No, but there has to be something . . ." Elaine starts scanning the room, looking for inspiration.

We're not in the same lineup as before, as we've tried to scoot our way toward the staircase. Unfortunately, we didn't make much progress in the past forty minutes or so. They really bound us tight to these chairs.

My stomach growls, but even if I had food, I'd probably throw it up at this point.

"See anything?" Margaret asks.

Elaine doesn't answer, which isn't a good sign.

But there has to be some way out. I can't let us starve and die in our own held-in urine. I was the one to get us into this mess and I should be the one to get us out of it.

How to do so is another story.

All there is in this room is the cuckoo clock and the weird statue with the swords.

My eyes widen. The bottom sword is basically wrist level for me. It's not that far from where I am now.

"The sword," I say. "Do you think it will cut through the rope?"

The rest of the group looks over at the statue.

"It's worth a try," Anderson says.

Scooting around in a chair while being tied to it certainly isn't easy, but my feet are secured enough to keep them down while still being able to move a little. It takes a long time, and the scratching sound is horrible, but I'm able to get to the statue. The sword is just a little high for my arms to reach, but I should be able to get it if I can lift myself up slightly. I try to land on my legs, which are tied together but not to the chair, but they are slightly crossed so I have no balance. I'll have to free my feet first.

Turning the chair around in little jumps, I lift my bound legs and stretch them up to the sword. Although the back of the chair digs into my skin, I pull my knees back and forth to rub the rope over the blade.

It starts fraying.

I keep going, and it takes a good amount of time, but finally, the ropes snap and loosen enough for my legs to be free.

"Bianca, you're a genius!" Elaine says.

"But why the hell couldn't you have been a genius an hour ago?" Anderson groans.

I don't respond to him or the encouraging comments from Terrance and Margaret.

Now I have to turn around and free my hands, which will be a lot easier now that I can use my feet.

I look at the sword, which is covered in a huge spiderweb.

Oh no. Do they not clean down here?

I scan the web to look at the sword edge. A large black spider around the size of a quarter is right there.

FEAR #2: SPIDERS

"Um . . . maybe someone else can do it . . ." I start.

"What?" Anderson asks. "Why? You're right there."

My skin is literally crawling. Even my scalp is itchy. I turn to face my head toward Anderson.

"There's a spider," I mumble.

"What?"

"There's a spider!" I say, voice now carrying through the room.

The four of them look at me like I suddenly did turn into a bird.

"Bianca, honey," Terrance says. "It's a little thing, it can't hurt you."

"Not to mention, your *sister might die*," Anderson adds, because a best friend calls someone out.

He's right. They both are.

It's a spider. It can't do anything to me. What's actually important is getting out of here and to the school before the musical finale.

I plant my feet on the ground to support my weight, leaning forward in a squat so that the chair legs lift. I feel around with my bound hands for the edge of the sword and manage to get the ropes in contact with the blade.

I move my arms up and down, willing the rope to fray quickly.

A little tingle moves onto my fingers, exactly like spider legs. Why why why?

My first reaction is to flail my arm out and hope the spider is thrown, but with them tied, there's not anything I can do. And I don't want to accidentally cut my skin instead of the rope.

Tears pour from my eyes as I force myself to keep sawing, the spider moving up to my forearm.

I swallow my scream, but there's nothing I can do about the crying.

Finally, right as the spider nears my elbow, close enough that I can make out a red mark, my wrist is freed, and I swipe at it and shake my arm.

"Is it gone is it off is it off?" I squeal.

"Yeah, I saw it fly off," Terrance says.

"Are you sure? Was it a black-and-red one?" My skin tingles up my back. Where is it? Is it still on me? It has to be. *No no no.*

"Yes, he's sure, look!" Anderson gestures to my side with his chin.

"Oh," I say, stopping my motion. I glance to the floor, where the spider scurries away, but that doesn't stop my skin from crawling and my body visibly shaking.

"Although if it was a black widow, it actually could have hurt you," Terrance adds thoughtfully.

All the blood feels like it drains from my face. "What?"

"You did it! Yay, Bianca!" Anderson interrupts and breaks out into whoops.

The four cheer from the back of the room as I remove the ropes around my stomach, and I'm finally free. Shaken up, crying, and wanting to burn a layer or two of skin, but free. I leave the chair behind me and walk back toward them. My vision spots black and I stumble a bit.

I've been sitting for too long, or it's an effect of being drugged.

I manage to steady myself and untie Elaine first. I have to get dangerously close to touching her butt when I work the rope around her wrists. My hand definitely brushes it, and I blush.

"Sorry," I say.

"Next time, buy me a drink first," she teases.

Now my face heats even more. "If we get out of this alive, sure."

Once she's free, we untie Margaret and Terrance, and then get Anderson last because with his one hand out of commission, he couldn't help with the untying.

Once untied, we sneak up the stairs, exiting into the Jamba Juice bathroom. Well. At least we know where we are.

We race into the store, moving as a group into the smoothie place. We're a sight as we enter from the bathroom hallway, worse for wear, half of us with head wounds.

"What time is it?" I practically scream to the person at the register. He's white and barely looks eighteen, staring with wide eyes and potentially some fear.

"Um . . . six fifty-five?"

The show already started. I think the run time is about two hours total, so they have to be somewhere in the first act. Still,

I'm not sure when in act two Kate's death scene is, so we have to get to the school fast.

Margaret walks up to the worker and pulls out a fifty from her wallet. "I will give you this if you get these kids a Lyft to their high school and call the police."

He blinks, lips parting a little before he swallows to speak. "I'll take it for the Lyft, but we'll call the cops for free."

Anderson gives the worker our high school information before running back into the bathroom.

"Why are you going back?" I snap.

"Do you want me to pee in the car?" he calls back as the door closes.

I twist to Terrance and Margaret. "You two can handle the police?"

"We'll handle it," Margaret says.

"In case you need to get back down there, the pass code in the bathroom is 2018. At least, it was."

Terrance nods. "Got it, now go save your sister."

The Jamba Juice worker gives Elaine and me the Lyft information, and Anderson is back before Steve K. picks us up in his white Toyota Prius.

Props to him for not saying anything about our appearances. He drives well, but doesn't ask much at all. I hope Terrance convinces the Jamba Juice guy to give five stars.

The parking lot of the high school is filled. We have no choice but to go in through the main entrance, as every other door will be locked. We try to keep back, and I peer around the corner to where the auditorium entrance is.

Jeffrey sits at the ticket table. *Of course.* Ms. Richards was volunteering for ticket sales—she was probably signed up to steal profits and recruited him to help. It must've made it easier for the rest of the cult to show up now.

"How do we get past him?" I ask.

"Bianca? Oh, and Anderson!" I turn to the musical voice calling out to us.

Queen Elizabeth. In an emerald-green dress and with her gray hair tied in a neat updo.

When we look back, her expression shifts into something of concern. "My dears, what happened to you?"

"It's makeup," I say, "to support, the uh . . . show." It's not a great excuse, so I try to change the subject. "What are you doing here, Florence?"

She smiles. "Why, I always support the local theater, I adore musicals." She clasps her hands together over the program. "And your sister is marvelous. The first act was wonderful. The second act is starting now, I believe."

Thank God, we just missed intermission. Audrey has to be alive. But we're cutting it super close.

"I'm so glad you came," I say, and I really mean it, as I don't think Jeffrey can do anything with Florence right here. "Why don't we walk you back in?"

"Oh, I'd love that," Florence says. "We must catch up after the show. Verdi and Poochie adore you both." She turns to Elaine. "Also, where are my manners? Hello, dear, I'm Florence. I'm a neighbor of Anderson and Bianca."

"Great to meet you," Elaine says.

Elaine is really adaptable.

Anderson holds out his good arm for Florence to take, and we huddle around her as she escorts us to the auditorium. I sneak a glance toward Jeffrey, but he's engrossed in something on his phone. Sure, there probably aren't many tickets to sell with the preview halfway over, but he's being a little obvious with how much he doesn't care.

I'm grateful, though, because it gets us into the theater unnoticed.

Florence returns to her seat with a promise to catch us after the show, as the three of us huddle in the last aisle. They're doing "Call Back in the Morning," the first song of act two, so we still have time.

"Do you see anyone else?" I whisper.

"They're harder to spot in normal clothes," Elaine mutters.

"Where the hell are they?" Anderson says, a bit too loud. He gets a few shushes from those seated around us.

That's when Jillian, sitting at the opposite end of the row, looks over directly at us.

"Shit," we all say at once.

Jillian gets up, pulls out her phone, and makes a beeline for the tech booth. She's a lot closer to it than we are.

"I'll go after her," Anderson says. He starts off.

"I'm going to go to Kate," I say as an automatic response. I look at Elaine. "Maybe go back out and wait for the police.

There's a side entrance that's usually locked, but you can slip out."

I point to where it is. Thank God Kate made me help with a few set builds.

"Got it," she says. Before heading toward the door, she looks back at me. "Try not to die, you promised me a hike."

"I wouldn't miss it." My heart flutters between nervous thumps. She starts to step off. "Elaine?"

She twists to me.

A few things I could tell her swim through my frantic mind, but I settle on a "be safe."

Elaine smiles and then she's off.

Now that Jillian knows we are here, she probably won't wait until the end to make her move.

I have to get backstage and warn Kate.

The music is loud in my ears. I try to make myself as small as possible as I walk along the wall down the outer aisle and slip behind the edge of the curtain. I have to climb onto the stage, and I shimmy closer to the back.

"Bianca?" Devon Hart, the stage manager, mouths as she sees me.

"I was never here," I whisper.

She's too focused on other stuff, throws her hands up, and lets me continue.

I wait by the wings. Once Kate exits the stage and comes back behind these curtains, I'll grab her. Even better if they go to black for a transition.

I try to peer around the curtain to see if she's anywhere near me.

And then I'm yanked into the large storage room backstage, a hand tight over my mouth as the door gently and silently closes.

"You're like a damn cockroach," Ms. Richards says. "We can't get rid of you."

THIRTY-THREE

EXIT, PURSUED BY A BIRD

My heart is in my throat as I look up at Ms. Richards. She's dressed impeccably for the performance in a silky low-cut jumpsuit and heels. Her hair is tied in a loose updo and her lips are bloodred.

My stomach lurches. Even though I saw the picture of her with Jillian, I didn't want to actually believe that she was involved. But there's no denying it now.

And as scared as I am, I'm hurt too.

"Well, it's not for lack of trying," I say. "Real team effort in teenage-kid murder."

Which is why I don't have the time to be doing this now. Not when Jillian is probably about to shoot my sister.

She blocks my path to the door.

Ms. Richards smiles. "Might as well put an end to it now."

She rolls her eyes. "Jillian doesn't have it in her."

Didn't seem that way when she ran up to the tech booth with a loaded freaking weapon.

"You actually believe that?" I ask. "That you will be birds in another life?"

"Absolutely not. The rest of them really got into it, though. Insane, isn't it?" Ms. Richards frowns. "I do, however, believe in the money it makes me. And I love Jillie. She's a nut, but I love her."

I almost feel bad for Jillian. Or, at least, I would if she didn't kidnap me and wasn't about to kill Kate.

Ms. Richards's little laugh twists into a grimace as she goes on. "She actually cared about you. If you weren't the neighbor of that nosy loser I killed, I think she would've convinced you to join. She's been planning it for months. She adores you." Her eyes catch mine. "Which is why I should kill you now."

Not only do I have to save my sister, I have to get away from this woman.

But the words escape out of me. "You killed Mr. Conspiracy?"

"The weird guy with the Post-its on his wall?" She pulls out a knife, like the one she used on him, from her purse and tosses the handbag aside. "Let's say I did."

I need to do something. I'm not sure I can outrun her. I have to open the door, but she's directly in the way. There's nothing around me I can easily grab—the closest thing is an old costume rack.

"All the conversations we had were fake?"

Ms. Richards steps closer, cornering me. I back up, and the hanging fabrics brush against me. She's nearly within reach, but I'm unarmed. I can't get to any of the bins of props or old set pieces lining the walls.

"Of course," Ms. Richards says. "Like I care about you and your little gender issues."

A bit of anger rises in me, but it's hard for the frustration to overtake my fear. I can't die back here, though. Kate is counting on me. Mr. Conspiracy is counting on me.

My friends are counting on me.

And I've never even had my first kiss.

What would Anderson do? What would Zoro or Luffy do?

As she starts to lunge forward, I snap one of the heavy dresses off the rack and toss it over her head. Her hands go up and I shift into fighting stance. Her momentary blindness gives me enough time to bend my knees and twist my hips to send a straight cross right to her belly. I'm not the strongest, but it lands, and the knife clatters to the floor as her breath expels.

I quickly reset and send a hook right to the side of her face.

Once I make contact, I drop to pick up the knife, whip open the door, and run out of the closet.

Holy shit holy shit holy shit.

A quick laugh escapes out of me, although that falls when I see Mr. Hawthorne from GLAOE—or, I guess, the Flock—preventing my backstage exit.

Which means there's only one way to go, especially because I hear Kate speaking in her Audrey voice on stage. I rush to the wings, knife in my hands. Cory starts his line, about two feet away from me, but Kate is all the way on stage left.

I run out onto the stage and shove Cory into the wings, out of the line of fire. Gasps sound from the crowd, and audience members erupt into murmurs.

The opening notes of "Suddenly Seymour" play. The big duet between Audrey and the male lead, Seymour.

Kate's eyes widen as she sees me, but otherwise she stays relatively in character. I look at her for a second, body frozen. I'm completely visible on stage.

I'm completely visible on stage.

Mom and Kate are going to kill me. But as long as they're alive to do it . . .

I quickly stick the knife in the waistband of my pants and hope it doesn't cut me.

I can't look toward the audience, who are audibly confused, although the stage lights are too bright to confirm it. It's certainly impossible to see what's going on in the tech booth.

And I'm visible. On stage. In front of everyone.

FEAR #1 (TIED): PUBLIC SPEAKING/HUMILIATION

It probably isn't a good idea to completely panic.

Before I know what I'm doing, I start singing the lyrics of the song. I've had to say the lines to Kate a billion times before.

It's hard to tell who is more surprised at my shaky but strong voice, my sister in her bright blond wig, or me.

As I continue through the lyrics, both hoping and not hoping that I'm loud enough, I grab Kate, and pull her in a weird kind of sightseeing dance tour that zigzags around the stage. She really excels at the whole Meisner "take the first thing" or whatever, because she goes along with it, probably making the awkward movements seem a little more planned.

As Kate takes over singing, I lead her behind set pieces that might not necessarily stop a bullet, but might at least make Jillian hesitate. As much as I'd love to run offstage with her, that probably would cause a panic, and even if I have a knife, there's Mr. Hawthorne and a pissed-off Ms. Richards in the stage-right wing. I also spot two cult members stage left.

They can't do anything to us in front of a nearly full house. At least I hope not.

We go behind the flower shop counter, despite it keeping us from being in full view, and around Audrey II.

Kate was right. The puppet looks amazing—way better than the morph suit.

I try to keep us moving as much as possible. It's not like the change in choreography really matters, I'm already ruining the show.

Despite trying to pay attention to the song, because I have to join in soon, my heart is pounding and my vision is spotty waiting in anticipation for a bullet to come spiraling at the two of us. Although part of that might be from being up here.

And the head wound. And potential drugs.

Well, there are a lot of reasons and I'm running on nothing but fear and the muscle memory of running lines and listening to this song with Kate.

The girls who are like the Greek chorus of the musical actually come out despite me making a mess of the show. I'll have to thank the trio, Yoneta and the two underclassmen who I haven't met, later for also going along with it, but I casually walk over to them with Kate still using the counter as a prop and get them to join in on constant movement.

I walk in front of the four of them, back and forth, although acting as a human shield for four people isn't exactly the best option.

If Anderson figures this out, I'll buy him Ben & Jerry's for life.

Even though I want to throw up, I focus on keeping everyone on stage moving behind something to shield them.

The song reaches the end, and on the hold of the last note, a gunshot cracks through the auditorium.

A bit of glass cracks and showers stage left as one of the lights goes dark.

The music immediately stops, and a few screams sound. None of the audience members seem to know how to react.

Kate and Yoneta look at me with wide eyes and the two other girls are ducked on the ground. All of them seem okay. The light shattered at the other end of the stage and we're closer to the right curtain.

A bit of relief passes through me, but it doesn't last long, because most guns hold more than one bullet.

Someone yells from the back of the auditorium, where the tech booth is—followed by loud footsteps and a big thud.

There's a long moment of silence. The stage lights are too bright to see what's happening. I don't know what to do without the music. I pull Kate closer to me behind the counter.

Suddenly, Anderson's voice cuts through the air. "Aha. It is I, the vengeful brother of the dentist . . . the . . . orthodontist!" He's walking up the center aisle, now holding the gun that Jillian had up high toward the ceiling. "I have come for revenge on Seymour!"

I wish I could better gauge the reaction to see if this really passes as part of the show. I don't want the Flock or even the cops to put Anderson in danger because of this.

He climbs up on stage, shrugs at me as his back is toward the audience, and then pretends to slip. He gives an exaggerated and prolonged "ohhh!" as he gently hands off the gun to me and tumbles into the mouth of Audrey II.

Whoever plays that role goes along with it. "Delicious," they say.

And the crowd claps and cheers, but I think that's because everyone must love Anderson, regardless of what they think of the play.

Now I'm carrying an arsenal, and the back of my neck sweats. I want to get rid of the weapons, but then one of the cult members could run and pick the gun or knife up. I glance down at the gun. The magazine is missing, so Anderson must have taken it out before using it as a prop, which makes it slightly easier to hold.

It still burns in my hand and I really want it to go away.

The tech booth starts playing the curtain call music, and the rest of the cast runs out on stage. They go through the bows as police start filing in from the front. I glance to the side and see two officers grabbing Ms. Richards and Mr. Hawthorne.

I finally let out a breath.

I gently place the weapons on the floor, since I don't really want to be seen holding them.

Anderson jogs from around the back and stands next to me.

I'm about to try to say something to him over the applause, but I don't get the chance.

Kate and Cory grab a hand from each of us and pull us downstage along with them to join in on the bows.

The roar is deafening, and I can kind of see why people like my mom and Kate enjoy this.

I, however, feel my vision fade as I pass out for the second time today.

THIRTY-FOUR

ALL'S WELL THAT ENDS WELL

After I wake up and the paramedics patch me together on the stage, I lie down flat over the black surface. I could sleep for a week.

My mom rushes over to me.

"Oh, honey," she says. "I'm so glad you're safe."

"Thanks, Mom," I manage to say through my dry throat.

"You were so good up there," she goes on, "a much better singer than that Cory boy. Honestly, they should have you sing the song every night, your range is absolutely brilliant . . ."

"Mom," I say. "Kate and I could have died."

"You didn't, though," she says. "What you did do is steal the show."

"Thanks, Mom," Kate says from next to her.

"Oh, you were amazing, honey, but who knew Bianca could

sing like that? We should really do an all-female production of this show. Or, oh my gosh, *Wicked*."

My headache returns in full force. "Okay, next. Who's next?"

Dad comes to my rescue by putting his arms around Mom and gently pulling her away. "Dear, she's okay, let's give her some space." He gives me a wink. "Ti amo, Bianca."

He usually doesn't say it outright, so it's kind of sweet that he did. The pronouns hurt, but not as much as my head, and I really had enough excitement without trying to start that conversation. As much as my dad works and doesn't usually have the right words, he definitely understands what's good for me as he pulls Mom away.

"Word on the street is you saved my life," Kate says.

"Maybe I did," I say. "Anderson, too."

"I just thanked him." She grins. "You're the best sibling ever."

Kate pulls me into a hug, squeezing a lot tighter than she usually would.

I sit up, since she kind of pulled me in that direction anyway.

Cory Kowalski stands upstage, where his mom is talking loudly to an officer about how money has been consistently diverted from the arts programs, there were strange volunteers working the show, and if they so much as look funny at Anderson or me, she'll sue the entire LAPD.

It's always good to have the blond rich white lady on your side.

"Is Cory mad?" I ask.

"Are you kidding?" Kate says. "You got him out of the line of fire. And don't tell anyone, but he told me that you did sing the song better than him."

I'm blushing now. "Don't tell Mom."

"No way," Kate agrees. "And I take back the many bad things I've said about Cory Kowalski."

We're not really the kind of siblings that hug a lot, but Kate gives me another one. I guess almost dying is one way to change that. "But seriously, you were the coolest."

"I don't know," I say.

"The assistant stage manager and a girl on props said they heard Ms. Richards threaten you and admit she killed some guy. They already told the police, too." Kate smiles. "By tomorrow, you'll probably have a fan club."

I roll my eyes and don't bother responding to that part. "They got all the cult people then?"

"I think so," Kate says. "But I doubt anyone else will get very far, especially not when you give them the evidence you found during questioning."

Ugh. That's the last thing I want to do right now, but if it will help, I should. I don't know if I have a choice.

At the very least, Jillian and Ms. Richards are in police custody. I can probably start sleeping in my own room again.

Anderson walks over, some gauze taped to his head. "Look who's alive."

I groan. "Define alive."

"Thanks again for saving my life," Kate says to him. She turns back to me. "I'm going to make sure Mom gives you your space."

She walks off, leaving me and Anderson.

"Paramedics said I'll be good," Anderson says, sitting down next to me.

"Same here." I tap the bandages I now sport. "Relatively."

"We might be sore tomorrow."

I rub the side of my head gently. "Could be worse." He gives a little laugh at that. I look over at him. "What was that?"

Anderson puts his good hand on my shoulder. "That, Bianca Torre, was us saving the day. Along with Elaine. And Ryan, who actually went to the cops first when we didn't come back from the hike." That helps explain why the police arrived so quickly. I'll have to thank Ryan later.

Now that the adrenaline is gone, a wave of tears rushes out, but I also start laughing. Anderson joins in, and we laugh and cry for a few solid minutes. He scoots closer to me so I can lean my head on him.

"What happened on your end?" I ask.

Anderson lets out a long breath. "It was a lot of being threatened, but I feel like Jillian didn't actually want to shoot anyone. I got her in a double leg and took the gun," he says. "Probably broke my wrist again, but hey. That's why you should try Jiu-Jitsu."

I try not to look too proud of myself. "Well, I punched Ms. Richards." I hold up my fingers to emphasize the point. "Twice."

"That was you?" Anderson asks. "I saw her face, that's gonna hurt tomorrow."

"You were right," I say. "I got a mean left hook."

"My little person is growing up so fast," Anderson says, squeezing his arm around my shoulders. "Rafael is going to be so proud. But you're not getting out of taking his class anymore."

"If I can stop a murderous cult, I can take a Jiu-Jitsu class," I say, even though I'm not one hundred percent sure about that.

Anderson looks a little too excited.

"*Maybe,*" I add. "No promises."

He chuckles again and falls back against the stage. "It's been a wild few weeks, huh?"

I lie down next to him. The stage lights are dimmed, so it doesn't hurt quite so much.

I feel like I've had enough happen since Mr. Conspiracy's murder to pass a lifetime.

"That's an understatement," I say, head turned in his direction. "I did want to show you something though."

He gives me a look. "Yeah?"

I reach into my pocket and pull out an envelope that thankfully survived. Along with a doodle of two birds, it reads BIANCA AND ANDERSON ANIME EXPO FUND. "Tickets for the summer don't go on sale until February, so I couldn't surprise you with them, but I'm going to help out my mom with filing and assignments to make some cash."

His eyes look a little glassy, but it might be the adrenaline. Anderson pulls me into a hug.

"I'm so excited," he says.

"Assuming you still want to go with me and not get some alone time with Layla," I joke.

He pulls away, expression serious. "First, we can all go. Second, she's going to be going in cosplay and I don't want to be left alone while she's taking pictures."

"At least you can tell people the two of us dragged you there."

Anderson smiles at the envelope. "I guess, but I don't really think I care what anyone would say. I might not be super open about what anime means to me, but I have people I can share it with, and that's what matters."

I grin. "Yeah. You're right."

Mrs. Coleman walks up to us. Her eyes are a little watery, and I know we definitely worried her a lot by being kidnapped and everything.

"Did the paramedics say you're both all right?" she asks.

"We're great," Anderson says. "Considering the circumstances."

I push myself back up into a seated position while Anderson rolls on his side.

Mrs. Coleman gets down on her knees to pull me into a tight hug.

"I'm so glad you're both okay," she says into my shoulder.

And honestly, me too.

She pulls away to hug Anderson. I take the chance to glance around the auditorium. The audience is pretty much gone. It's over.

I'm not sure if I'll get in trouble for punching Ms. Richards, but I'm not going to worry about that now.

For now, we all survived, and everything is good.

A lot of the cast and crew of the musical, along with their

families, are around, as the police are getting statements from anyone with a parent or guardian present.

Elaine is talking with one of the paramedics in the front row, also with a wrap on her head.

"They're going to want to hear from us too," Anderson says.

"Do I need a lawyer or something?" I ask.

"I mean, you're not accused of anything, so I don't think so," he says. "Your mom is probably scarier anyway."

"You're not wrong."

Mrs. Coleman gives me a quick pat on the back. "You can take your time though. Once you're ready, we can get your parents."

I look between the two of them. "There's one thing I want to do first."

I slowly stand, trying not to move too quickly and get woozy again. The last thing I need to do is throw up when I already fainted in front of everyone. My cheeks heat, but I clench my fists as I keep walking forward.

I don't stop until I'm about two feet away from her.

FEAR #6: INITIATING CONVERSATION

"Hey, Elaine," I say. "Can we talk for a minute?"

The paramedic nods and steps aside, and Elaine turns to me. "How are you feeling?"

"I'm fine," I say. "You?"

"Not bad for narrowly escaping a murderous bird cult," she says with a smile. Even in our current states, she's so freaking beautiful. Her hair is a mess and stained with dried blood, and my heart still beats rapid-fire at the sight of her.

FEAR #13: BEAUTIFUL PEOPLE

"I have something to ask you," I say, my chest squeezing as I rock on my feet.

"Okay," she says.

FEAR #32: NOT BEING LIKED

I force myself to look directly into her eyes, and she doesn't look away. My heart thumps higher in my chest.

FEAR #44: PROLONGED EYE CONTACT

"I think you're the most amazing person I've ever met," I say. The words come out so quickly, tumbling over each other, but I keep it going. "And I've had a massive crush on you forever, so would you maybe consider going on a date with me?"

I take a breath.

I can't believe I did that.

Elaine's face goes bright red.

"Um, yeah," she says. "I've had a crush on you forever, too."

For a second, I'm not sure I heard her correctly. I feel so light, and I want to cover my lips before they split into a smile.

"Really?" I ask.

"Well, since I met you. I thought it'd been obvious lately." We can barely look each other in the eye now. "And, you know, I'm in the market for new people to go hiking with. Turns out my birding group was a cover for a money-stealing cult."

"Mine too," I say. "It's perfect timing."

"What a coincidence," she says through a smile.

"So . . . I'll text you?" I ask. Because she probably doesn't want to plan out our date right here and now.

"Yeah," Elaine says. "I'd like that."

"Okay," I say. "Do you have a ride home?"

"My parents are here, I should go meet with them, but we'll talk soon. About our date." She rubs her arm.

My skin burns, but in a good way. "Our date, yeah. Just me and you. Totally. Yes. Um . . . get home safe, and, yeah, talk soon!"

I turn away quickly so she doesn't see how much I'm smiling. I can't believe I have a date with Elaine Yee. And she actually likes me back.

I glance up at the stage, to where Mrs. Coleman, Anderson, and even Ronan stare at me with huge smiles on their faces.

"Were you three listening?" I ask.

They don't try to deny it.

"It was adorable," Ronan says.

As if I wasn't already blushing enough before. I can't look back at Elaine, so I'll have to text her an apology later. Anderson and Ronan both give me little shoves, saying how proud they are. Mrs. Coleman pulls me into another hug.

"Ready to talk to the police?" Anderson asks.

"I guess," I say.

Ronan holds out the flash drive. "I brought this in case you want to turn it in."

I look between the three of them and back to the flash drive.

"You think it'd be all right if we give them that tomorrow?"

TO THE GIRL WITH THE TELESCOPE

I'm not sure why I'm leaving this to you. I don't know if you'll ever read this, and I'm sure not making it easy for you to find it. Even if you do decide to help me, there's no guarantee you'll get this far, and I wouldn't blame you. But I have hope.

Maybe it's because I don't know what else to do.

Maybe it's because I don't have anyone else.

Maybe it's because, in some weird way, you remind me of him.

Nate always loved ornithology. He was most himself when he was surrounded by birds, and he would constantly message me about them. When he went missing, I knew I would do anything to find out what happened.

Even die for it. Even involve you.

I saw you the day you saw me, peeking through my curtains. I had the feeling I was being watched, so I took a page out of your book and used binoculars to try to find out why. At the time, you were actually birdwatching, which is why I started leaving you those drawings.

It was like I got a piece of my nephew back in some ways.

But to be honest, you don't just remind me of Nate. You remind me of myself. When I noticed you looking in at all these different lives, I wasn't mad.

Because I get it.

You look through glass like I do, only I use a computer screen.

It's so easy to be afraid. To feel like you are too much or not enough, or a combination of both. It's comfortable to stay away, as much as it is lonely. I saw loneliness in you. Probably because I'm so used to feeling it myself.

If you're reading this, you already have the information on the Flock and their Valley Quail scheme. I hope you can do something about it, and I truly hope nothing bad happens to you as a result of this. I can barely live with myself to think that I am directly putting a teenager into the line of fire. To be fair, I won't have to live with it for much longer.

I hope you can do what Nate and I failed to do. I don't necessarily have a reason, but I believe you can. And I'd like to tell you one thing before I go.

Do not get so absorbed in your fear that you let it prevent you from being yourself. I know how hard it is, but try to put your happiness first. You will make mistakes, you will feel pain, you will even have major regrets, but those things are beautiful, because they mean you actually lived.

I didn't realize this until it was too late, so maybe you can live on my behalf.

It's a short life, and the worst thing to do is go through it alone.

With hope and thanks,

Steven Lebedev

THIRTY-FIVE

NEW BEGINNINGS

It's kind of weird to have a couple chilling in my bedroom with me, but since it's my best friend and my newest friend, it kind of works. Anderson and Layla sit next to each other on my bed, backs against the wall, Puck curled up at their feet.

I turn slowly in front of them, dressed in jeans and a short-sleeve button-up with little cats all over it.

"Okay," Layla says. "I love the shirt, but I'm kind of feeling the first pants option."

Anderson puts his hand on his chin, looking down at my jeans.

"Yeah . . ." he starts. "I mean, you look chill. But I think you want to look more than chill on your first date."

Just the thought of it makes me blush. I try to distract myself by walking back into my closet to peel off my pants.

"Where did you two go for your first date?" I ask. "You didn't tell me on Thanksgiving."

"In front of my nana? Really?" Anderson snorts. "Did you not decide where you're taking her yet?"

I peek my head out from the closet door to glare at him. "I already told you. We're grabbing food and then going to the Getty."

"So Los Angeles," he says.

I'm back in the closet changing into the black pants I tried on for the first option, but I manage to stick my hand out to flip him off. "What was your first date, then?"

"We got ramen," Layla answers. "Then watched *Demon Slayer.*"

"So weeb trash," I respond, imitating Anderson's voice.

I step out of the closet in the cat shirt but with the original pants.

Layla puts her hand on her chin, looking over my appearance. "Wait, tuck the shirt in, if you're comfortable with that."

I unbutton my pants to tuck the shirt in, forcing it down so it's smooth. Then I adjust the waistband.

"And unbutton the top button of your shirt," Anderson adds.

I do kind of have it high enough that I could be going to church. I undo the top button.

Both Anderson and Layla practically jump up from their seats.

"That's it!" Anderson says at the same time Layla exclaims, "You look so good."

My face heats.

"Thanks," I say. "I'm glad you didn't think it was weird I invited you both over to help me get dressed."

"First of all," Layla says. "You invited us over to watch the new episode of *One Piece*."

I mean, that's true, we did do that. We planned it after last Sunday's group meeting, where I managed to publicly mention I had a date and not throw up and pass out. A huge win for me.

"Second, I wanted to show you my new comic concept," Anderson adds. "And third, we would have come even if it was solely for helping you decide what to wear."

His sketching has been really improving, and Anderson is a great storyteller. I loved his idea for a comedic slasher comic. I really hope he actually makes it, because I'm already more than a little invested.

"And your concept is brilliant." I glance down again at my outfit. "I really look all right?"

"Saying you look all right is like saying the weird murder cult was *a small annoyance*," Layla teases. "You look amazing."

I blush. Though it's only been two weeks since everything went down with the cult, it feels like a different lifetime. I can't complain that the most stressful November of my life is over, but it is strange. If anything, the worst part of it is knowing that I totally fell for Jillian's lies. I trusted her. I looked up to her.

Ms. Richards, too. As much as I hate to admit it, it has been a lot harder to pay attention in English class since she was replaced.

Ms. Richards is a terrible, trash person, but she really wasn't a bad teacher.

Jillian being gone is a different story. Not only did I lose her, but I lost the entire GLAOE. It was basically a scam from the start, sure, but it was a community for me. Without that, it's like there is a little something missing.

But, thankfully, Terrance and Margaret are starting their own birding group with a focus on marginalized birdwatchers. One that is actually a birding group, and not a cover for anything. They've already invited Elaine and me on their first walk next Saturday, on the ninth.

Plus, Elaine and I can always go on our own hikes, too.

"You look great, you're ready, and you can totally do this," Anderson says.

"Okay," I say. "I look great, I'm ready, and I can totally do this."

I catch a glimpse of myself in the mirror and smooth my hair, the longest waves now only falling to my right ear. I force a smile. My body doesn't quite follow along, as it's still jittery and shaky.

"You are Bianca Torre. You punched a killer in the face. You can impress a girl on a date," he continues.

"I punched a killer in the face," I repeat. "I did that."

The doorbell rings. I stay frozen in place, stomach churning.

"Now what do you do?" Anderson asks.

I twist to him and Layla. "Throw up," I say.

"Oooh," he says. "So close. But no. You answer the door."

"Right," I say. "Of course."

I start walking out of the room. "Are you staying here?"

"No, that'd be weird," Layla says. "But we'll wait until you leave."

"Cool," I say. "Right. Of course."

I exit my room.

"Text me everything after," Anderson calls from behind.

My heart is beating quickly and my body is filled with nervous energy. I shake out my hands a little bit like I've seen Kate do in her warm-ups.

It doesn't really help.

I take a deep breath and pull open the door. Elaine is there, hair down and straightened, and she wears a navy-blue romper that is incredibly cute.

"You look amazing," we both say at the same time.

And then both blush at the same time, too.

"You ready?" Elaine asks, reaching out with her hand.

"Yeah." I take it in mine. "I'm ready."

BIANCA TORRE'S LIST OF FEARS

1. PUBLIC SPEAKING/HUMILIATION

    1.5. TIED: GUNS

2. SPIDERS

3. MURDER

4. PANDEMICS

5. DEAD BODIES

6. INITIATING CONVERSATION

7. MY MOM READING MY SEMI-EROTIC FANFIC

8. BEING ALONE

9. WILDFIRES

10. BLOOD

11. TELLING MY PARENTS I'M A RAGING LESBIAN

12. THE FUTURE

13. BEAUTIFUL PEOPLE

    13.5. ASSUMING IT'S A DATE WHEN IT ISN'T

14. ZOMBIES

15. LOSS OF CONTROL

16. GETTING CAUGHT DOING SOMETHING BAD

17. BEING THE CENTER OF ATTENTION IN ANY CIRCUMSTANCE

18. HAVING RUMORS SPREAD ABOUT ME

19. GETTING BAD GRADES

20. PHONE CALLS

21. *DOKI DOKI LITERATURE CLUB!*

22. PEOPLE IN POSITIONS THAT GROSSLY ABUSE POWER

23. BEING WATCHED

24. SHEEP

25. SNAKES

26. DANGEROUS SITUATIONS IN GENERAL

27. BEING WATCHED THROUGH MY LAPTOP CAMERA

28. BEING NEEDED IN A CRISIS

29. FALLING

30. FALLING ONTO AN UMBRELLA AND DYING (THANKS, *ANOTHER*)

31. BEING RUDE

32. NOT BEING LIKED

33. MOUNTAIN LIONS

34. VENTRILOQUISTS AND ESPECIALLY THEIR DUMMIES

35. ELEVATORS

36. OPENING UP TO FAMILY

37. OPENING UP TO STRANGERS

38. CLOSE CONTACT

39. MASCOTS

40. PEOPLE MAKING A BIG DEAL OUT OF THINGS

41. RABBITS

42. PISSING OFF MY MOM

43. ACTING CLASSES

44. PROLONGED EYE CONTACT

45. ACCIDENTALLY SAYING "YOU TOO" TO CUSTOMER SERVICE WORKERS WHEN THAT DOESN'T MAKE SENSE

46. SWEAT AND OTHER BODILY FLUIDS

47. ~~BEING CAUGHT IN A LIE~~

48. ~~SKIN CANCER~~

49. ~~DYING BEFORE THE CONCLUSION OF *ONE PIECE*~~

50. ~~DRIVING (AND INEVITABLY FAILING AT IT)~~

51. ~~GETTING CALLED ON IN CLASS WHEN I'M NOT PREPARED~~

52. ~~IMPROV~~

53. ~~LARGE OBJECTS FALLING UNEXPECTEDLY ON ME~~

54. ~~ESCAPE ROOMS~~

55. ~~BREAKING INTO A DEAD GUY'S APARTMENT~~

56. ~~ANIMAL CARCASSES~~

57. ~~HAVING TO TALK TO ANYONE I DON'T ALREADY KNOW WELL~~

58. ~~WHATEVER THE FUCK THIS IS~~

   ~~58.5. ANDERSON'S "GREAT IDEAS"~~

59. ~~GETTING MY ASS KICKED~~

60. ~~RINGWORM~~

61. ~~OPENING UP TO FRIENDS~~

62. ~~CULT MEMBERS MURDERING THE GIRL I LIKE~~

63. ~~CULT MEMBERS MURDERING ANYONE I LIKE~~

64. ~~ANYTHING BAD HAPPENING TO RYAN PÉREZ, GODDAMNED HERO~~

65. ~~TELLING PEOPLE ABOUT THIS LIST~~

66. ~~CULTLIKE CHANTS~~

67. ~~NOT BEING ABLE TO SAVE MY SISTER~~

68. ~~THAT THE CULT THAT TRIED TO MURDER ME DOESN'T GET TIME~~

69. ~~FIRST DATES~~

70. LETTING MY FEARS HOLD ME BACK

JUSTINE PUCELLA WINANS IS THANKFUL TO EVERYONE

1. First, to my mom, who has supported me since I was writing full-length books as a teenager and dreaming about seeing them on shelves one day. Even if that meant reading an entire draft of a sapphic pirate fantasy with a somewhat explicit scene and pretending that didn't leave you with questions about me. I wouldn't be here without you, and I definitely wouldn't be this funny. (But not as funny as you, I know, I know.) Thank you so much, and I love you more.

2. To Alex Brown, for being the best writing friend and supporting this book when it was still Lesbian Sheep Idea??? Thanks so much for checking yes on my Do I Write This? note, and for being the first person to really believe in *Bianca*. You (and your incredible books) are amazing!

3. To Thomy, my love, my soul mate, my best friend. Your support means everything to me, and I could write pages of how much you mean to me and how none of this would be possible without you, but I'm not going to make you do all that reading. Te adoro, mi amor. You are my everything.

4. To Jasper Fidencio and Twinklepop Mauricio, the world's finest writer's assistants and handsomest cats. Jasper, you have chewed on my outlines from the very beginning, and your jumpiness and penchant for spying on both birds and the neighbors inspired a lot of *Bianca*. Twinklepop, you're newer to this, but I love you all the same. You two are the best boys.

5. To Jordan Hamessley, an absolute rock star of an agent. Thank you for first believing in *Bianca* and supporting me and my work. Even if I feel like I'm your most annoying client, you never make me feel that way, and I appreciate everything you do. I am one lucky author to have you on my team!

6. To Lily Kessinger, editor extraordinaire, for being so passionate about this book from the beginning, and accepting my silly emails and Pokémon references. The entire editing experience was so fun, and with your notes, this book really became something to be proud of. Thank you for the guidance, support, and the much-needed love for our best boy, Ryan Pérez.

7. To both cover designer Joel Tippie and artist Mariia Menshikova for putting together an absolutely stunning cover that I couldn't love more. I am still in shock over how perfect it is for this book!

8. To the amazing team at Clarion: Mary Magrisso, Erika West, Emilia Rhodes, Mary Wilcox, and my wonderful copyeditor, Megan Gendell.

9. To my sensitivity readers, including Shadae B. Mallory, for providing honest feedback that not only improved the characters, but improved this book as a whole.

10. To Jasper's Write Squad: Elle Gonzalez Rose, Danielle Simonelli, and Hailie Kei (and by extension, Chloe Lauter and Mary Feely), you all inspire me so much and your writing is brilliant! I'm so lucky to have had you all as mentees and, more importantly, as friends.

11. To Eiichiro Oda, who will probably never read this, but who created a world that I was able to escape to in my darkest times, and whose story inspired me to keep writing when I was ready to quit. If my books can mean something to a reader even a fourth of what *One Piece* means to me, everything would be worth it.

12. To Kay Choo, thank you for your support and friendship! I can't wait for us to (hopefully) meet in person, but I'm so glad to have you to geek out over both writing and *One Piece* with. You are an amazing writer and an even better friend, and I'm always happy to see your messages!

13. To the Italian family I've always had and the family in Costa Rica I've gained: ti amo and te amo, grazie mille and muchas gracias. I'm so grateful to have all of you in my life.

14. And to my nonno. You won't get to see me as a published author, but you always supported me as an artist. I love you forever and I miss you more.

15. To Ben and academy readers Helen Needham, Renee Jones, and Kyra Horvat. Thank you for first giving this book a

chance and being (or introducing me to, in Ben's case) my first teen readers!

16. To other early readers: Christen Young, Kara Kennedy, Erin Sullivan, Honni van Rijswijk, Tea Belog, and David Girbino. You all first read this at different times, but I'm certain it wouldn't be the same book without any of you. Thank you so, so much for convincing me I'm funny. (But really, you are all amazing!)

17. To my amazing QS debut group: Jen St. Jude, Ronnie Riley, Caroline Huntoon, and Kate Fussner. And to the rest of the 2023 debuts, especially Trang Thanh Tran and Kaylie Smith for winter debut support! I couldn't share a better year to debut with so many incredible stories and I am grateful to be here with all of you.

18. To my writing group friends for allowing me to share updates and motivating me: Sandra Proudman, A. J. Sass, Camille Baumann-Jaeger, Shannon A. Thompson, and Jennifer Honeybourn. To Traci Chee for answering all my publishing questions and being so amazing and kind. And to other writing friends (I'll probably forget some of you, ahhhh) who always inspire me: Riley Swan, Anca Demeter, Shelly Page, Morgan Ashbaugh, Zach Humphrey, Sydney Langford, Leanne Yong, Birdie Schae, Elle Grenier, and so many more! I have the best writing community and I love you all.

19. I have to mention my Mayfield Middle School and Mayfield High School Science Olympiad teammates, who got me into

ornithology because no one else wanted to do it, lol. Even if we didn't keep in touch, you are all awesome and I hope you're doing amazing.

20. To the girl who was always writing stories, even if she didn't really know herself yet. I know you wanted to give up so many times, but you never did. And I'm grateful for that. I know how hard it is and I'm proud of you. Thanks for letting us become the person we are today. Someone who can love and be loved and, yes, even publish a book. I'm still learning to love you, but thinking back to where we were and where we are now . . . I think I'm pretty close. I wish I could tell you to not be so afraid of who you are and where you can go. It gets so much better, kid. Just keep going.

21. To you, the reader, above everything else. For taking a chance on this silly, weird book of my heart. For taking a chance on me as a writer. Sure, I hope you were able to see a piece of yourself in this book. I hope as you finish this, you have a smile on your face and clutch it to your chest and think *wow, I loved this* or *this was actually really funny* or *finally, a book for the anxious queers with a sense of humor*. But even if you think none of those things, or nothing even remotely close to those things, I'm grateful to you and I'm so happy you're here. Thank you, thank you, and remember: it's okay to be afraid of everything, just don't let that stop you from soaring. (I feel like I had to end this on a bird pun, right?)